Way
of the
Serpent

To Kevin

A NOVEL

Here's to our future!

Donna Dechen Birdwell

Donna Dechen Birdwell
donna.birdwell@gmail.com

Cover art and design by Donna Dechen Birdwell.

Here's to all the unexpected good fortune that has come my way in this life and in particular to the best of it, namely Brendan and Rebecca.

Way of the Serpent

Serpent

A NOVEL

Donna Dechen Birdwell

When Jenda Swain – youthful and vigorous at the age of 111 – encounters an incongruously old woman at an out-of-the-way café, her life veers in a new direction amid unsettling questions about her own identity and her role in the corporation-dominated culture of 2125. Her journey takes her into the arms of a Latino artist, who has a quest of his own. Answers come together as their world falls apart.

Available on Amazon and at select bookstores.

Contact the author!

www.donnadechenbirdwell.com

donna.birdwell@gmail.com

      @wideworldhome

"She couldn't remember having gone out of her house that day; she had the feeling that she had made the trip without a car or a carriage, a trip full of mysterious shadows, and that she had woken up on a road lined with trees that smelled like Australian pines where she had suddenly found herself making nests for birds."

--Silvina Ocampo, "Forgotten Journey" (1937)

Part I:
Eternal Youth, Disrupted

1.

The café was down a couple of side streets, in an area of Dallas Jenda never went to, but she thought she might have been to the café once before. She couldn't remember. Without looking at the menu, she ordered a grilled cheese sandwich with fried potatoes and sweet tea. It was plain food, but she liked it. She was halfway through her meal, savoring the anonymity afforded by this out-of-the-way eatery as much as the greasy food, when she noticed the woman who had turned on her stool at the café's counter to stare.

The woman was old. That in itself was disturbing. Nobody got old anymore, not since Chulel – the drug that prevented aging – had come on the market a hundred years ago. Jenda, at 111, was as fresh and vigorous as she had been in 2035 when, at the age of 22, she had received her first annual Chulel treatment. Jenda's grandmother was 165, but appeared no older than she had when she began taking Chulel in her mid-sixties. What was this old woman doing in Jenda's world?

Jenda turned away, but she could still feel the woman's dark eyes boring into her, probing. Jenda couldn't help herself; she looked again. When the woman saw her looking, she smiled.

"Zujo!" Jenda swore, quickly returning her attention to her unfinished sandwich. It was too late. Taking the smile as an invitation, the woman dropped down from her counter stool and shuffled over to Jenda's table.

"You're Jenda Swain," she said, cocking her head to one side and narrowing her eyes. "God, you look the same as you did in high school."

"Excuse me?" Jenda sat up straighter and used her best business voice.

"Of course you don't remember," the woman said, dragging out the chair across from Jenda and sitting down heavily. "Nobody remembers much of anything anymore." She shrugged and looked down at her hands. Jenda looked, too. The woman's hands were wrinkled, misshapen, and covered in brown and red splotches. "I remember you, though," she continued, looking up into Jenda's face. "My god, you were a firebrand back then. I idolized you and your boyfriend, you know. Such temerity! The things you did..." The woman refused to turn away. "Do you still paint? You always had your mom's gift for art."

"I think you must have made some mistake," Jenda said quietly, fighting to modulate her voice against the tightening in her throat. "You may know my name, but you clearly don't know me. Nothing you are saying makes any sense at all." Jenda felt her cheeks warm as she flashed on an image of herself with an easel and paintbrush. Her last bite of sandwich seemed to have lodged somewhere near the base of her esophagus. "Now, would you please go on your way? Leave me alone." Jenda blinked, shuttering herself away from this intrusive presence.

The woman's face clouded and she leaned forward, looking Jenda squarely in the eye. "You need to ask more questions." She spoke the words clearly and forcefully. Then she pushed her chair away from the table with a loud scraping noise. As she leaned over to pick up the leather bag she had dropped under the chair, the pendant around her neck clanked on the table top. It was an old fashioned timepiece, the kind with a round face with numbers and moving hands. Jenda reflexively reached up to grasp her own necklace, a cluster of plexiform flowers in the latest style from her favorite recyclables boutique. The woman took in a deep breath, as if rising from the chair had taxed her strength. She looked at Jenda again. "You're the one who doesn't know who Jenda Swain is." Her voice was gentle, maybe sad. Then she turned and walked out the front door.

Jenda's impulse to run after the woman and ask her name was unexpected. Holding it in check, she sat rigidly, staring at her cold, greasy food. She swallowed hard, trying to dislodge that last bite of sandwich. Her hands trembled. She quickly finished her dilute, not-so-sweet tea and left the café, looking up and down the street as she exited. There was no sign of the woman.

Jenda looked back over her shoulder as she made her way back to the main street, back to reality. "What possessed me to go to that café anyway?" she scolded herself, shoving her fists deeper into the pockets of her fashionable jacket.

All afternoon at her desk in the Dallas offices of Your Journal, Jenda's mind kept wandering, pacing back and forth across the odd feelings, trying to tamp them down. How did the old woman know Jenda's name? What was that about idolizing Jenda in high school? What boyfriend? Firebrand? Ridiculous. Jenda's personal records with Your Journal clearly indicated that her high school career had been quietly unremarkable. She had been a good student with good marks who never made trouble. The woman must have gotten Jenda mixed up with someone else. That was it. Old people did that sometimes, didn't they? But Jenda had enjoyed painting in high school. And her mother had been a sculptor of some note before the accident.

"Are you okay, Jenda?" It was her office mate, Weldon.

"What?" Jenda started, realizing she was probably scowling at her desktop. "No, no, I'm fine," she said. "Maybe something I had at lunch disagreed with me a bit." She gave Weldon a wan smile and waved him off. It was nearly quitting time.

Jenda's discomfort followed her home. "It's just an attack of cognitive dissonance," she told herself. There was a pill for that. But when she got home, she didn't take the pill. Instead she poured a glass of wine and pulled up Your Journal on her home screen, accessing her high school years. There wasn't much, but the pictures were all precisely as Jenda remembered them – she had the same golden blond hair, the same flawless fair skin. She stopped for a moment to examine the picture of herself with an easel and paintbrush. Why had she ever stopped painting? "To make a living," she told herself, "and a contribution." She had majored in art at Perry University, but her course of study focused on digital design and graphic psychology. With that, she had secured her position at Your Journal. That was 90 years ago.

Jenda loved her job with Your Journal, loved being part of such an important corporate institution. Everybody relied on Your Journal as a secure repository of their personal photos, stories, thoughts and feelings. People interacted with it every day, experiencing pangs of guilt if they failed to respond to the reminders on their digilets. You could also put photos and comments on LifeBook, but these were shared with everyone in your loop. YJ was personal and people often referred to their YJ files as their "exomemories".

Jenda was due for her next sabbatical in a couple of months and she had already booked into a resort in the Republic of California. The social order under Chulel had done away with retirement, moving instead to a system in which every worker received a one-year sabbatical every ten years. Technically, of course, a "sabbatical" should occur every seven years, but the term had a nice feel. Nobody questioned such verbal technicalities.

Jenda pulled up some pictures of the resort, which suddenly struck her as mundane and boring and not somewhere she wanted to spend an entire year of her life. Maybe she should try something different. Maybe she should try painting again. Jenda vaguely recalled a place where her mother had gone a few times, a place that used to be considered something of an artists' colony. Maybe in Mexico. Jenda searched through various mediazones and finally came up with a town in central Mexico called San Miguel de Allende. She wasn't sure that was it, but she decided that was where she would go. She did check to verify that there would be tennis courts. She always said tennis was her favorite activity.

Within a few minutes Jenda had cancelled her reservations for California and made new ones for San Miguel de Allende, Mexico. Then she drafted a memo to her supervisor, asking to begin her sabbatical early. She would lose a few weeks of leave, but she felt an odd exhilaration arising from these rash decisions. It felt good.

2.

2125 marked the centenary of the entry of the miracle age prophylaxis Chulel into the marketplace. The occasion probably should have been marked by a celebration of some sort, but so few people remembered what life was like before Chulel that it would have seemed rather like commemorating the invention of water or air. So the year would come and go without fanfare.

Two people who did remember life before Chulel were the inventors of the drug, Drs. Max and Emily Feldman, who had lost their only child to Hutchinson-Guilford progeria syndrome (HGPS) back in 1977. "Progeria" referred to a set of diseases that caused premature aging due to a genetic anomaly; HGPS had been its most common (though still extremely rare) form.

The Feldmans had delayed "having a family" as people used to say, until after they both completed med school. Following their daughter's death, they had devoted their careers to finding a cure for progeria. It had been a long haul. The first significant advance had come from another lab, which announced a promising new avenue of research in 2014. Pharmakon Corporation, and specifically the Drs. Feldman, built on this and in 2017 published preliminary results of a drug they named according to its active chemical components. Nobody now remembers that name.

The drug was ready for human trials by early 2018, and a dozen or so families from around the world came forward, traveling to the Pharmakon headquarters in Atlanta to let the Feldmans try out the drug on their afflicted sons and daughters, who had been diagnosed with either HGPS or one of the other, even rarer, forms of progeria.

What nobody knew was that Max Feldman was also testing the drug on himself. Even Emily didn't know. Max Feldman was already 78 and although he checked out healthy enough, he had a family history of heart disease and atherosclerosis and there were certain aspects of the lab tests on the new drug as well as its effects on a small test group of bonobos that had irresistibly piqued his curiosity.

By the time the tests on human progeria patients were declared unequivocally successful in 2021, the people closest to him were beginning to notice something about Max. One of those people was the Feldmans' lab assistant, Winslow Morris.

In the third month of the trials, Winslow noted that there seemed to be a couple of vials of the drug missing. He questioned Dr. Max about it, and was told it must be a mistake. When Winslow re-counted the next day against the numbers in the computer, he found no discrepancy. It happened again a couple of months later and this time Winslow kept his observation to himself. Again, the numbers mysteriously rectified themselves within a matter of hours. Then one day Winslow thought he saw Dr. Max slipping a vial of the medicine into the pocket of his lab coat. That's when it clicked. Winslow started observing Dr. Max more closely. On the day before the results of the progeria field tests were formally announced, Winslow missed work. And then he disappeared altogether.

Winslow hadn't needed to steal any of the medicine. He knew how to make it. His destination was China and within six months a new drug started showing up on the streets. It was called "Fontana" and it was touted as the "fountain of youth". It was outrageously expensive and sold mainly to customer lists Winslow compiled by irrupting into databases of dermatologists specializing in cosmetic surgery. He was an instant millionaire.

Winslow did not know that Dr. Feldman had altered the dosage for his own use. Fontana consumers were overdosing, and before the drug had been on the street for a full year, its reputation went into free fall. People who were self-medicating with this black market miracle potion started to develop strange skin disorders, unexplained neuropathies, and a vulnerability to infection, all of which ended up on the list of warnings regarding possible side effects when the first generation of the real drug went on the market in 2025 under the name "Chulel." A number of younger women who took Fontana had died.

Winslow was sorry about all this. It cut his income stream down to nothing. But he took his multi millions and his remaining stocks of Fontana and fled.

3.

Jenda's spontaneously rescheduled sabbatical began on the first of May, 2125. Her grandmother had issued dire warnings about the risks of traveling anywhere other than to the purpose built resort centers, but Jenda was resolute. She was going to the old artist colony of San Miguel de Allende in Mexico.

The nearest airport was in León and it wasn't exactly up to 22nd century standards, but Jenda found the ambience pleasant and the staff friendly and helpful. She accessed an autocar to navigate the remaining 150 km from León to San Miguel.

The older model autocar bounced uncomfortably over potholes. The attendant at the airport had apologized for these in advance, blaming recent heavy rains. As the car hit an especially large hole, Jenda began to doubt the wisdom of her choice of destination, wondering if San Miguel de Allende might indeed be as unpleasant as Granny El had predicted. A part of Jenda felt excited, thrilled by a sense of impending adventure; but another part of her kept wondering, "Why ever would you want to do anything so silly?" That thought came in her grandmother's voice. "I can always leave and go somewhere else if I don't like it," Jenda reassured herself.

The road was awful, but Jenda found the views enchanting and, traveling by autocar, she could give the views her full attention. Jenda watched the landscape as it slid by, like a series of pictures on a digiscreen – fields and small lakes, hills and valleys. She passed through a few villages that would have been picturesque if not for the disturbing presence of dogs and children on the streets. In the primary corporate population hubs, nobody kept pets anymore; they had such short life spans and could carry disease. Efforts to come up with a veterinary form of Chulel had failed. As for the children – through Gen5, they had been considered a rather charming novelty. By Gen7, they were frowned upon as a thoughtless aberration.

Jenda awoke from a brief nap just as the town of San Miguel de Allende was coming into view. She could discern on the near horizon the outline of the iconic old neo-Gothic church. In the distance was a line of mountains. She knew that the town was not nearly as prosperous as it had been in its heyday, but she hoped it still had its charms. These were not apparent on the main artery into town, where the usual corporate recharge stations, quick meal establishments, and roadsteads predominated. But as the autocar slowed into the center of town the streets narrowed and these generic institutions gave way to antique brick and stone facades, adorned with digital skins advertising small cafés, bars, and shops with Spanish names.

Jenda had booked a room at a small hotel near the Jardín Allende. The autocar stopped at the specified location and its service arm hefted her large suitcase out of the trunk, setting it upright on its little wheels on the pavement. The autocar pulled away and Jenda watched with some trepidation as the bulky case navigated over the old paving stones that led to the main hotel entrance.

A quarter hour later, as Jenda began unpacking her clothes in a spacious courtyard-view room, she reflected on exactly why she was here. Her distressing encounter with the woman in the café had aroused a yearning to reconnect with art and to try painting again. "I'm here to paint," Jenda told herself. Then she went through a checklist of her impressions of San Miguel. The roads – it was worth repeating – were awful. The town was attractive enough in a quirky sort of way. The hotel seemed pleasant, despite its limited amenities. The staff were friendly, although their English was something short of fluent; Jenda guessed they had become unaccustomed to receiving English speaking guests. On balance, Jenda decided to leave some of her things in the suitcase, which she zipped closed and slid under the bed. "I should try the food," she decided.

At the recommendation of the receptionist cum concierge at the front desk, Jenda walked a few blocks to a restaurant called La Mazorca Loca, which supposedly had "the best huitlacoche tamales in all of San Miguel." Jenda studied the menu intently and then ordered the huitlacoche tamales with pipian sauce, green chile rice, and a cold beer. Jenda noted that she was one of only a few patrons in the establishment.

While she waited for her food, she unfurled the digilet that she always wore on her left wrist. Granny El called it her "slap bracelet", insisting that there had once been an accessory much like the digilet that had been marketed to children. Of course, it hadn't had a flexible digiscreen or a whole computer with colloidal drive inside. "Hi, Gran. Just want you to know I arrived safely," Jenda spoke into the digilet as it turned her words into syllabic symbols to pulse to her grandmother's digilet, where they could either be read from the screen or re-formed into speech. "Love the place so far. Exclamation." That was somewhere between a slight exaggeration and a lie – Jenda hadn't decided yet – but there was no point in worrying Granny El. Or, worse, giving her reason to pulse back "I told you so."

After finishing her meal – which Jenda mentally awarded four stars – and a second three-star ice-cold beer, Jenda decided to take a walk through what her NaviGiz claimed was the primary arts district of San Miguel. The street was shaded by ficus trees, most of which looked to Jenda like the fabricated variety, which had become popular after the droughts that devastated much of the planet in the late 21st century. A fabricated ficus only required an occasional shower of water to remove dust, making no demands on dwindling underground water tables. The newest models even had miniaturized 3-D printing devices that produced new leaves according to a convenient timetable, letting fall the old ones in coordination with the schedule of cleanup crews.

Jenda located the first street of art galleries easily enough and went inside a few. She was not impressed. The work was nice but seemed hardly different from what she could have had printed up in Dallas at 3Dec, the three-dimensional printing company that dominated the interior décor industry.

She was on her way back to her hotel, on the verge of disillusionment, when a building down a side street caught her eye. The storefront, instead of exhibiting the popular digital skin with color-changing geometrics, looked as if it were hand painted with something like a surrealist landscape. The sign read "Galería Kukulcan."

The door to the gallery opened to the tinkling of small bells and Jenda found herself alone and surrounded by paintings that, although clearly recyclable 3D facsimiles, were a departure from the boring scripted fractals and formulaic abstract landscapes that prevailed in most of the commercial galleries. As Jenda examined each painting first from a distance and then close up, she became aware of someone else entering the room from a rear door.

"These are nice," she said casually, without turning around. "Do you ship internationally?"

"Nice." The answering voice was deep and resonant, but the tone was flat, perhaps sarcastic.

Jenda turned to see who was there. He looked like a native, with his tan skin and dark hair and eyes, but he was taller and more muscular than most of the Mexicans Jenda knew in Dallas. He was clean shaven, but his longish hair made him look a little unkempt. What caught Jenda's attention, though, was the streak of blue paint on the side of his white shirt. That and the fact that he was stunningly handsome.

"Yes, we ship to most places," he said, answering the question that Jenda had forgotten she asked. "Where did you have in mind?"

"Oh, I'm from Dallas. Texas. But I may be around for a while. Sabbatical, you know. No rush."

"Hmph." The man folded his arms and leaned against the door frame. "Not many people come here for sabbaticals. What made you choose San Miguel?"

"Well, the art I guess." Jenda paused. "I paint... a little. Or I used to. And I like to be around art. My mother was a sculptor." She was surprised that she had added that last statement.

"Really?"

"She worked in plexiform and plastimold, of course, but also in bronze. Quite a lot in bronze." Jenda was being somewhat reckless in disclosing her mother's penchant for bronze sculpture in an era when making things with intentionally limited lifespans was much preferred, keeping the economy ticking along as it did with recycling and remanufacturing.

"Bronze sculpture is hard to come by these days," the man responded.

"I really do like these paintings," Jenda said. "Who is the artist?"

"That would be me," he replied, with a slight bow. "Luis-Martín Zenobia, à la orden."

"I suspected as much," Jenda chuckled, turning to smile at Luis-Martín Zenobia.

"What gave me away?" he asked, returning Jenda's smile with one of those full-on smiles that crinkled his cheeks and lit up his eyes and made Jenda blush. "Was it my scruffy artist hair?" He ran his hand through his hair, looking like a mischievous schoolboy.

"Well, maybe that. But mainly it was that streak of blue paint on your shirt. Probably Phthalo blue."

"Argh! I thought I'd found one shirt with no paint on it, but it seems I failed." He looked down and scrubbed at the paint stain as if this might make it go away. "How long have you been in our beautiful little city?"

"I've only arrived today."

"And the first thing you did was come to the art galleries? That shows a bit of dedication," he said. "Maybe you would let me show you around to some of my favorite galleries."

Jenda cocked her head to one side, looking at the painting but seeing in her mind the captivating smile of Luis-Martín Zenobia. "That might be nice."

"How about Monday? The gallery will be closed then. About eleven?"

They said goodbye and Jenda went back to the hotel and finished unpacking her suitcase.

It turned out that Luis-Martín was an artist of some note, although his first career had been in anthropology, studying the traditional arts and crafts of the few surviving native populations of Mexico. As people had lost interest in adding to their burden of knowledge about the past, he had abandoned anthropology to devote himself to painting.

Luis-Martín produced a constant stream of novel images in the recyclable materials that society and the economy demanded. Some of his best customers were ready to buy a new piece at least once a month, blithely submitting one of the old pieces for recycling as they hung the new in its place. Luis-Martín had a finely tuned sense of what colors and shapes and patterns were most popular from week to week. He also had a finely tuned sense of how to please a woman, which was something Jenda discovered before she had been in San Miguel for a full week.

Jenda had always found a companion, a lover, on each of her previous eight sabbaticals. The first was the only serious one, leading, as it had, to her marriage to Benjamin Cohen. That marriage had lasted only until Ben's next leave. All of Jenda's subsequent sabbatical relationships had been carefully circumscribed. In light of this experience, Jenda was finding Luis-Martín Zenobia unnerving.

Luis invited Jenda to dinner at a restaurant that he promised would be much better than La Mazorca Loca. "Did you know the receptionist at your hotel is the son-in-law of the owner of Mazorca Loca?" he asked.

Jenda recalled having awarded that meal four stars. The restaurant Luis took her to, however, made her wish she had given Mazorca Loca only three stars, so the five she wanted to give El Piñal would be more meaningful. During dinner, Luis kept her entertained with stories about the history and culture of San Miguel, interspersed with jokes and personal tales of the local populace. Jenda loved listening to his stories. It gave her ample opportunity to study the way his eyes sparkled, the way his hands danced, the way his perfectly formed lips would suddenly part to let her glimpse his perfect teeth. Jenda felt that she had never known such a perfect man. Her mind tried to caution her about letting this potential relationship slip out of her control. But when Luis laid his hand casually over hers she yielded to a shiver of joy that passed all through her body, settling into a pleasing moistness between her legs. When Luis asked if she would like to come up to his apartment to sample some coffee liqueur he had acquired that day, Jenda's only gesture at control came in trying not to sound too eager.

They laughed the next morning as they looked at the unopened bottle of liqueur. Jenda realized she had not taken her usual tablet of Femozem, a pill designed to facilitate and enhance the feminine sexual experience. She hadn't had sex without it in at least 40 years and had come to believe it was essential. She didn't recall Luis having taken a pill either. She wondered how she could feel so satisfied, yet so eager for more.

This was not what was supposed to happen. Jenda needed to regain control. She hoped Luis wouldn't notice her sudden withdrawal, her cool silence over breakfast, the flimsiness of her excuse for going back to her hotel, for not being available for lunch. She did concede to let him walk her back to the hotel. She agreed to meet him for dinner.

Jenda lunched on her own. It was only a couple of tacos from a street vendor. They were bland and she ate them while sitting on a broken park bench. Jenda didn't know how to think about what had happened the night before, so she just let it replay. It left her – mind and body – wanting Luis. What she didn't want was this sense of being out of control.

Jenda's eyes settled on a woman seated at a corner of the park. The woman sat on the ground, trying to attract the attention of passers-by, trying to entice them to purchase what she was selling. Absently, Jenda rose from her bench and walked toward the woman. As Jenda approached, she saw that the woman was selling pieces of white cloth adorned with colorful stitched patterns. "Embroidery." The word came to Jenda, even though she was uncertain she had ever seen such work before. She picked up one of the pieces and turned it over in her hands. She could see that it was stitched entirely by hand. It was not perfect, but it was beautiful.

"You made this?" Jenda asked. She heard the note of incredulity in her voice.

"Sí, señora," the woman answered. "¿Lo quiere comprar?" She held up her digiscreen to show Jenda the price.

Jenda did want to buy it. She had no idea what she would do with it – it was only a piece of embroidered cloth – but she felt drawn to it. She wanted it. So she bought it and as she walked away, she studied the pattern, trying to discern some kind of meaning. All she saw was a display of flowers. Flowers and a little blue bird. But as she folded the cloth and tucked it inside her bag, she felt her mind settling and she began to look forward to dinner with Luis-Martín.

Before the end of another week, Luis invited Jenda to move into his apartment above the gallery and Jenda accepted. Luis' apartment was spacious by contemporary Dallas standards. There was an open living area and a balcony overlooking the tree-lined street. There was a tile-surfaced table with several brightly painted chairs for sit-down dining just like in a restaurant. There was a well equipped kitchen. The bedroom had a large bed and a huge window, which unfortunately opened onto a neighbor's rooftop terrace. Jenda insisted on hanging curtains, but contented herself with a diaphanous fabric that obscured the view without blocking the light.

A few days after Jenda settled in, Luis introduced her to what he called his "real art" studio, in the attic above his first floor commercial studio (which, he said, was really more of a factory) and his second floor apartment. Jenda didn't know what to think. The images were no different from the ones in his commercial pieces, since they served as prototypes for the recyclable, 3-D printed replicas. But there was something about the richness of the colors, the subtle detail, the texture and sheen of the surfaces that kept drawing her more deeply into the images. She didn't particularly like the smell of oils and turpentine, but she quickly fell in love with the work. And with Luis-Martín.

Luis was what had become known pejoratively in the commercial art world as a retrogressive, painting in real oil paints on traditional archival canvases that he carefully crafted himself. Of course, the commercial art world in 2125 only knew his 3-D replicas, which fetched premium prices. His originals were known only in an underground art world. The oil paints and rolls of natural canvas and pots of gesso Luis needed for his work were acquired from this underground network of people devoted to preserving the knowledge of how to produce durable fine arts and crafts. In a socioeconomic order in which high consumption was de rigueur, producing anything that was not intended to be readily and willingly recycled was anathema.

Jenda experimented with the oil paints in Luis' clandestine studio and, under his loving tutelage, began to rediscover the joy of painting. She wasn't sure whether the pleasure derived from the rich oil colors or from seeing her mental images take form on canvas. Or perhaps it came from the exhilarating sense of freedom she found spending time with this beautiful man in this secret place.

As Jenda fell into the rhythm of life in San Miguel and her new relationship, she almost forgot about the odd experience that had prompted her decision to come here. "Does it really matter?" she asked herself. The old woman in the café down the side street in Dallas had told her she needed to ask more questions, but when things were going so well, why should she? The only questions she felt like asking were the ones that helped her get to know Luis.

The man himself was a beautiful enigma. Jenda found his dissident tendencies exciting. He evoked something in her – a frankness, a creative assertiveness – that she found surprising. He invaded her dreams, although in her dream world Luis sometimes seemed darker and a bit shorter than her real world Luis. Once or twice he was accompanied by a lady in blue, a lady hidden in the shadows. Jenda thought she knew the lady. She thought she saw the lady beckoning her, entreating her to look behind the curtains, to find out what lay in those shadowy places. The lady in blue had a kind and tender countenance and Jenda found her terrifying. She wanted to tell Luis about this dream, but when she tried to remember it and put it into words, the images slipped away and she could think of nothing to say.

"What made you decide to do oil painting?" Jenda asked Luis one afternoon, as she stood back to examine her own small painting on the easel, trying to decide if the central image wanted a trace more Quinocrodone magenta somewhere offsetting the shadow to the right.

"It was never a decision," Luis said. "It just happened. When I was at boarding school in the US, one of my art teachers showed me some oils and real cloth canvases one day and I felt it was something I had to do. Some of us were already finding the trend toward recycling everything – and only making things that were intended to be recycled quickly – more than a little offensive." He paused and glanced at Jenda, as if anticipating some reaction. Then he continued. "I guess my attitude was a bit ungrateful, given that my education was being paid for by my father's success as an engineer and product designer for one of the major recyclables manufacturers."

"But you make recyclable paintings, too." Jenda wondered how he reconciled this.

Luis frowned. "It supports my real art. And I'm good at it. I can give people what they want. Is it wrong to make them happy?" He paused as the frown softened into a half smile. "My secret aim is to make my consumers feel at least a tiny twinge of regret when they drop one of my paintings off for recycling."

Jenda wasn't entirely sure she understood. Or maybe she didn't want to understand. Luis' motivations were at odds with the dominant culture in which she moved so successfully back in Dallas. The whole economy in 2125 hinged on the motivation to buy lots of things, use them for a short time, surrender them for recycling and buy more. Everybody agreed it was more satisfying to design new things, build new things, and buy new things than it was to deal with a lot of old stuff sitting around needing repairs and maintenance and eventual restoration. Anything worth keeping could be digitized and stored at Your Journal.

"So you did an art degree at university?" Jenda decided there was quite enough Quinocrodone magenta on her painting and she picked up a tube of Dioxazine violet.

"No," Luis responded. "I took lots of art classes in secondary school, but by the time I got to university I'd developed an interest in primitive and traditional arts, so I decided to do a degree in anthropology. And then one degree led to another." He stepped back from his own large canvas and turned to look at Jenda's painting.

"What do you think?" Jenda tilted her head side to side as she examined her work. It showed a female figure, her arms flung out, her head tilted skyward, as if dancing to a tune that emanated from the swirl of colors surrounding her.

Luis stepped closer to her easel, closer to Jenda. "I like it," he said. "It has great emotional intensity. Your color choices are excellent. It's a charming self-portrait, Jenda. And I like the slightly metallic quality…"

"Wait. What? Why do you say it's a self-portrait?" But as Jenda looked again at the painting, seeing it through Luis' eyes, she realized there was a strong resemblance.

"Didn't you intend it as a self-portrait?" Luis asked. "It sure looks like you – perhaps a more child-like Jenda, but I think this is definitely you."

"Well, it wasn't intentional. But I see what you mean." Jenda stuck her paintbrush between her teeth to adjust the band holding back her hair. "Who knows where these images come from anyway, Luis. You've said yourself that sometimes they seem to well up from nowhere. I'm glad you like it." Jenda dunked her paintbrush into the cleaning solution, deciding she was finished for the day.

"So in anthropology you had to do – what? Fieldwork? Where did you do that?" Jenda picked up the thread of their conversation, settling on the sofa.

Luis sat down next to her. He explained that he had done his doctoral dissertation fieldwork in Guatemala, working in some Mayan communities in the mountains and befriending a few contemporary Mayan artists who were practicing their ancestral arts. "One of them was also a shaman, an artist of ritual as well as a visual artist. He became my primary guide and friend."

"You call them informants, right?" Jenda tried to recall an anthropology text she had read in an introductory class in college.

"Oh god no!" Luis shook his head vigorously. "We stopped using that term long ago. Although, when I was in graduate school, there were still some heated discussions about it. No, that term…I hate it. The way I see things, field studies have to be cooperative. The people have to be full participants in putting together the stories that naturally belong to them." Luis paused, staring at his left hand and stretching out all its fingers, then massaging it with his right hand. "The first day I met Armando – the shaman I mentioned – he was sitting under a ceiba tree with his hand wrapped in a bloody cloth. I thought he looked like he was about to pass out, so I went over to see about him. It turns out he was trancing. I apologized for bothering him, but he laughed and said that he was taking advantage of the opportunity to make an offering to the vision serpent."

"The what?"

"A deity among the southern Maya – southern Mexico, Guatemala, Honduras. In ancient times they made ritual blood offerings. And one of their most important deities was the vision serpent, which connected with the Aztec Quetzalcoatl and Kukulcan among the northern Maya."

"So that's where you got the name of your gallery?"

"Exactly. Kukulcan – by whatever name – is a flying snake. Literal translation is 'feathered serpent'. I've always liked that image. Anyway, Armando had accidentally cut his hand on a machete in the field and decided since he was losing blood anyway, he'd just as well say the prayers of blood sacrifice. He was quite a character. I don't know how I would have gotten through my research without him." Luis paused, looking thoughtful. "Did you know that one of the Mayan words for the life force – which they identified with blood – was Chulel?"

Jenda hadn't known, although she had occasionally wondered how Pharmakon came up with such an odd name for their most profitable drug. Jenda always seemed to be learning something new from (and about) Luis. She liked that. Most of the people she knew were so predictable. They had so few stories of any interest about their past – most of them trivial, although sometimes amusing. But once you had known them for a while you knew all their stories. Of course, Jenda was just getting to know Luis, but there was something about his stories, something about the way they fit together that told her he was different.

~~~

Jenda and Luis began going dancing. At first Jenda objected, claiming that she didn't dance. But once Luis got her out on the floor, she wondered whether that was true. "I honestly didn't think I could dance, Luis," she said, after he insisted that she must have taken lessons. "I've always refused to dance, for as long as I can remember. But with you, I have to admit I'm really enjoying it."

She also enjoyed spending time fussing over a painting and trying to comprehend that it was not going to be digitized and tossed into recycling at the end of her sabbatical. Mostly Jenda enjoyed being with Luis. They frequently shared dinner in small cafés and loved going back to El Piñal, where they first ate dinner together. Occasionally they met up with one or more of Luis' friends for drinks. They took long evening walks through the parks. And of course there was their intimate time in bed, although Jenda was developing a predilection for sex on the studio sofa, where the scent of hers and Luis' aroused bodies blended with the odor of oil paints, producing sheer intoxication.

"You know I'm in love with you, don't you?" Luis said one evening, as they lay sprawled on that sofa, savoring the intoxication. He brushed back the strands of perspiration dampened hair that clung to Jenda's forehead and cheeks.

"Then I guess," she said, tracing the line of his jaw with her finger, "we're in love with each other." Luis leaned closer, his face almost touching hers. And then they kissed - a gentle, lingering kiss, expecting nothing beyond the moment.

Jenda and Luis spent many hours together in his commercial gallery and work space – Luis' "factory". Sometimes Jenda took the gallery's open hours as her time to wander off on her own. Once a week an art student from the local institute came to mind the studio and Jenda and Luis could take off together. Luis also had talked Jenda into minding the gallery on her own from time to time when he went out to meet with "people", which Jenda assumed meant clients or materials providers, although Luis didn't always say. She liked spending time alone in the gallery and she liked listening to the admiring remarks of the not infrequent visitors. She made some good sales.

"Did I ever tell you why I decided to come to San Miguel?" Jenda asked Luis one afternoon as they sat in the commercial gallery together waiting for customers.

"You said you came for the art."

"Well, yes, that's true. But there's a little more to it." Jenda screened off the book she had been reading and rested her forearms on the work table. "I had made reservations to go to a resort center in California. And I was supposed to leave in July, not May."

"You obviously changed your plans."

"Yeah. Because… Well, I was having a sandwich in a little lunchroom. One of those cafés that professionals don't go to, you know? Anyway, this woman – an old woman – started staring at me and then she came and sat down at my table. She knew my name. She said she knew me in high school. She asked if I still painted. And she knew my mother was an artist. But she also said other stuff – crazy stuff – about how she had idolized me and my boyfriend in high school. How we had been such… What was the word she used? 'Firebrands'?" Jenda suddenly felt this might all sound foolish and looked up at Luis to check his reaction. He looked serious.

"Really? And you didn't recognize her at all?"

"No. But she looked so old. How can you tell for sure when someone looks that old? But the upsetting part was when she got right in my face and said 'You need to ask more questions.'"

Jenda looked directly at Luis as she said this and the dramatization made her shiver, remembering. "And when I tried to tell her she didn't know who I was, she said that I was the one who didn't know who I am."

"And on the strength of that you changed all your plans?"

"Yeah. I can't explain why the experience affected me the way it did. It just made me want to do something different. To break out of my routines, I guess. Anyway, now I'm glad I did."

"Me too, querida."

Jenda was relieved that Luis now knew that little story. She was grateful that he hadn't asked questions because she felt certain she had no answers.

A few days later, Jenda was once again minding the gallery by herself. She looked up from the novel she was reading on her digilet at the sound of the tinkling bells and saw that it was Luis returning from one of his meetings. He was carrying a package that bore the distinctive shape of a bottle of their favorite tequila.

"Celebration time!" he announced. "I've signed a contract with Marvaworld to supply all of their corporate offices in Texas with a regular rotation of paintings. That should keep us in oils and canvases for quite some time. And, by the way, provide ample excuses for me to travel to Texas."

Although it was still an hour until closing time, he tasked off the "Open" sign and locked the door, grabbing Jenda's hand and giving her a quick kiss as they headed upstairs. It took them a while to get changed to go out for dinner, because Luis had been unable to resist joining Jenda in the shower. Her hair was still damp as they headed out into the early evening to their favorite café, having already shared shots of tequila as they got dressed.

As they lingered over dinner – which entailed a couple of margaritas each – Luis told Jenda the details of his contract and how it would mean taking on a regular employee to replicate the required paintings in the required numbers at the required intervals. Luis seemed excited about the contract, but Jenda also detected an edge of contempt in his voice as he related the frequency with which Marvaworld would want the paintings to be switched out.

"You're sure this won't take you away from your oil painting?" Jenda asked.

"No. Oh, no, not at all!" Luis said. "God, if I thought that I'd never do it. The only reason to produce these recyclables is the fact that it supports my real work. This is going to make our life better, I'm sure of it." And they gazed at one another, letting the fact that he had said "our life" sink in.

Both Luis and Jenda were slightly drunk as they headed back to the gallery apartment, but they decided to have one more shot of the celebratory tequila Luis had bought for the occasion. Jenda's was more like a half shot and she put it in a glass of orange juice. They went onto the balcony. By resting her head on Luis' shoulder, Jenda found that the world didn't wobble quite so much.

"Tell me more about your mother the sculptor," Luis said. There was a warm breeze and the lights from the street became fireflies amid the dancing leaves. "You told me about her that first day, but... The way you talked about her made me think..."

"My mother is dead," Jenda said. "You remember that spate of autocar accidents back in 2080? When there was that fault in the script update? My mom was one of the fatalities."

"I'm sorry," Luis said. "That must have been awful."

"Don't be sorry." Jenda felt the muscles of her shoulders and neck tense, as if trying to make up for the lack of mental discipline that was letting feelings about the loss of her mother bubble to the surface. "She had gone completely mad so it was possibly for the best." Jenda heard her words slurring slightly and her voice trailed off. The bubbles of sentiment were coalescing into images, memories. "She was delusional. She would get into these rants, claiming that people she was friends with had disappeared off her LifeBook chapters and Your Journal logs. She accused my father of drugging her and lying to her. Stuff like that." Jenda shook her head and the world wobbled. "The worst was this story she came up with about how I had gotten pregnant in high school. We showed her all the YJ records to prove that never happened, but she got crazier and crazier."

Jenda's eyes were having a hard time focusing and she was unclear whether it was the tequila or the pull of resurgent memories drawing her away. Maybe it was her tears that made everything blurry. "Mom was such a good sculptor. A wonderful artist. I wonder sometimes whatever happened to all of her beautiful work. It was so stupid. Her wreck was only two days before the script fix came out. She flipped out on a curve at full speed. She never knew." Jenda began to sob. "Poor Mommy. Why did she get so crazy? She was so good. I wanted her to know how much I loved her." Jenda surrendered. Luis held her gently as she wept, whispering quietly that he loved her, that surely her mother knew how much Jenda loved her. "There's nothing wrong about feeling sad," he said.

"I'm sorry, Luis," Jenda said, with one more jerky intake of breath as she wiped her eyes and nose with the back of her hand and searched for a tissue. "I don't know why this suddenly hit me like this." She wondered vaguely why she had never entered anything about it in her Your Journal files. Her files, she knew, contained only a bare mention of the circumstances of the death of Tessa Jenkins Swain and nothing at all about the descent into madness that had preceded it. "It must be the tequila." Jenda forced a smile. "I shouldn't drink so much." But she couldn't help wondering if this was the kind of thing the old woman had meant she should question.

"How about a cup of manzanilla tea before bed?" Luis said, standing up, still holding Jenda's hand.

Jenda looked up at him. "Yes," she said. "Thank you." She hoped he understood that she wasn't just talking about the tea.

33

4.

Amid mounting evidence of the success of their Chulel formula in 2040 – the year Max and Emily Feldman both turned 100 – the two researchers had decided to retire. It would be another decade before the concept of retirement gave way to the ten-year sabbatical.

The Drs. Feldman watched from afar the unfolding of the new world they had helped to create. When people had started turning 120, it was kind of a big deal. When their offspring started turning 100 it was an even bigger deal. When people were still around to celebrate their grandchildren's century mark, they began to wonder where it would all end. As the Drs. Feldman began to think that they would easily reach their 200th birthdays, they started having second thoughts about the great gift they had bestowed on humankind.

The big question that began to occur to observant and thoughtful people like the Feldmans was whether this present trajectory would end at all. It wasn't that people had become immortal; they were still vulnerable to physical violence and the few remaining infectious diseases that could kill you if not treated in time. But the medical professions were as diligent as ever in defending against all of these potential calamities. If anything, they had become even more adept at keeping people from dying of all kinds of things. Even violence, whether intentional or accidental, rarely resulted in death. Many of the tragically mutilated survivors of the last great wars were still alive, reminders of an incomprehensible time most people preferred to forget. Increasingly, death required deliberate intent. The new normal – the kind with Chulel – was for all the intact cells and organs of the body to continue regenerating in an orderly and reliable fashion, staying perfectly healthy and youthful indefinitely. The decline of cancer had been a pleasant side effect.

Reproduction had declined. As the generations piled up one after another, it seemed unnecessary. And then, of course, there were those unpleasant and potentially fatal interactions between Chulel and natural progesterone that at first interfered with and later discouraged reproduction. Fertility was near zero in all the primary corporate hub regions. The few children who were produced were seldom seem, being generally sent away to boarding colonies where they could be raised by professionals.

The pharmaceutical industry had been impacted rather severely by the decline in demand for the lucrative drugs that had addressed the chronic maladies of old age. There was a concomitant uptick in demand for mood drugs, and then after the so-called "War on Drugs" was finally brought to an end with the legalization of almost everything, big pharma found its new calling in the manufacture of all kinds of designer recreational drugs, which merged imperceptibly with the mood enhancers.

The Feldmans closely monitored their own health as well as that of the small colony of bonobos that had been receiving Chulel treatments longer than any humans, even Max. The bonobos occupied a forested reserve near the Pharmakon labs outside Atlanta, where they were cared for by one of the Feldmans' former assistants. The bonobos had been largely forgotten by Pharmakon, but the assistant continued to faithfully cater to all their needs and to provide their annual Chulel infusions and physical checkups. It was in the bonobos that Max and Emily first noted the slight deterioration in the beta chains of hemoglobin. A few years later, they detected the same deterioration in their own blood. The changes were very slight, but they bore an odd similarity to sickle cell disease. Max and Emily also noted that the effects were cumulative and that they were most pronounced immediately after an infusion of Chulel.

The health and demographic implications of the new order had been superseded in the Feldmans' minds by concern over an apparent side trip into memory management via cognitive photonic therapy. Max and Emily knew perfectly well that the widely touted memory loss that had come to be associated with Chulel was a fabrication. They had been taking the drug longer than anyone else – entirely self-administered – and they knew exactly what its effects and side effects were. Memory loss was not among them. And yet, in 2045 there had been a worldwide panic as FlixNews and Corporate News Network suddenly began reporting alarming memory loss associated with Chulel, stampeding people into enrolling in a digital storage corporation called Your Journal and receiving Chulel exclusively in spa-like clinics that promised memory maintenance and restoration. Max and Emily knew that Chulel maintained the brain in peak health, the same as any other physical organ. Their own memories of both distant events and recent occurrences remained remarkably clear. However, their interactions with people who were availing themselves of the "memory restoration" treatments that were offered at the Chulel spas caused them growing concern. It seemed to be producing some form of collective dementia.

The Feldmans had been more than happy to leave Pharmakon behind. They had felt some solidarity back in the early 2000s with what was originally called the "Occupy" movement, which had briefly tried to rally people against the domination of society, culture, and politics by big corporations and plutocrats. There were rumors that their movement had precipitated a clandestine reaction within the corporate world under the code word "Preoccupied." If it was real, it would indeed have been a clever tag for a project designed to keep people so self-absorbed and emotionally dependent on entertainment, novel material goods, and selected, media-hyped "causes" that they had no interest in real political involvement. They might even be convinced (as indeed they had been) that less government was best government. It was easily recognized by anyone who paid attention to such things that corporations and corporate alliances had become the only meaningful centers of power. Most people complacently accepted the idea that corporations were more reliable than governments in giving them what they wanted and needed for happy lives. As the true elites had become fewer and more powerful, they also had become more brazen. The advent of Chulel and, fortuitously, cognitive photonic therapy had been all they needed to solidify their hold.

There had been a campaign back in the late 21st century: "The best days of your life haven't happened yet. Make room for what's to come!" This had encouraged people to get rid of their last remaining boxes of mementos and artifacts from past eras. It was a cooperative venture between Your Journal and the recyclables manufacturers. The real estate corporations were also on board, as they were squeezing more and smaller residential units into limited urban space. Naturally, these smaller residential units had less and less storage space. The leading home décor company had followed up with their own campaign: "Why live in the past when you can have today's most gorgeous home?" So people had tossed out the last of the Tiffany lamps and the Hepplewhite dining room sets in favor of the latest limited-lifetime items from 3Dec.

The leading 22nd century economic sectors entailed the manufacture of recyclables, renewable energy (which had been wrested away from the off-grid delusionists and placed safely in the hands of the plutocrats who knew how to make it generate wealth), entertainment providers of all kinds (a category that included foodstuff producers and pharmaceuticals), and advertising. Of course all of it was done in the context of electronic/ digital/ computerized wizardry, but that had ceased to be considered an industry in itself. It was simply how corporations did business. And really, the less the populace knew about how it worked the better. Digital communications and information sharing had been on a dangerous trajectory around the start of the 21st century, with ordinary workers having access to almost everything across what was called the internet, as well as the ability to communicate with one another in an unregulated manner. They had tried to argue that this was their right. Heroes had risen up, disclosing the ways in which corporations and governments were attempting to manipulate and intrude upon these communications. Fortunately, the corporations had been able to consolidate their control by convincing people it was the governments that were the greatest threat. Before long, governments became practically irrelevant, conceding all authority to the corporations.

Max and Emily Feldman's first stop post-retirement had been Buenos Aires, where they intended to indulge their lifelong love of the tango and other things Argentinian. They had a fondness for old paintings and books and owned a couple of small works by Argentine painters such as Carlos Alonso and Xul Solar as well as books – physical books printed on paper – by Argentine writers including Jorge Luis Borges, Julio Cortázar, and Silvina Ocampo. In Buenos Aires, they discreetly pursued the possibility of acquiring a few more precious books and possibly even a new painting or two. They adored Buenos Aires and, although they lived briefly in many more places over the next seven decades, they kept returning to Argentina. They thought they just might stay this time. They had well and truly fallen in love with the porteños of Buenos Aires.

By the time they settled there for good in 2125, Max and Emily had been witness to many changes in their beautiful city. For one thing, the underground tranvía subterraneo or "subte" had been closed after the devastating floods of 2077, replaced by a solar powered elevated monorail winding its silent, serpentine way through the city. Its exterior was of an alloy that reflected back the colors and forms of its surroundings, but never the glare of the sun. The buses known as colectivos had been done away with. The corporate-owned tranvía alta was much more satisfactory, generating wealth as it did for the corporations and the plutocrats.

Max and Emily were pleased to find that their favorite little Buenos Aires art gallery – the Galería Picaflor – was still in existence, occupying a modest store front on a side street near where the now defunct Contemporary Art Museum had been.

All the public museums had disappeared. As weakened governments found it increasingly difficult to extract revenue from the globally peripatetic corporations that monopolized wealth, public institutions were put on austere budgets. Naturally, the corporations had come to the rescue. National parks went first. In Texas, California, and the USA, park lands had been sold off to corporate interests. Then the artworks of the major public museums, including the once venerated collections of the Musées de France, had been "deaccessioned" at cut rates as even corporate collectors and plutocrats lost interest in the so-called "old masters." The great libraries had been corporatized and subsequently reduced to mere facades for digital collections.

When Max and Emily first encountered the Galería Picaflor in the 2040s, many of the paintings were already being printed in unlimited editions on the increasingly popular recycled and recyclable canvases, but there also had been some traditional oils and even a few bronze sculptures. Now the gallery's inventory of paintings and sculptures appeared to be entirely of the recyclable type. Max and Emily were delighted to find that the woman who had taken over the Galería Picaflor shortly before the Feldmans' last visit to Buenos Aires in 2105 was still there. She was a sprightly woman by the name of Isabel Hernandez.

Isabel's English was as fluent as her Spanish and Emily's conversations with her tended to make use of both languages in about equal measure. "Where did you learn to speak such good English?" Emily asked one day, as she watched Isabel hanging some new pictures for an exhibit.

"Oh, you know," Isabel answered brightly. "Just around."

"No, really, Isabel. Your English syntax is far more sophisticated, your vocabulary much more extensive than what we hear from people who have learned from casual interaction with tourists and sabbaticos. Did you attend University in an English speaking country? You have a bit of a North American accent, you know. Kind of California even," Emily said. Languages and dialects were a hobby of hers.

Isabel's shoulders dropped a bit and she spoke without turning toward Emily. "I honestly don't know," she said quietly. "I guess I've just... forgotten."

"Oh, well," Emily said. "Probably not important. I was only curious."

Isabel finished straightening the painting she had just hung and turned to face Emily. "Actually, it is important. I wish I knew. They say it's the Chulel. I've never been able to get the treatments at the clinic where they give you the memory restoration. Some foreigners seem surprised that I haven't lost my memories altogether."

Isabel took a few steps back to look at the paintings she had hung. She shook her head. "Estas pinturas que se reciclen… ¡Que mierda!" Isabel glanced quickly over her shoulder at Emily, although she was pretty sure Emily would not judge her for this outburst.

Emily was laughing. "You used to have some real paintings, too," she said softly. "¿Que pasó?"

"Oh, I still have some. I'll show you once we get this exhibit over with."

That evening, over their usual restaurant dinner, Emily told Max what she had learned on her visit with Isabel. "The woman has always self-administered Chulel," she told him. "And yet she seems to have some huge memory gaps. What do you think that's about?"

Max looked thoughtful. "You know, there were rumors back in – oh, maybe around 2030 or so? – about some experimentation with photonic memory restructuring going on here in Argentina. Do you think maybe she could have got mixed up with that?"

"Could be," Emily replied. "I think she might be amenable to some assistance in finding out where she lost her memories." Max nodded thoughtfully, and Emily could see that he was already plotting a research strategy.

5.

"Do you want to go to a party tomorrow night?" Luis asked Jenda one evening around mid-July.

"Sure! What's the occasion?" Her mind went reflexively to considering what to wear.

"It's just a group of friends. We get together occasionally," Luis replied.

Jenda bought a pair of dark blue form-fitting pants and a sheer, billowing ivory-colored blouse over a lace camisole with a deep neckline. She complemented it with shiny dark blue high-heeled sandals and plexiform pearls. And of course she dropped off some things in the recycling, choosing one of her least sexy outfits.

When they arrived at the party, Jenda realized that she had already met most of the guests, although she had never thought of them as constituting a "group of friends". She didn't know that they knew each other. Luis introduced Jenda to a couple that she hadn't met previously – Tao-Min and Meli.

"Anything to report?" Meli asked, raising her wine glass to clink amiably with Luis' and leaning against Tao-Min's shoulder.

"No, nothing new from me," Luis replied. "What about you, Tao-Min, didn't you just get your annual Chulel? When, last week?"

"Last Tuesday, in fact," Tao-Min replied, her brow furrowing. "So far I'm not finding any discrepancies in my exomemories. Do you think maybe they're onto us and have stopped messing with records of Recall people?" She paused. Her smile was met with concerned looks.

Tao-Min and Meli were a beautiful couple. Tao-Min was taller with onyx hair, deep brown eyes and creamy skin over a spare, muscular frame. Meli was darker, a little plumper, with a round face and soft, sparkling gray eyes. There was something about Meli's face that Jenda found vaguely familiar – maybe like something in a painting she had seen somewhere. Looking at Tao-Min's and Meli's flawless faces and bodies, Jenda wondered absently what generation they were, or even if they were of the same generation. It was impossible to tell anymore. There were now at least five adult generations of people living together and, with the exception of Gen1 and to a milder extent early Gen2, they all looked much the same. Those first two generations had already been on the downslope toward old age when Chulel became available and the drug only arrested aging. It couldn't reverse it.

They also reminded Jenda of her brief engagement to Sandra and of Sandra's unfortunate disappearance in a mountain climbing accident. Homosexual and heterosexual had ceased being absolute categories some decades ago. It was understood that some people were unequivocally one or the other, but it was widely accepted that there was a broad middle ground as well.

"I still have a few more months of records to compare with what I wrote down in my handwritten journal," Tao-Min continued. "And then I'll need to compare the drawings in my sketchbook that I made from some of the original photographs."

Luis produced an exaggerated startle response. "Wait. You mean you've actually been following our advice and keeping handwritten records? And making drawings? Did we finally convince you to take this seriously, Tao-Min?" And he raised his wine glass to touch hers.

"My generation does still know how to write," she laughed. "In longhand script even. And – not meaning to brag – but I even know a good smattering of traditional Chinese characters. Poor Meli, here, on the other hand…" She tousled her partner's hair affectionately.

So Tao-Min could be late Gen2. If so, she was remarkably youthful and likely part of the earliest group to begin using Chulel, judging by her somewhat more robust frame and jawline, a feature that had ceased to develop once the artificial progesterone had been fine tuned. Meli must be at least Gen3 like Jenda, although she could just as easily be Gen4 like Luis or even Gen5. Nobody remarked on cross-generation partnering anymore, although it had initially seemed a bit scandalous.

Jenda started to say something about her own ability to write in longhand script – a habit rare among Gen3 and almost unknown Gen4 and beyond. But since she had no explanation for why she had developed this particular ability, she let the thought pass. Written languages, including English, had all evolved into layered forms of digital syllabic symbols. It was easy enough to input to a screen, but hardly anyone tried to replicate it by hand.

As the evening progressed, Jenda drank more wine and conversed with more of Luis' friends, all of whom shared a deep concern about the reliability of their exomemories at Your Journal. She noted that Luis was introducing her simply as an artist from Texas and not mentioning where she was employed. Everybody Jenda met had a story. A woman from Portland, Oregon, claimed that she still remembered being engaged in 2067 to a dissident writer who abruptly disappeared from her life and subsequently from her Your Journal file and LifeBook loop. She had no proof. A man from Mexico City told about a friend who claimed to have quit his job at Your Journal after he was asked to alter some photographic files. He had no proof either. His own YJ files suggested he had never had such a friend. Then there was the man from Montreal who showed Jenda a print photograph that included one more person in the group picture than was shown in the same group photo he showed her in his Your Journal file. He had no memory of who this person was.

As Jenda listened to the stories, she felt flattered by this evidence of Luis' trust. But she began to wish he hadn't trusted her with so much. Luis knew she worked for Your Journal, and yet here he was introducing her to people who appeared to think that YJ was intentionally messing with their memories. Is this what he thought, too? It was true that Jenda had joked with him a couple of times about a work colleague who had her office in the restricted area between the 12th and 34th floors where banks of primary digital termini were housed. Admittedly, she had waxed a bit melodramatic about how this woman was always vague when the conversation turned to specific aspects of her job. But it was just collegial teasing, and even the employee in question participated in the jokes. And then, of course, there were her own mother's chaotic memories that had begun to diverge so drastically from her YJ exomemories in the months before her death. And there was the old woman in the café.

Jenda leaned on Luis-Martín's arm as they walked back to the gallery after the party. Jenda's head was spinning, and she knew it wasn't just the wine.

"I like your friends, Luis," she said. "Of course, I'd met most of them before, but they seem different when you put them all together." She wanted to talk with him about all the stories she had heard from these friends, but she decided that could wait. Maybe tomorrow. Tonight she wanted nothing more than a warm cup of manzanilla tea and to cuddle up in Luis' arms for a long, restorative sleep.

Jenda woke the next morning to a bright sun blasting through her eyelids. She squinted, placed a hand over her eyes and turned lazily to reach for Luis. His side of the bed was empty but still warm. She opened her eyes and looked up to see him offering her a steaming cup of coffee and a smile.

"Come on, sleepy one," he said. "It's a beautiful day and I offer you a cup of real, authentic café." Jenda propped herself up on her elbows. The fragrance emanating from the cup was glorious.

"Why do you always call it 'authentic'?" she asked.

"My friends in the mountains grow coffee beans that are handed down from before Gen1," he said. "Their coffee may not have all the added benefits of the redesigned brews, but you have to admit, it tastes wonderful."

Jenda inhaled the heady steam once more and then took a cautious slurp. She closed her eyes. "Mmm. Delicious." Luis had put in a touch of honey and cinnamon, the way Jenda liked it.

He held out his hand and Jenda took it, letting him lead her out onto the balcony, where the glare of the sun was filtered through the shuddering leaves of the ficus and bougainvillea that lined the street. They settled into the wicker bench and the comfort of brightly printed cushions.

As they sipped coffee, Luis talked about the various trees and flowering plants they could see from their perch and what they were called both in Spanish and English and often in one of the Mayan languages as well. This was the kind of thing Jenda had always loved about a sabbatical. Nothing to do but revel in small things in the warm company of a new friend. But this particular sabbatical was different and she still felt uncertain about what might lie ahead.

"So, can we talk about the party?" Jenda asked.

"Cierto, mi amor. What shall we talk about? The wine? A local vintage from…"

"Let me guess – from your friends in the mountains who grow grapes from vines handed down from before Gen1," Jenda interjected.

"Actually, yes," Luis responded, pulling Jenda closer. "It was good, don't you think?"

"Pukka," Jenda agreed. "And the food was marvelous. And the house was beautifully decorated. And everybody was wearing the most amazing outfits. And…"

"Okay, okay," Luis grinned. "You want to know how I came up with a whole room full of people who have big questions about the place where you work ¿verdad que sí?"

"Sounds like a good start," Jenda said, sitting up straighter and moving a little bit away from Luis so she could better see his face. "Just start talking." It came out a little harsher than she had intended.

"Am I in trouble?"

"No. Sorry. It's just… I don't even know what questions to ask. Let's try, 'How did you meet these people?'"

"Ah." Luis took a deep breath, giving Jenda a look that seemed to say he hoped she could handle this next level of trust and wouldn't decide he was a madman. "We're all part of an informal group," he began, explaining that the group was known locally as Trivial Pursuit. They got together usually in

47

small groups, but occasionally in larger gatherings like last night's party. Luis told Jenda that they took their name from an old board game people played back in the 20th century. It made them seem innocuous enough, even a bit ridiculous, and certainly worthy of being ignored. They had found one another in various ways, but all were connected through a zone known as Recall and a communications portal called Interloc, all linking via what Luis called the infranet.

All this was new to Jenda. She was curious about why they did these things. But this wasn't what she most wanted to know about.

"What's your story, Luis? I heard lots of stories last night – some more believable than others – but I haven't heard yours yet, and I'm kind of assuming you have one."

"Mine's a little complicated." Luis paused. "Hard to know where to start."

"The beginning might work."

Luis settled back into the cushions, drained his coffee and set the cup down. He flexed his shoulders as if he were at the gym, about to begin some heavy lifting. "I will tell you the story as close to the truth as I can," he said, "although it may not be exactly the one stored with your office."

Luis' story was about his maternal grandmother who, he said, had taught English in Mexico and Spanish in Los Angeles, California, back in the first quarter of the 21st century. "When I was young, my mother used to talk to me from time to time about my grandmother, and the one thing I knew from early on is that my abuela died in Argentina when I was about six or seven. We were living in Merida, Yucatan, at that time. I remember very little about my grandmother, since I was just a little boy when she died. She had lived in California, and my mother was born there. That's where she met my dad – at Zuckerberg University."

Jenda shifted impatiently, wondering exactly where this story would link up with the whole matter of what did or did not occur at Your Journal.

"Anyway, when I was about six, as I said, my grandmother and my Uncle Julian – my mother's older brother – went away and my mother told me they had gone to Argentina. After a while – many months, I think – my mother went, too. She was gone a long time, or so it seemed to me. I remember being unhappy. My father was an engineer and was always at work, leaving me with minders. When Mama finally came back, she took me and we moved to California. She said my abuela had gone to be with Jesus."

"What does all this have to do with the idea of the unreliability of exomemories at Your Journal?" Jenda asked.

"Right. The thing is that my mother's YJ files have no information about her going to Argentina. Of course Abuela kept no YJ files at all. Yes, yes – I know. I'm not supposed to be able to access someone else's files. Anyway, my mother never liked talking about Argentina and after about 2045 she never spoke of it again. Even when I would ask her about it, she didn't seem to know what I was talking about. Recently, though, I found this little notebook that belonged to my mother, and it had some addresses in it that turned out to be in Argentina – in and around Buenos Aires. When I searched out the exact locations of the addresses from the little book, I learned that they were jails and prisons. So now I have to conclude that is where my grandmother ended up – in prison in Argentina. And I think my mother must have been down there trying to take care of her by bringing her things. There were little lists in the book – things like soap, hand lotion, toothpaste – personal things a woman might need." Luis ran his finger around the smooth lip of his coffee cup.

"And your mother doesn't remember any more about being there, other than your grandmother's death?"

"And even that isn't in her YJ files."

"Odd." Jenda was trying to come up with an explanation. "Have you talked to your mother recently about this?"

"I can't talk to her, Jenda, because my mother is dead." Luis' gaze wandered off toward the mountains, to the far horizon where the morning mists still lingered.

"Oh, I'm sorry, Luis. I was wondering… from what you said…" Jenda leaned a little closer to him and covered his hand with hers. "How did your mother die?"

"I don't even know." Luis told Jenda how he had received a notice from his mother's habitat management indicating they had received word of her death and that the unit was passing into the hands of someone whose name Luis didn't recognize. "Probably a member of the Christian organization she joined. Once I was in high school, she moved off with them and we lost touch." Luis said that first his father and then he himself had made payments on his mother's habitat unit, hoping she might return, but the right of occupancy passed to this stranger rather than to him. There were legally executed papers.

"Didn't that make you angry?" Jenda asked.

"A little. But mostly it made me sad. At least I was able to go through her stuff and salvage some things – especially that little notebook about my grandmother." They sat silently for a while, holding hands.

The sun suddenly glinted off a glass lantern on the balcony and Jenda blinked. "I was in Argentina once," she said.

"Really? When was that?"

"Oh." Jenda dug the heels of her hands into her eyes. "I don't know. Maybe I went. Maybe a long time ago. It doesn't matter. Wasn't there anything else in your mother's little book?" Jenda suddenly felt angry and she didn't know why. She got up and walked the few steps to the railing, leaning into the breeze that stirred the leaves and scattered the sunlight.

"Her notebook did have some other entries – more like little diary notes. She wrote about being worried that my grandmother was becoming forgetful – even senile – and she thought she was being mistreated in the jails. Poor Mama. All of this must have been distressing to her." Luis paused. "There were also a couple of names with addresses in the little book, and one of them led to an old fellow who remembered a few things about Abuela and her activities there in Argentina."

"Old? How old?" Jenda returned to the settee.

"It's hard to say. He hadn't been taking Chulel. Maybe he had had some treatments earlier on, but he was definitely showing his age when I contacted him in… I guess it must have been three years ago – in 2122."

"So you talked with this man? Where? In Argentina?"

"Well, yes. Querida, once you lose faith in the corporate records and the corporate communication channels, the only thing is to go and see with your own eyes and hear with your own ears."

"So what else did you learn from your old man?"

Luis said that the old Argentine was named Silvestre Ocampo. "His memory was faltering a bit with age, but when I mentioned my grandmother's name – Isabel Hernandez – he started telling stories."

"'La bella Isabela,' he called her. He was only a kid when Abuela Isabel was in Argentina, but he remembered her. Silvestre told me that she liked him because of his aunt, Silvina Ocampo, who she claimed was one of her favorite authors." Luis chuckled softly. "Silvina was more likely Silvestre's great-great-aunt, but who's counting? Or in fact they may have just had the same last name. Makes little difference to the story."

"And that's all you know about your grandmother?"

"I know that she received a degree in languages and literature from the Universidad Nacional Autonoma in Mexico City in, I think, 1996. That part is – was – still on record. There is still a lot I don't know. I haven't even been able to find a photograph of her. I searched everywhere. And my own memories from early childhood are of course pretty vague."

"There's a bit more that I learned from Silvestre." Luis resumed his story. Silvestre had told about going with Isabel to an estate off in the countryside, behind a tall fence. "He said they never went in through the main gate – there were guards with big guns. They knew a way in through a place where a fallen tree had broken down part of the fence. Silvestre said he would wait near the fence until Isabel returned and that she always came back carrying a little package. And then Silvestre told me that one day Isabel simply disappeared. Later a woman showed up looking for her – that would have been my mother, Juana."

Jenda and Luis sat in silence as Jenda processed what he had told her. Luis watched her face.

"And there's nothing at all in your mother's Your Journal files about being in Argentina?" Jenda asked. This was the part she was having trouble with. Mysterious buildings in the countryside and imprisoned teachers of language and literature couldn't even be entertained as real until she dealt with this question. Jenda's professional life for the past 90 years had centered on writing and producing compelling advertising campaigns about how Your Journal helped you remember, how it protected your privacy, and was "Your Lifeline to Your Life's Story". That one had been her campaign and she had felt great pride in its success.

"How could that happen?" Jenda continued. "Maybe the old man had her mixed up with somebody else. Maybe she didn't go there." She was feeling irritated again.

"But I remember her going. We used to talk about it."

"Yeah, but you were just a little kid. Maybe…"

Luis inhaled deeply. "What about the book?"

"Okay, I guess that's kind of hard evidence, isn't it." Jenda stared intently at the blossom on the banana tree below the balcony. She wondered how long it might take for the blossom to turn into ripe bananas and if perhaps Luis had some ripe bananas in the kitchen that they could have for breakfast. She watched her mind doing its best to run away from where Luis was trying to take it. She watched herself trying to evade the wave of anger that seemed to be coming from nowhere.

"I talked to Silvestre's wife, too. She remembered Abuela Isabel being there, even though she was only ten or eleven at the time. Silvestre and his wife are still there," Luis said. "You could go talk to them if you want."

"Really?" Luis' whole story felt somewhat surreal. It was disturbing. Jenda slumped back into the cushions.

"Okay, let's say maybe I believe all this. Most of it." Jenda sounded tentative. "Damn it all, Luis. You're going to have to give me some time. Let me think about it, alright?"

Jenda felt there was something in Luis' story that resonated with something she had forgotten, yet every time she tried to identify what that might be, it slipped away. It was infuriating.

6.

Over the next several months of her sabbatical, Jenda listened to more stories and her mind began to formulate clearer questions. Answers were elusive, and her body reacted to her mental disarray with a whole host of symptoms - headaches, dizzy spells, and loss of appetite.

Luis jokingly accused her of being pregnant. "Isn't that what used to happen to women when they would become pregnant?"

"At the age of 111?" Jenda rejoined, with a weak smile. Luis gave her hand a reassuring squeeze.

"Do you need me to get you some more meds?" he asked.

"No. No more meds, I think. Nothing but fresh bananas and some more of that pre-Gen1 coffee from your friends in the mountains," she replied.

"So now you're craving bananas?" He dodged the bed pillow Jenda swung at his head. Maybe she was recovering.

By late that afternoon, Jenda was feeling even better. Good sex always made her feel more centered. As she and Luis snuggled under the damp sheets, she asked one of the questions that had been forming in her mind for several weeks now. "What can I do about all this?" she said softly. "My sabbatical is eventually going to end and I'll be expected to go back to my job at YJ. If it's as bad as you and your friends say, maybe I should give notice and find some kind of work that's less distasteful."

Luis stroked her cheek and secured a stray strand of her golden hair behind an ear.

"Let's think about that," he said. "Tell me more about what it is you do at Your Journal."

Jenda reminded him that she was in the advertising department, one of several people tasked with coming up with new campaigns to keep people mindful of how important it was to screen in and journal on a regular basis.

"So you don't actually have access to any customer files?" Luis asked.

"Sometimes I do. When I have a particular project in mind, they let me sift through recent files to get a better idea of what's on people's minds, what they're currently interested in. You know," she said. "Research."

"Market research," he countered. "Do they give you some kind of general access phrase that gets you into the files?"

"I guess it's a general access. But I don't enter it myself. Somebody else always gets me in and then I work away until I have what I want."

"This is okay. This could work." Luis lay back on his pillow and stared at the ceiling.

"What do you mean, Luis? Work how? What are you thinking?"

"I'm thinking, " he replied, "that if you're up for it, you might be able to help us get access to some information that would help the Recall network understand more about what goes on at Your Journal."

Jenda raised her eyebrows. She was getting a twinge of that sensation she had felt right before she switched her sabbatical from California to San Miguel de Allende.

"It would be better if you had some kind of access phrase. Of course if they gave you something like that, it would probably be changed the minute you screened off. So never mind. This is okay. There are ways of detecting when files have been altered. I could teach you how to look for those indicators."

Jenda looked away.

"But we can do that tomorrow," he said. "And only if you want to. Today you rest and tonight we'll go to a nice café for some supper. Tomorrow we can work."

Jenda woke the next morning with a sense of dread. She tried to recapture the brief thrill she had felt the day before, but it was gone. Did she want to get into all of this? She felt Luis' arm steal across her torso and pull her closer. "Let's not work today," he said. "Let's close the gallery and go for a walk and

56

let you recover some more. It's a good day for a walk. It's a holiday in some of the old neighborhoods and we can enjoy the fun."

Jenda was relieved. "What holiday? What day is today anyway?" She had lost track.

"It's the second of November – el Día de los Muertos."

"Well, that doesn't sound like much fun. Dead people day?" Jenda pulled the covers back up around her chin and glared at Luis.

"Sorry, mi amor. I guess it's not a very important holiday in your culture." He shrugged. "Not even very important in mine anymore, but some of the people still enjoy it." And he explained that it was a day when people honored their ancestors – the deceased ones. "Of course, not so long ago, almost all of one's ancestors were deceased."

"Not like today, when you can go visit your grandparents and great-grandparents at their habitat instead of at the cemetery. Even your great-great-grandparents if you happen to be Gen4 or 5. Nobody goes to cemeteries anymore."

"Well, some of these people do. For most of them, though, it's just a day to get together with family and friends and enjoy music and dancing and good food and sweet cakes shaped like little skulls."

"Ewww!" Jenda hid her face in the pillow. "You're trying to make me sick again."

"No, no! I promise you, querida, they are delicious cakes and the skulls don't look realistic at all. They look more like… like little clown faces."

"Luis! You know I hate clowns."

"Oh, come on. Get over yourself and come along and see if you can have some fun doing some of the crazy things your crazy partner's crazy people do."

Luis stood up and held out his hand. His smile was that warm, engaging, big-as-the-world smile that had attracted Jenda to him from the outset. Jenda held back for a moment, then grasped his hand firmly and raised herself slowly from the bed.

"Okay then. Let's go play with your crazy dead people."

The day turned out far better than Jenda anticipated. They strolled at leisure along shaded streets through neighborhoods she had not been to before, neighborhoods where people still lived with their families. Whenever she got tired, they would stop at a sidewalk bar to sip fruity rum punch or they would sit for a while in one of the little parks or plazas along the way. They spent more time sitting than walking.

Luis took her to a few small art galleries, most of which had special displays of Día de los Muertos curios for people to buy and take home with them. Luis knew all the gallerists and shopkeepers. One of the gallerists invited them into the back of his space, to a locked room where he kept what he called his real art – oil paintings and sculptures in stone and bronze. Jenda recognized a few of the paintings as Luis' work. They lingered over a graceful small bronze of a girl reading a book.

"I love this artist's work," Luis remarked. "So sensitive."

"You know this artist?" Jenda also found the piece captivating.

"Not personally. We know her name, though – Setha Tica."

A little further down the street, they entered a small shop selling old paper books, maps, and printed photographs. Jenda picked up a few of the books and found the feel of them in her hands had a curiously comforting effect. She felt the urge to sit down on the floor and open them up one by one and read. One of the books had a warped cover and water stains on its faded binding. When Jenda opened it, she found that many of the pages had stuck together. She felt sad, thinking how whole sections of the story had disappeared into those ruined pages. She wondered why no one had tried to pry the pages apart. She returned the book to the chaotic jumble on the table and picked up another one.

"What are you finding there?" Luis asked.

"Oh…" She looked at the book's cover. "It's something called *The Wonderful Wizard of Oz*. I was wondering if maybe I had seen it somewhere before. Probably not. Look at these strange characters on the front – a little man made of metal and another stitched together out of rags." She ran her fingers over the figures and then laid the book back on the table. Jenda had suddenly thought of her brother Jonathan and wished Luis could meet him; she thought they would probably like each other.

As they made their way toward the door at the front of the shop, Luis stopped abruptly and looked around at all the books and other things on paper. "You know," he said, "Sometimes I feel like we and our things have been evolving in opposite directions – human beings becoming more enduring while the materials we use to record our memories become more temporary, transient." He picked up a tattered paperback in one hand and a well preserved leather-bound volume in the other. "Of course, nothing lasts forever. It all changes. But I keep thinking – wouldn't it be better to encode our memories on a more human scale? Something more than the momentary digital image but less than the bronze and stone objects we call permanent?" He put the books back on the table, still lost in thought.

"Thank you, Dr. Anthropologist." Jenda hadn't meant to be dismissive of Luis' comments, but the experience of being in the bookshop had made her feel like a kid again and she was having a hard time remembering to behave like an adult.

"So let me tell you more stories about my ancestors," Luis smiled, taking Jenda's hand as they made their way back onto the street. "Día de los Muertos is one of our distinctively Mexican holidays," he said, "a mezcla of old Spanish Catholic customs with even older native ones. Our ancestors believed that crying and mourning would insult the dead ones, and so they celebrated, with lots of good food and drink and music and dancing and entertainments of all kinds."

"I like that part."

"You know, not so long ago, people considered death to be part of life, not so different from birth, childhood, growing up. So on this day, they celebrated as if those who had died were still part of the living community."

"So now that our ancestors are mostly still among the living, I'm not sure I get the point," Jenda said, although she was enjoying this glimpse of the world according to Luis.

"Well, just go along with it at least and let's have fun," he said, as another group of troubadours marched down the street in their calaveras masks, dancing to the raucous sounds of a mariachi band.

The next morning Jenda was feeling better than she had in weeks. She and Luis lingered over mugs of steaming coffee on the balcony.

"Are you ready for your first lesson?" Luis looked ready.

"Ready as I'll ever be."

They passed through the kitchen to refill their coffee mugs and then settled in front of Luis' large digiscreen.

"What I'll show you first is how to recognize that a photograph has been altered."

"How do you even know about these so-called indicators?" Jenda was becoming more skeptical than she had been before meeting Luis, who didn't mind when she aimed her skepticism at him. He seemed to like questions.

At first, he said, they had used a specialized script to analyze files for evidence of tampering, but since personal digiscreens were kept under surveillance by the corporations, these extraneous scripts had a tendency to disappear overnight. Then one of the Recall geniuses had come up with a way of adapting some standard scripts to the task. They also designed gizmos to masquerade as something else, something harmless and trivial. It made analysis more tedious and time consuming, but it was more secure. Luis screened up some of his own Your Journal files and opened two pictures in PhotoStyle.

"Hey, I didn't know you could do that." Jenda had always understood that Your Journal files could only be opened in Your Journal and not with any other script.

"Some of us can do that," Luis replied, looking smug. One picture showed him with a beautiful woman at one of the more popular restaurants in San Miguel. "That was before I knew you existed, mi amor," he said, grinning at Jenda. "She was only a harmless diversion." Jenda silently hoped that she wasn't going to be described the same way in another ten years or so, but all she said was "She's very pretty." The other picture showed Luis by himself in front of an art gallery. It didn't look like San Miguel.

"Where was that taken?" she asked.

"Buenos Aires."

"So now we play 'What's wrong with this picture?' Right?"

"Right." He clicked through a complex sequence of processes for each image, some of which Jenda found familiar, but others she didn't recognize. The way he quickly ran through the sequence suggested that he had done this many times before. He ended up with each image transformed into a screen full of dots. He scrolled through the picture from the local restaurant. "This is how things should look," he said. "See how smoothly the dots align? But now look at this." He pulled up the picture from Argentina and, once Luis pointed it out, Jenda could see some dots that didn't align with the surrounding area. Luis placed a dark line along these vaguely defined margins and then zoomed out.

"Wayee!" Jenda's eyes widened. What she saw was the ghost outline of another person, apparently a woman. "So I guess your girlfriend must have been in this picture, too."

He shook his head. "No. It was Rosalí. Silvestre's wife."

"Okay, now I'm getting confused. You're saying Your Journal altered your photo but you still remember who was in it before? I thought that memories were reconstructed because of the things you forgot due to the Chulel."

"You know better than that, Jenda. You've heard other people's stories, seen their pictures."

She knew. She knew things she desperately did not want to know. Her mind kept resisting, reverting to her old ways of thinking, shielding some last few tenuous scraps of reassurance that she had not been employed for the last 90 years in convincing people to surrender their minds and life stories to a pack of carefully crafted lies.

"You know," he continued, "that Chulel doesn't actually affect the memory at all."

That was the most difficult piece, the one that threatened the last shred of self-respect that Jenda had been hanging onto.

Luis was relentless. "The forgetting is part of the little show you get that is supposed to be helping you remember. Anyone who uses off-market Chulel knows this." He reminded her that it was after the big lost memories scare back in 2045 that people had become afraid to take Chulel at home and had eagerly signed up at the new Chulel clinics that offered memory restoration using the customer's own Your Journal records.

"So you self-administer Chulel?" Jenda hadn't known about that. Why did knowing about it annoy her so? "But how do you avoid your appointments – and all those reminders?"

"I self-administer, as you say, and I always have, so I've managed to stay off their appointment calendars. But others go in for their appointments as expected. They smuggle in earplugs and opaque contact lenses so that they're shielded from the photonic memory reconstruction process."

Remembering her own invariably pleasant experiences of Chulel spa days with memory restoration, Jenda felt her defenses and her ire rising. But had they really been so pleasant? She felt sudden sparks, electric pricks throughout her body. Small white explosions. Fear.

"Really, Luis? Come on. That's ridiculous!" Jenda knew her anger was irrational, but it felt real and it was keeping her focused. "No, really. Now you're making stuff up. No, that can't be. I refuse to believe it!" The questions had been bad enough; the answers threatened Jenda's mind like a jackhammer. She wanted to get away. She shoved her chair toward Luis.

As he started to speak again, Jenda raised her hands in front of her face. "No!" she shouted. "Enough! Leave me alone. I don't want to hear anymore." She grabbed up her shoulder bag and, shoeless, stomped out of the house, down the stairs, and into the midday sun. Tears were coming, but she refused them. "No," she told herself. "I've let all this get to me too much already. I've had enough. I want my boring, trivial little life back." The graveled walkway was hurting her feet and it felt good. Her mind was in turmoil.

Jenda stopped next to a fountain in the heart of the little park. The grass under her feet felt cool and soft. She stood there, listening to the splashing water. She watched it spurting up, spilling over the first level, the second level, disappearing somewhere beneath the ground to emerge again through the little spout at the top and continue its monotonous cycle. Some of it splashed out onto the ground and disappeared, nourishing the thick carpet of grass. Jenda sat down. The sun was warm on her face and arms. Almost too warm on this sunny November day, but every once in a while a cloud passed overhead and Jenda clung to each deliciously cool shadow. She didn't want to think, she only wanted to feel the sun, the shadows, the cool grass, and listen to the fountain.

By the time the sun approached a more oblique angle, Jenda had given in to her tears. She clasped her arms around her bent knees and put her head down so that no one would see as she wept silently. When her tears finally ran out, she lifted her sweater to wipe her face. "What was it Granny El used to say?" she mused. "You can't put the toothpaste back in the tube." However much she might want to un-know what Luis had shown her, she knew that was impossible. She might have been able to live with a delusion imposed from outside, but she couldn't – she wouldn't – delude herself. She did want to know. She did want to ask questions and whatever the answers might be, she wanted to know.

Jenda sat a while longer, feeling cleansed by the sound of splashing water. Then she rose, brushed herself off, and began to walk slowly back to Luis' place, keeping to the grassy patches and the smooth paving stones.

She half expected the door next to the outdoor staircase to be locked and her suitcases on the top step. Instead the door was slightly ajar and when she went inside she saw a glass on the table filled with sweet hibiscus tea and some mostly melted ice cubes. The glass sat in a puddle of condensation.

"So you finally decided to come back?" Luis was standing in the shadows by the door that led to the balcony, his arms crossed. His voice was tense.

"What made you think I'd come back at all?" Jenda countered, with a covert sniffle.

"I guess I hoped you would."

"What, so I wouldn't mess up your crazy subversive plot to expose some incredible conspiracy?"

"No, Jenda, I just... I've pushed you. I'm sorry."

"No, Luis. No apologies. Why should you apologize for showing me the truth? I don't understand why I got so angry. There are things I can't explain. But I want to, Luis. I want to know the truth."

Jenda took a couple of steps toward him and stopped. She looked up into his moist eyes. This was her life now, and she was ready to embrace it.

Luis reached his hand toward her and she took it. They each stepped forward, then leaned together, their arms around one another.

7.

Despite her new resolve, Jenda continued uploading daily posts and photos to Your Journal throughout her sabbatical, largely out of habit, but also due to what she now suspected was an implanted sense of guilt if she failed to give YJ something for the day. Her posts became increasingly cursory and her photos were now more likely to be pictures of streets or shops or trees in the park rather than of anybody or anything of significance to her personally. She spent long hours in the art studio, painting.

One afternoon, she became a bit stuck with the painting she was working on and began exploring a far corner of the studio that she had not paid much attention to previously.

"What are these?" she asked, picking up a thin but colorful paper book encased in a translucent envelope. There seemed to be a large stack of similar items.

Luis looked over his shoulder to see what had caught Jenda's interest. He smiled. "Those," he said, "are my prized possessions."

"Oh." She looked puzzled.

Luis placed his brush in the container of solvent and wiped his hands thoroughly with a clean white cloth. He walked over to where Jenda stood holding the book gingerly as if it were some strange specimen. Luis took the book from her and lovingly removed it from its envelope.

"This, mi amor, is a Batman comic book." He took Jenda by the hand and led her back to the shelf where she had found the book. "On this shelf, I have an almost complete collection of Batman comics, all carefully preserved in archival sleeves." His face radiated pride.

"What is a batman?" Jenda asked.

"¡Ay, pobrecita! How could you live so long without making the acquaintance of the Dark Knight, the incomparable Batman, el Hombre Murcielago? Come here, querida." He sat down on the floor in front of the shelf and motioned for Jenda to join him. "Sit here and I will introduce you."

First he pointed to the figures on the cover. "This one with the black cloak – this is Batman, the Dark Knight, champion of all that is good, protector of the weak. His real identity is… but we'll get to that later."

"What about that one?' Jenda pulled her knees up close to her chest and pointed to another figure.

"That," Luis said, "is the evil trickster known as The Joker, Batman's nemesis."

"I can see how evil he is. He has a clown face."

Luis opened the book. The first couple of pages were just pictures without words. Jenda followed Luis' finger and the story began. On the next page, there were little white bubbles representing speech, pointing toward the person who was speaking. Luis read aloud, using different voices for Batman and Joker and the other characters. When they came to a page with a woman speaking, he attempted a falsetto to read her words.

Jenda laughed. "No, silly, let me read that one." And she read the woman's words in her best theatric voice. And so they proceeded through the entire story, reading the various voices, alternating between melodrama and laughter. Luis was especially good at reading the sound effects.

When the story finally ended, he closed the book and asked, "So what do you think?" He replaced the book in its protective cover.

"I think that's some pretty scary stuff," Jenda said. "But I like your Batman. I think he's my new hero. Can we read another one?" And so they read another. Reading comic books became their second favorite break activity in the studio.

~~~

Jenda would have let her 2025 birth anniversary pass unnoticed if Luis had not become aware of it when he joined her LifeBook loop. It was on November 18. Luis remembered something he had read about Texas birthday traditions and decided he would buy her a cluster of brightly-colored helium balloons, a bouquet of real fresh-cut flowers, and a cake with tiny candles. After considerable effort, he had located sources for all of these items. On the morning of her birthday, Luis said nothing to Jenda, having ascertained that an element of surprise was part of the tradition. He was relieved when she announced she was going shopping, as he had not yet settled on a plan to keep her out of the house while he gathered the requisite items from their various sources and arranged them for her.

"No problem," he said, indicating that he would be available to mind the gallery himself all day if necessary. "But on your way home, would you mind stopping by Federico's gallery for me and pick up a pot of gesso? If you do it last thing, you won't have to carry it far." Luis had at least figured out how to determine when she was on her way home; Federico would pulse him.

Jenda agreed. She kissed Luis goodbye and left by the front door, to the sound of tinkling bells. She was looking forward to a shopping excursion. She had been worrying again about her eventual return to Dallas and Your Journal. She hoped shopping would help calm her mind.

It didn't. If anything, the process of sifting through rack after rack of recyclable garments made her feel even more agitated. "It's all so temporary," she thought angrily. "It's what they want us to do – keep buying more and more things every day and feeding their recycling machine. Bright colors, flashy patterns – it's only to attract our attention. Some of these things are just ugly!" Jenda wondered if the so-called fashion trends weren't somehow included in the memory reconstruction process, herding consumers into buying exactly the things the corporations had already decided to produce. She needed clothes, though, so she bought a few outfits, fully aware that she was selecting what would likely be considered the least fashionable items on the racks.

Her shopping trip didn't take long and Jenda was already on her way back to the gallery apartment when she remembered the gesso. She didn't want to disappoint Luis. Perhaps she didn't want to have to discuss her agitated state of mind with him, which her failure to keep her promise might reveal. Better to backtrack the few blocks to Federico's gallery and get the gesso.

As she finally opened the door to Galería Kukulcan, the sound of the bells gave her a welcome sense of safety. "Luis?" Jenda called. Luis was not at his usual place behind the little desk that gave him a view of the gallery from his factory space. Then she heard him running down the stairs. He looked a bit breathless. "I got your gesso." Jenda held out the package wrapped in brown paper.

"Gracias, querida," he said. "I see you have a few more packages, too. So you had a good morning?" He didn't wait for her to answer, but took her hand as he said. "Let's close and go up for some lunch."

"You made lunch?"

As they entered the apartment from the stairwell, Jenda saw the reason for Luis' excitement. The place was filled with balloons and flowers. And there in the middle of the little tile-surfaced table was a sugary cake inscribed "Happy Birthday Jenda." There were tiny candles on the cake.

"Surprise!" Luis said, looking pleased with himself. "Happy birthday, mi amor!"

Jenda was speechless, barraged by a contradictory set of feelings, thoughts, and vague memories. Tears came to her eyes and she couldn't have said whether they were tears of joy, anger, or sadness. She sat down heavily on an arm of the sofa, facing the table with its disturbing cake, her hand over her mouth, her eyes wide.

"Oh, Luis, you shouldn't have," she said.

"Really?" He looked crestfallen. "I thought it would make you happy."

"No, I mean... it's so sweet. And you went to so much trouble." Jenda got up and threw her arms around Luis, "Thank you. You are a dear, precious man."

Jenda was beginning to understand that if she ever expected to come to terms with memories that might have gotten rearranged in her own mind, she should welcome these ambiguous moments and try to let them move freely through her. It wasn't easy.

Luis pulled out a lighter and began to light the candles.

"Oh, do we have to," Jenda began, her brow furrowing slightly.

"But I thought there was a custom about making a wish," he responded. "You don't want to miss your wish, do you?" He was grinning, apparently enthralled by the whole process, not noticing her discomfort.

"Okay. Of course." She did seem to remember something about wishes. It all reminded her of her mother and she felt a strong urge to be held.

Luis lit all the candles – there were ten of them – and stood back. "I think there used to be a song to wish the happy birthday," he said, "but I couldn't find it. So I'll just say 'Happy birthday, Jenda!' And now you wish something and blow out the candles, right?"

Jenda paused, watching the candles burn, trying to decide what to wish. "I wish…"

"No, no! I don't think you're supposed to say it out loud – your own private wish." Luis took her hand. Jenda looked up at him then and felt what he was wishing for; she silently wished the same thing. Then she blew out the candles.

"And now," she said with a laugh, "I'm pretty sure we're supposed to eat a piece of cake before we have lunch."

The next day Jenda told Luis she needed to go look for some new shoes to match the outfits she had bought. Truthfully, she just wanted to get away on her own. She didn't understand why the odd candle-bedecked cake had upset her and she needed some time to reflect.

Without thinking, she found herself following the route that Luis had shown her on Día de los Muertos and within a short while she was deep into the neighborhood that belonged to the native Mexican inhabitants of San Miguel. She found a sidewalk café that she remembered visiting with Luis. She sat down at one of the tables and picked up the plastiflex menu screen. She was a little hungry, so when the waiter came to see to her needs, she ordered a taco de nopalitos and a glass of rum punch. She was pretty sure that was exactly what she had ordered when she had come here with Luis. Jenda sipped the cool citrusy punch and watched the passers-by, letting her mind wander.

There was a park across the street with lots of open space where the grass was worn thin. On one of the thinnest patches of grass there was a little seat attached by long ropes to a tall frame and a child was sitting on the seat as it moved forward and back like a pendulum. As Jenda watched, she felt the child's sense of the ground rushing closer, the feeling of flying up into the sky, falling back to earth. Jenda realized she was smiling. Had she ever been on one of these devices herself as a child? A woman who had been sitting on a bench near the device got up to give the child a push. "¡Mas alto! ¡Mas!" the child shouted, laughing. There was something odd about the woman's appearance. She had a slender frame but her body seemed strangely round. Jenda realized the woman was pregnant and her hand went involuntarily to her own flat belly. How odd it must feel, she thought, to have something alive inside your body. She ordered another punch when the waiter brought her taco. The day was warm and she was thirsty.

She looked across the street again and saw that the child had left the swinging contraption and was walking alongside the woman, holding her hand. Another woman rose slowly to her feet to join them. This second woman had a body that was frail and bent. She was old. How old? "Without Chulel, she's likely not even as old as I am. How can it be that there are still people living like this? Living without Chulel, having babies, growing old? We should do something to help them." Jenda scowled. Then her expression softened as she watched the two women walking arm in arm, the little boy holding his mother's hand.

8.

"What do people around here do for Christmas or New Year's?" Jenda asked one morning as she and Luis sat on the balcony enjoying the December sunshine.

"Ah. I guess that will be coming up soon," he replied. "Well, there used to be elaborate celebrations, but now we have only a couple of days of Posadas. And a few decorated trees, I guess."

"Posadas?"

"Commemorating Mary and Joseph's search for lodging. There are processions leading from one church to another. There used to be a lot of churches. Now there are only three. The rest have been turned into shops and restaurants and hotels. More profitable, you know."

"We used to decorate a tree, I think." Jenda tried to remember. "Maybe with lights. And sparkly things. And gifts are always nice."

"We could do a tree. Shall we? And gifts?"

Jenda smiled. She already knew what she would give to Luis.

The next afternoon they went in search of a tree, which they purchased from a temporary street vendor in an old neighborhood. It was an asymmetrical and ungainly thing, but they liked it. They found some strings of tiny lighted tin lanterns shaped like stars and some glittery paper flowers for decoration. They set the tree into a bucket with rocks and a little water and placed it next to the doors that led onto the balcony, laughing at its insistence on remaining just off vertical. Once it was decorated, they switched off the lights and sat on the sofa, admiring their glowing handiwork.

In the week before Christmas, they studiously avoided questioning one another too closely about the intent of their various errands. They watched the Posada processions and enjoyed the spectacle of people – including a few children – swatting away at piñatas in the park. They took evening walks to enjoy the various lights some of the people had put up to adorn their houses and gardens. Jenda found the entire spectacle familiar and was pleased that, for once, something that seemed to awaken old memories wasn't distressing.

The final Posada terminated in front of the temple of San Juan de Dios. "Do you want to go inside?" Luis asked, as the crowd began to disperse.

"Sure." Jenda was curious. She had never been a church goer, as far as she knew. These buildings looked so wise. She expected the stone interior to be cold, but instead it felt warm with the glow of fragrant candles and incense, the press of bodies. Individual candles flickered and danced, but the glow was steady, unmoving. Jenda reached for Luis' hand.

As one group of pilgrims parted, revealing the object of their devotion, Jenda caught her breath. It was a lady in blue, like the one she dreamed about. She tugged at Luis' arm and gestured toward the statue.

"Who is she?"

"Her?" He looked in the direction Jenda indicated. "Ah. The Virgin of Guadalupe," he said, pulling Jenda forward for a closer look.

Jenda held back. "She frightens me. I think I used to have dreams about her. I can never quite remember."

Luis placed a comforting arm around Jenda's shoulders and, as they left the church, he explained how important the Virgin of Guadalupe was in the history of the Mexican people.

On Christmas morning, Jenda woke early, but tried to keep quiet and still so as not to disturb Luis, who was still snoring softly. Carefully, she turned to face him. Just as she was closing her eyes to settle into her pillow, Luis let out a huge snort. "You goof!" Jenda laughed. "You're not asleep at all. God, you almost scared me to death." They smothered their laughter in a Christmas kiss.

"No gifts without coffee," Jenda commanded. They went to the kitchen to make coffee, then placed their steaming mugs on the little table in front of the sofa. Each one disappeared to retrieve a carefully hidden gift.

"Now what?" Luis asked, looking at Jenda for guidance. "Do we go have breakfast and come back later?" He grinned.

"No, no," Jenda instructed. "We definitely open gifts before breakfast. You go first." She handed Luis her present, using both hands. "Merry Christmas, Luis!"

"It's heavy," he observed. "But I think you should go first, querida."

"Okay, I'll tell you what we'll do. First, we'll take turns removing the ribbons. Then the paper. Then – you know, whatever comes next."

Luis handed Jenda her gift. "¡Feliz Navidad!"

So they each removed the ribbons, savoring the anticipation.

"This paper is so pretty. I don't want to tear it," Luis said. He folded the paper and then set his unopened box in his lap and looked expectantly at Jenda.

She could tell her gift was a book. As she removed the paper and turned the book over to reveal its cover, a smile lit up first her eyes and then her whole face.

"Oh, Luis," she said quietly. "I remember this. We saw it at the old bookshop. You know, I think I do remember it from when I was a child. It's about a little girl, isn't it? And she has a dog. And they fly through the air to a magical place." She leaned over to give Luis a kiss. "Thank you," she said, stroking the cover of the book.

"I thought you might have some connection with it. I remember reading it when I was a kid, too."

"Time for you to open your box now," Jenda said, hugging her book to her chest.

Luis lifted the cover of the box and reached inside, giving Jenda a puzzled look. He pushed the box aside and set a tissue-swathed object in front of him. Then he carefully removed the layers of paper.

"¡Ay! querida," he whispered, and then fell silent, mesmerized by the sculpture that sat before him. It was the small bronze of a little girl reading a book.

Jenda saw that his eyes were moist. "I noticed how you admired it when we went to your friend's gallery that day – the day of the dead people. Do you remember?"

"Oh, I've admired this little piece even before that," he confessed. "I can't believe you got it for me. ¡Qué milagro!"

He lifted the figure up to admire it at eye level. He looked at Jenda and then back at the sculpture. "You know, she's sitting exactly the way you sit when we're reading Batman comics in the studio," he said. Then he set the figure under the tree and reached to embrace Jenda. "Mil gracias, mi amor." And they followed up with another Christmas kiss.

"Now breakfast," Jenda said. But she made no move to extract herself from their embrace.

~~~

During the final months of Jenda's sabbatical, her days became more balanced between painting, learning useful digital skills, and enjoying spending time with the man she knew she was going to miss more than she had missed anyone in a very long time. She noticed that Luis was absent more and more frequently, leaving her to mind the gallery on her own.

On an unusually rainy afternoon in late March, Luis returned from one of his unexplained errands soaking wet and out of sorts.

"Why did you have to go out on a day like this anyway?" Jenda admonished, helping him out of his wet jacket and shirt.

"I had to go, Jen."

Jenda stood back, holding his wet things. "Because…" she prompted.

"Okay. Sorry. I guess I owe you more of an explanation of why I've been out so much lately. Let's close up and go upstairs. I could use some hot cocoa."

Dry clothes and a mug of steaming sweetness put Luis in a better state of mind.

"I've been meeting with various Recall people," he explained. "There are plans afoot."

"Plans?"

"Mmm." He took a big gulp of hot chocolate. "They're not telling us any details yet, but they've been asking us to make some test posts on various mediazones and then monitor how they're dealt with. Honestly, Jenda, I don't fully understand what it's all about. At first I figured you'd be better off not knowing anything about it. Now I think that was probably unfair. I trust you, querida, and I also have confidence in your intelligence and discretion. Why shouldn't I tell you everything I know? Even though, as I said, that's not a lot."

Jenda smiled at him and then kissed his cheek. "Thanks, Luis. I'm glad to know you've been attending to important matters. And I'm glad to learn that, as you say, there are plans afoot. Maybe we should get you some kind of costume to put on when you take on your Recall identity and go out to save the world." They spent the next half hour imagining elaborate superhero costumes and identities for one another, laughing as they became increasingly ridiculous.

As the time neared for Jenda to return to her job at Your Journal in Dallas, she and Luis worked out a project for her. It was a loose plan whereby she would devise an advertising campaign for Your Journal that would require her to get access to a wide range of files. Luis supplied her with a tiny wireless device she could use to draw down these files for subsequent analysis off site. It was a rather open-ended assignment.

"You'll have to come up with a great proposal to convince them, I think," Luis said.

"Not a problem," Jenda sniffed. "You are looking at the queen of Your Journal advertising campaigns. Well, not officially. But still, definitely not a problem."

Jenda felt comfortable and happy in San Miguel. She had even resigned herself to the idea that the company she worked for engaged in activities she found objectionable. But when she thought about the fact that she would be returning to work there soon, her serenity faltered. She worried about the fact that she would be due for her Chulel spa day upon her return to Dallas. Sabbaticals and Chulel days were generally synchronized such that the spa treatment was perceived as a welcome re-entry into working life.

"Is there any way to avoid it?" Jenda asked Luis one day. "I've always looked forward to my Chulel spa days in the past, but now, after what I've learned…Luis, I don't want to forget even one moment of the time we've spent together."

"Well, if you worked for anyone other than YJ, I'd suggest you start self-administering," he answered. "But in your case, your employers would notice and it could put your job in jeopardy."

"You told me that some people have found ways of protecting themselves from the memory reconstruction. Could you help me do that?"

"Of course, mi amor. They tell me it's not that hard, since they leave you alone in the room during the photonic treatment. They can't monitor it on camera because of the photon bursts. And I guess it would be dangerous for anyone else to be in there. They might come out thinking they were you." He laughed. Jenda didn't.

In the past, whenever she had approached the end of a sabbatical, Jenda would begin to distance herself from whatever lover had been her companion for the duration. This time was different. Missing Luis would be painful, she knew, but she also knew they would be together again. A lot. For a long time. They had a joint project and an immediate plan to meet in Houston in just over a month. Jenda already had made plans to attend a tennis tournament there, so her travel would require no explanation. Luis would try to arrange a Marvaworld trip to coincide.

When they finally said their farewells at the León airport, they agreed to say only "hasta luego" – "until later". But Jenda cried a little, and Luis held her as if he would never let her go.

Part II:
Questions

9.

"Increase speed!" Jenda commanded, addressing the control panel of the autocar. A red light flashed and the voice admonished: "The speed limit in this zone is …55 …kph. You may not exceed... 55...kph." Jenda glared at the panel's clock. It was her first morning back in Dallas and she was running late for her appointment at the Chulel spa. Also, she didn't like the voice's prissy tone. She fiddled with a hangnail and finally bit it off.

"Zujo!" Jenda swore, as a tiny spot of blood rose up on her cuticle. Jenda was more nervous than she had been before her first Chulel treatment back in 2035. That one had been a celebration of her college graduation.

"Pull yourself together, Jen," she said, which didn't help at all because she hated taking orders, even from herself. She felt once again for the earplugs and opaque contact lenses she had stashed in the pocket of her trousers. They formed what she hoped was an undetectable bulge hidden under her loose shirt. She removed the band holding back her long hair and shook the hair down over her ears. She didn't think the earplugs would be noticeable, but she thought this would help. It was one less thing to worry about, anyway.

Arriving at the spa, Jenda passed her digilet in front of the registration point and took a seat. She searched for something to read, even though she didn't feel like reading. When her digilet buzzed, Jenda went into the next room and entered the first unoccupied cubicle. She arranged her body in the exam chair, settling her arms and legs into the supports that would read her vital signs and analyze her blood composition. A few minutes later, the results came up on her digilet. Jenda thought her blood pressure looked a little high. She was instructed to report to room 217 in the spa wing. A medical attendant arrived, holding a digiscreen containing all of Jenda's medical records. She asked a few questions about the state of Jenda's health.

"And your medications? Is everything satisfactory, or do you wish to schedule a consultation?"

"No, everything is fine," Jenda said. She hadn't been taking most of her allotted medications, but she didn't want to be burdened with an appointment for a consultation and all the questions that would entail. The attendant ticked off each medication on the screen.

"Room 217 is all set up for you," she chirped. "Right this way."

As they walked through the soft lights and soothing music that filled the walkway, Jenda felt her blood pressure rise another few points. She wondered if any of the other clients they passed in the walkway were carrying earplugs and opaque lenses.

"Here we are," the smiling attendant said. Jenda was struck by how much her voice resembled the synthetic voice in the autocar.

Jenda placed her right hand on the entry pad and the door opened. Jenda knew what to do. The attendant helped her adjust the recliner to the position she found most comfortable and gave her two quick and painless infusions. The first was the Chulel and the second was a drug designed to make the memory restoration process maximally effective.

As soon as Jenda was sure she was on her own in the room, she inserted the earplugs and contact lenses. She was glad she had tested them out at home, because the loss of sensory input was unnerving. Luis had suggested she use the time trying to recreate the plot of a favorite novel or flick or remembering the lyrics of some of her favorite songs – anything to keep her mind focused and diverted away from what was happening around her. As the second infusion began to take effect, Jenda found it was becoming difficult to concentrate on anything at all. Her mind kept popping from one image to another and she was only able to drag it back to her selected storyline by force of will. She had to remember to keep her eyes open, too, so that if for any reason the attendant popped in, she would not be caught napping. The process would last three hours, and Jenda had set her digilet to vibrate and remind her to remove her protective gear.

She removed the lenses first, and was immediately inundated with images from the past year being shown on the 360 degree floor to ceiling screen. She closed her eyes as she removed the earplugs. The sound was white noise, but Jenda knew from her conversations with Luis' friends that it supposedly contained abundant subliminal messages. "Or maybe not," she thought. Jenda was exhausted from the effort of maintaining her focus during the treatment, but, recalling that in the past she had always felt relaxed and exhilarated, she did her best to appear that way when the attendant entered to take her to the snack room, which clients simply called "re-entry." Jenda was glad it was over. She hoped her efforts had protected her memories of San Miguel, her memories of Luis.

Jenda had the rest of the day free. She decided to take the monorail home instead of an autocar. She had time and submitting herself to the efficient confinement of an autocar was not appealing.

The rail station was not particularly crowded and she had only a brief wait before a stage going her direction glided in. She found a seat near the middle of the stage and unfurled her digilet. She didn't want to engage with her fellow passengers, although she found their physical presence somehow comforting. Rails were used primarily by lower level workers. Jenda thought about the backstreet lunchroom. She looked up from her digilet to scan the faces in the stage, to see if the old woman might be there. She wasn't. But there was one woman who seemed to have been staring at Jenda. She had turned her attention quickly to her digilet as soon as Jenda looked toward her. Her perfect hair and erect posture made Jenda vaguely uncomfortable. Everyone seemed thoroughly engrossed in their own digilets, with the exception of one young man – an adolescent, by the look of his soft face and slender build – who was reading a paper book.

Jenda disembarked at the station nearest her habitation complex and emerged into the April warmth. She noticed the woman with perfect hair get off, too. Then, as Jenda headed toward her habitat, the woman went back inside the station. Jenda's endurb was built for autocars rather than pedestrians, and she had to choose whether to walk in the edge of the roadway or on the manicured lawns. She chose the lawns.

Back inside her own habitat, Jenda set about rearranging things. She felt different and she wanted her surroundings to reflect that. She moved a few small pieces of furniture. She placed the book that was her Christmas gift from Luis on the table next to the sofa and hung one of the small oil paintings she had made in San Miguel on the wall next to her home screen. She might seem like the same old Jenda when she was at work or meeting friends somewhere, but at home she wanted to be able to be herself, whoever that might turn out to be.

The next day Jenda went back to work at Your Journal as if nothing of any consequence had transpired over the past eleven months. She joked with her friends about the sexy Latino she had met, but she refused to give him a name. Jenda knew it was for her own and Luis' protection, but she let her colleagues believe it was because he was nothing more than a sabbatical flirtation, someone she had no intention of seeing again or remembering much about, other than the fun they had had. And the sex.

Coming back from sabbatical was always a delicate transition and companies had learned to reserve a simple assignment for returnees to let them slip into routines again without becoming overwhelmed. Jenda busied herself with her assignment as she also began working on the plan she and Luis had devised.

In her free hours at home, Jenda spent time on the Recall zone. She had learned how to access the inner depths of Recall, where she screened in to Interloc under a persona Luis had created for her. The messaging system was decidedly old fashioned and cumbersome, but since it took up far less bandwidth than visual or live audio communication, it was easier to blend in unnoticed. On one of her first tentative forays into Recall, Jenda found this item:

Time was when memory existed solely in the minds of men and women, and the elders of the society were its treasury. As humankind evolved, art became the handmaiden of memory, encoding in images – and in stories that were recited or sung or danced – the episodes and values that defined a people. Writing was the next revolution of memory. The printing press was another. Digital electronic storage took memory to the next level but also put it at risk as never before. In every age, people believed their encoded memories to be somehow infallible, unassailable, invulnerable. They were always wrong, but the notion was pervasive and reassuring. It still is.

The item was written by someone calling himself "HombreMurcielago" – Batman. It was Luis. Although this was an old item, Jenda responded: "Sometimes the short-term memories, shared only with one other, are the best." It wasn't profound, but she knew Luis would understand. She didn't care what other readers might think.

Jenda quickly developed favorites to follow on Recall. Number one, of course, was HombreMurcielago. Then she added Crone1 and HillBill. Crone1 was a woman who had decided, after some 40 years of Chulel treatments, to retreat into an enclave where she was now experiencing aging and reporting on it in eloquent detail. Jenda found her accounts a bit frightening, but she liked the wise insights that Crone1 often put forward. HillBill was the most entertaining. He had a way of cleverly ridiculing almost everything about the current cultural ethos, and especially the penchant for recycling everything, which he termed "destroy and reinvent." He exhorted people to resist the mindless submission of all their old books and printed photos for recycling.

Jenda found some of the items posted in Recall confusing or disturbing, prompting her to screen up a game or a flick or go to the kitchen for a dram. Increasingly, though, she found herself picking up a bound journal of paper pages and writing. At first she only wrote brief notes such as the ID tags of particular entries or pictures that caught her eye. Gradually, her journal entries became longer and more rambling. Jenda wasn't sure what some of the things she wrote meant. She wasn't even convinced they made any sense at all. Maybe they didn't need to. She only knew it felt good to write things down on paper.

By the weekend, Jenda was more than ready to get away from Your Journal. On Friday (the first day of the weekend) she had a tennis date with her grandmother. As usual, Jenda was running late. Granny El was ready and waiting and, as she slid into the leftside seat of the autocar, Jenda reached across to give her a quick hug. Then she pressed the "resume" button on the car's control panel. "Sorry I'm late, Gran, but…"

The autocar voice interrupted. "Proceeding to next destination. Lakeland Sports Complex. Time to destination…12...minutes." Their reservation slot began in eight minutes.

Jenda sighed audibly. "I'm sorry, Gran. I know we've been looking forward to getting back to our weekly tennis dates."

"Never mind," Jenda's grandmother said. "I wasn't nearly as interested in the tennis as I was in finally getting to spend a little time with you. Why don't we just go to the Food Strip and get a glass of tea and catch up. You've been way too busy since you got back from sabbatical. You've been back… what? Almost a week now?"

"Almost," Jenda said. "Gosh, it's good to see you Gran. I've missed you."

"Redirect." Jenda addressed the autocar. "New destination Hydra Delect at M Court."

Although she had put off their reunion longer than she should have, Jenda was deeply fond of Granny El, her mother's mother, who was her only family in Dallas, the only family she still had regular contact with anywhere.

"So tell me all about the sabbatical, Jen. Your pulses have been awfully brief, so I really have no idea. How was it?" Granny El began, as they settled into a courtyard table with their icy drams.

"Sabbatical was good, Gran."

"So, what was his name this time?" Granny El gave Jenda a sly look.

Jenda pursed her lips and stared into the distance as she struggled unsuccessfully to suppress the smile that seemed to surface whenever she thought of Luis. "Let's just say he was Latin and beautiful," Jenda said, taking a long draught of her NutriQuaff.

"So your inexplicable choice of San Miguel de Allende was not a total disaster?"

"Not a disaster at all, Gran. I made some new paintings." Jenda was unsure how much to share with her grandmother. "The weather was lovely," she said.

On Saturday, Jenda met up with her friends Eldred and Yeshe to visit a new experiential museum that had recently opened. As people had lost interest in the past, museums for all ages followed in the footsteps of early children's museums, providing engaging interactive exhibits and activities. A couple of times, Jenda thought she saw the same woman she had caught staring at her on the monorail her first day back in Dallas. She had the same perfect hair and erect posture. It was that posture Jenda found slightly unnerving. The woman carried herself like a member of the corporate police.

As Jenda and her friends sat in the museum snack shop enjoying cold drams after an exhausting romp through the exhibits, Jenda broached a question that had begun to nag at her during the visit.

"You know," she said, "museums used to provide people with information about the past – about history, evolution. Do you think it's important for us to know about things like that?"

"I seem to remember some of those," Eldred responded. "I always found them kind of boring. These new interactive museums that focus on vanguard culture are a lot more fun."

Yeshe frowned. "Past, future – not important. The Buddha taught us to always live fully in the present moment." Smiling, she added, "And these activities sure do keep me in the present moment!"

Jenda stared at her dram, stirring it thoughtfully. She was trying to recall a conversation she had had with her brother Jonathan shortly after he came back from Tibet. "Didn't the Buddha also teach about…What is it called? Dependent origination? You know – cause and effect. How can we understand where we are if we don't know anything about the causes? And causes have to be in the past."

"I don't know about that," Yeshe said. "But I do know that the Buddha taught that reality is only a construction of the mind. So I like to engage in activities that help me construct a happy mind."

Eldred leaned back in his chair, studying the colorful kinetic sculpture above their heads. "You know I'm a fan of the Buddha. But I also think sometimes we might be missing something by never looking back at the past or thinking where our present actions might be leading. What do you think Jenda?"

"If I knew what I thought I probably wouldn't have asked the question." Jenda knew she was being evasive. "I guess I get a little weary of just running around creating happy mind. No offense, Yeshe."

Jenda was troubled. There was undeniable appeal in living in the moment with no thought for the past or future. And if the neo-Buddhists were right about all reality being a construction of the mind, where did that leave Luis and his Recall crowd?

On her way home, Jenda sent a pulse to the last contact phrase she had for Jonathan, her brother who had left home at the age of 14 to follow a Buddhist guru and who eventually ended up spending years at a monastery in Tibet. One of his gurus had pronounced him a reincarnation of a 20th century monk known as Khentsy Norbu, who had been a modestly successful producer of flicks. It was because of him that Jonathan had become a flickmaker.

"Been thinking about you lately." Jenda spoke into her digilet. "How are things? Are you still in Denver?" Jenda had seen a brief flurry of advertising hype while she was in Mexico over the release of Jonathan's latest flick. When she later searched for it to draw it down from the atmosphere, she couldn't find it. Jenda also was shocked to see that Jonathan had somehow disappeared from her LifeBook loop. She was certain she had not erased him herself. Jenda was worried. The last few times she had spoken with Jonathan, he had tried to talk to her about things that happened when they were kids – things Jenda couldn't remember. Now she thought she might want him to tell her more. She checked her digilet. There was no immediate response to her pulse.

Jenda felt restless. She missed Luis and the world they had inhabited in San Miguel. She needed a new activity. Maybe a dance class. But not couples dancing; she knew she wouldn't enjoy that without Luis. She did a mediazone search and found several dance classes at convenient locations. She decided on a class in a building she knew, which also housed an odd little boutique where she had shopped a few times. The boutique, of course, had clothing in many of the popular recyclable fabrics and materials, but it also had some unusual accessories, including neck pendants with old watches and lockets.

The dance studio, it turned out, was on the floor above the boutique and was run by the same owner, a woman by the name of Leticia Poole. Leticia didn't have the dancer's body Jenda anticipated, but as Jenda watched her move about the shop, she had to admit there was a certain grace and strength in her short, roundish body. She sold Jenda a form-fitting outfit with a wispy skirt, assuring her that it would be perfect for the class she was signing up for. Shoes would not be needed, Leticia said.

At the start of her first class, Jenda felt awkward and self-conscious, but as she followed the instruction to stop thinking and to let her body reflect Leticia's movements, she began to relax. When they reached the end of the class and Leticia put on a solo cello piece and told the students to move in their own way to the music, Jenda felt transported. She wondered why she had never tried this before – or had she? There was something about the free movement to music that felt so familiar, that seemed to be stirring some forgotten feelings.

After class, Jenda chatted pleasantly with Leticia as they changed into their street clothes. As Jenda picked up her shoulder bag to leave, Leticia turned to her and laid her hand gently on Jenda's arm. "A word of advice: If you want to get the most out of this class, don't mention it on LifeBook or in Your Journal." Then she turned and went inside the shop.

Jenda walked back to her habitat, thinking of Leticia, thinking of how the dancing had made her feel, and thinking that whatever was hiding in those forgotten recesses of her mind, not all of it was bad. Her heart ached for the good friends she might have forgotten and she wondered if Leticia might be one of them.

She came to look forward to her weekly dance classes. Her favorite moments, however, came when she was alone in her habitat, chatting with Luis on Interloc.

"How long do you expect to live?" Jenda pulsed Luis one day, when they were both on Interloc, where Luis was identified simply as "Murcielago." Jenda was "Polilla." Luis had tried to select "Mariposa" for her, in honor of her butterfly-like qualities, but too many people already had claimed some form of that, so he chose "Polilla" – clothes moth – in honor of her constantly morphing wardrobe of fashionable clothes.

"I don't know," Luis replied. "What about you?"

POLILLA: Not fair. I asked first.

MURCIELAGO: Okay. Let me think.

There was a long pause. Jenda liked that Luis took her questions seriously. Unlike herself. She would probably have made some clever or sarcastic comeback and hoped the question would go away. Or at least, she used to do that. She knew Luis would give her a thoughtful response.

MURCIELAGO: We're in a strange place, mi amor. Nobody I know from Gen1 or Gen2 ever expected to live nearly as long as they have. But it's happening. The scientists are not reporting any deterioration in our bodies' ability to continue regenerating themselves indefinitely under the Chulel regime. It's only the memory thing that gives most people doubts, and you and I and a few others know that is a false fear. Of course

88

we are all subject to being killed in accidents or dying from some lethal disease. But as our futures seem more and more unlimited, you can see how people shy away from risky behaviors. When people figured they were going to die relatively soon anyway, why not risk your neck for the pleasures of fast driving, rock climbing, scuba diving, traveling to foreign places with strange diseases? "Nobody lives forever," right? Well – now maybe we do. And maybe we find that disturbing.

Jenda didn't respond. She was thinking.

MURCIELAGO: You still there?

POLILLA: Still here.

POLILLA: You haven't answered my question yet.

MURCIELAGO: Okay. I'll try harder.

Another pause.

MURCIELAGO: I expect to live to be a very old man.

POLILLA: That's it? What's that supposed to mean? Nobody gets old anymore!

MURCIELAGO: Exactly. What I mean is, I think humankind may have pushed it too far. Living forever is not natural. And it's not some eternal bliss of heaven-on-earth as some of the Sanguinists would have it. The demographics are already getting unmanageable and potentially disastrous.

POLILLA: I think I only wanted to know how long YOU expected to live. You know, so I can make plans to live that long.

MURCELAGO: Then you'll have to accept the answer I gave you. And the fact that I love you. Unto death.

POLILLA: I love you, too. But let's not get morbid about it.

MURCIELAGO: How's the research going?

Jenda was grateful that he recognized her cue that she wasn't in the mood for further philosophical and social scientific analysis of the current state of the world, even though she knew her question had clearly invited it.

POLILLA: Pretty good. I can send you a full report by the end of the week.

Jenda's research had, in fact, been proceeding nicely. Three weeks after her return from sabbatical, she had proposed an exciting new idea for an advertising campaign featuring a series of photos from customers' files. It was part of the contract that personal photos could be used for advertising purposes, but without identifying the persons in the photo, which of course would be an invasion of privacy and YJ deeply respected people's privacy. So Jenda had been sifting through people's YJ personal files for several weeks and surreptitiously drawing down large segments of the files to the wireless device Luis had given her, carefully timing her work to blend in with high activity to avoid detection.

Once Jenda received access to these private files, she couldn't resist examining them in the evenings on her home screen. She intended to look through only a few of them, but she found herself staying up late in order to go through just a few more. She was noticing a lot of empty walls behind people. Or finding the same boring prints of the same popular commercial artists of the day. She painstakingly applied the transformation process Luis executed so expertly and found telltale signs of alteration. She made notes.

On the fourth night, as she was flipping through photos, barely aware of what she was doing, she suddenly startled awake. "Wait, what was that?" It wasn't the picture currently on the screen that had caught her attention. She backed up. Not that one either. One more back. There. What was it about this picture that seemed so odd? She looked at the people. She looked at the wall. There was nothing strange there. Then she looked at what the young person on the left was wearing. She zoomed in. What were those big stitch marks on his shirt and pants? And how had she noticed something so small when she was half asleep? Fully awake now, Jenda put the photo through the steps for analysis. The only thing she found that had been changed was the young person's hair – not the shape, so possibly the color. And maybe something had been hanging around his neck. What color had his (or it could be her) hair been before it became the rather unremarkable chestnut brown it appeared to be in the YJ photo?

And what kind of objectionable jewelry had she/he been wearing? Jenda wished that the analysis could restore what was originally there, but unfortunately all it could do was reveal that something had been changed. She stared at the photo for another couple of minutes. Finally, she shook herself and, after noting in her book a few details about the picture, she screened out.

Luis cautioned her that sleep deprivation might attract undue attention. He reminded her that she needed to give her creative attention to making her project a successful one. Besides, Luis was going to be coming to Houston soon and they could meet there and analyze things together. Jenda tried to be patient.

~~~

The next Friday afternoon as Jenda and her grandmother were sipping drams after tennis and swapping stories about their latest fashion finds, Granny El told Jenda about a friend who had recently returned from a sabbatical that had included a wonderful voyage aboard a brand new vessel called "Oceans Celestial".

"She's come back all refreshed and happy to be part of the corporate world again. Especially after that wonderful Chulel memory refresher."

"Yeah," Jenda ventured. "You know some people think they do more than just refresh and restore memories, Gran."

"Oh, I know about that," Granny El responded, with a laugh and a wink.

"You know… what?"

"I know what you people do," she replied, stirring her drink vigorously. "Hell, girl, when you reach my age and have an additional 50 years or more of memories to deal with, you'll be grateful for clever folks like your YJ people to help you keep things, you know, kind of pruned back into something manageable."

Jenda was unable to swallow her mouthful of NutriQuaff and it dribbled back into her straw. She stared at her grandmother.

Granny El took a more serious tone. "Gosh, Jenda, if your YJ didn't help us get shed of some of the old memories, we'd be like… like a bunch of reptiles trying to live out our lives always in the same old skin. You have to move on and not be always living in the past. Especially these days, when we have no idea how much past we might still have to look forward to."

Jenda was surprised, but not exactly shocked. She knew that Granny El had always been one of the "science-can-solve-everything" types. She had scoffed at the nay-sayers when Chulel first became available. She was quite a beauty in her youth and in 2025 when the earliest Chulel was offered, she had been nearly 65, although a well-cared-for 65, having benefitted from good nutrition and exercise, as well as the best dermatological treatments available. She admitted to having been tempted to try Fontana when she received that suspicious pulse about it, but a bad experience with a street drug when she was a teenager back in the 1970s had made her cautious. She was glad she had waited.

This was a new insight into Granny El, Jenda thought. It was also a new perspective on YJ.

10.

Jenda grew giddy with anticipation as the date approached for her long weekend in Houston with Luis. She was careful to make everyone think it was the big tennis tournament that was making her eyes sparkle. Keeping her relationship with Luis secret might have been unnecessary, but Jenda was unwilling to give him substance in a world she increasingly rejected.

Jenda wanted them to stay at her favorite boutique hotel, but Marvaworld was paying for Luis' room at one of the big chain hotels and Jenda conceded the point. She didn't care so much where they were, as long as they were together. Although, she mused, the surprises of the ever-changing décor in her favorite hotel, and the constantly novel menu in the restaurant, and the elegantly presented room service – all of that had contributed to her frequent daydreams over the past weeks. Magnum Hotel would have to do.

Jenda checked in several hours before Luis was expected. Time enough to unpack and enjoy a shower and put on one of her new outfits bought for the occasion – a pair of loose trousers in a deep red and a flowered top with a provocatively draped neckline. She wished vaguely that she still had one of the outfits Luis had admired in San Miguel, but those had all long since hit the recycling bins.

When Luis finally pushed open the unlatched door, Jenda almost tackled him, pushing the door closed behind him, knocking over his suitcase, and locking him in a fully reciprocated deep kiss. They murmured some unintelligible greetings to one another. Jenda knew Luis would be tired out from travel, so she had figured sex would wait until later. But as Luis' hands gently moved from her face to her neck to her shoulders to her breasts, she decided now was good, too.

"I was right," Jenda whispered later, gently stroking Luis' new beard at close range, watching him sleep. "The poor dear is exhausted. But damn you're good even when you're tired." She could have sworn she saw a faint smile cross Luis' face.

Jenda dutifully attended what she calculated to be a respectable minimum of her tennis events, trying to appear enthusiastic while also trying to avoid her old tennis friends. She didn't want to be constantly making excuses about why she couldn't meet them for dinner and drinks. The first morning at the tennis venue, Jenda thought she saw the woman from the monorail stage again, the one with the military posture. She decided maybe it was time to mention these encounters to Luis.

"What do you think, Luis? Am I being followed?" Jenda asked, after she had told him about all three sightings of the mysterious woman.

"Are you sure it's the same woman?"

"Pretty sure. But I think the most disturbing thing is that every time I've seen her, I had some sense I was being watched and then I look up – and there she is. And then she disappears."

Luis looked troubled. "Well, if it's the corporate police, you know they can get pretty ugly. Let's stop drawing down files for a while. And if you see her when we're together, please let me know. It's probably nothing to worry about."

Jenda could tell Luis didn't believe that, but she nodded and smiled. "Right," she said. "Now can I show you what I've found?"

She screened up the photos she had identified as altered during her first sleepless week of spy work. Luis hypothesized that the missing or altered backgrounds probably contained either photographs showing someone best forgotten or else paintings or prints that were the work of dissident artists or any artist no longer in favor.

"How can art be that big a deal?" Jenda asked. "Sorry," she backtracked. "Don't mean to imply artists are insignificant."

Luis nudged her with his shoulder, almost pushing her off the chair. "I know most people today think art is just for entertainment or personal therapy, but not so long ago there were some artists using it more politically."

Jenda's attempted "Hmmm..." as an expression of mild interest somehow came out more of a "Hmph!"

94

"No, really," Luis said. "One of our early heroes was a fellow called Ai Weiwei – an artist working during the declining years of Chinese state capitalism. There are photos of some of his work on Recall. You should check it out sometime."

They looked at a few more of Jenda's selected pictures. "Good work, Jenda," Luis said, with a note of finality. She could tell he was impatient to get on with his own expert analysis.

"Let me show you one more," Jenda said, checking her notebook for a number. She reached over Luis' arm and entered the number on the keypad. The photo of the family with the youth in the oddly mended clothing popped up.

"So what did you find on this one?" Luis asked, placing his hand on Jenda's thigh and massaging gently.

"You tell me," she said. "I want to know what you see." His pressure on her thigh lightened.

Luis sat back in his chair and squinted at the picture. His mouth curled into a smile and he began running through the transformation steps, zeroing in precisely on the youth's hair, then moving to his/her neck area.

"Good eye, Jenda." This time he seemed genuinely pleased. "What did you notice first about this one that made you decide to analyze it?"

"It was the odd stitching on the guy's clothes. And I have no idea how I noticed it, since I was half asleep at the time. What do you think was altered about the hair, Luis?"

"I can tell you exactly what was altered: The color. This guy – or it could be a girl, it's often hard to tell with these youngsters – was a 'Vintie.' This is a particularly sloppy alteration. YJ is usually more thorough."

"A what?" Jenda rejoined. "Like a twenty-something? That doesn't help." She looked disappointed.

"No," Luis laughed. "Not 'veinte' – 'Vintie.' She – or he – was part of a political movement that called themselves 'Vintagonists'. They were opposed to the destruction of anything old. That was a big trend during the late 2020s or so.

Surely you knew some of them. This would have been when you were in high school or early college."

"But I don't remember anything about them. Maybe there weren't any Vinties in my school. Probably not in my circle anyway," she said lightly.

"They were pretty much everywhere, although not always in large numbers. You don't remember them at all? Do you have some old high school photos we could look at?"

"Sure. Although not a lot. Screen up YJ." Luis did and Jenda reached over and put in her access phrase.

"Let's try 2028," Luis suggested.

As Luis began flipping through the photographs, Jenda muttered, "That seems an odd cause for a group of young people to get behind."

As Luis scrolled through the pictures, he began to frown. He leaned toward the screen with his chin in his hand.

"Not finding anything?"

"Al contrario, querida. I'm seeing at least some evidence of Vinties in almost all of your pictures."

"What?"

"Let me show you." Luis deftly processed a photo and showed Jenda the results. "You see there?" he said. "The hair color has been changed. And see these little marks on the clothing? Evidence of mending has been removed. And in the neck area – these Vinties always wore some kind of pendant, usually old-fashioned things like timepieces or lockets. Also, on this one, some makeup has been added to the face."

"I don't remember ever having even heard of these Vinties." Jenda looked troubled. "Tell me more, Luis."

So as the two of them stared at the screen full of tell-tale misaligned dots, Luis explained that it had been a time when recycling everything was the message coming from the great corporations and their media affiliates. In opposition to this, the Vintagonists advocated the preservation of printed books and photographs, physical works of art, and any clothing, decorative items, and furniture that they termed "vintage."

"Much of what they were preserving was of dubious merit, but they didn't care. Vinties were considered to be dangerously conservative, even retrogressive." Luis explained further that Vintagonists dyed their hair in pale shades of sepia and wore old clothing salvaged from the recycling bins. They repaired these items with crude hand stitching and the more an item could call attention to inferior materials and shoddy workmanship, the more they liked it. Every once in a while, however, someone would come up with a trove of items from earlier generations, items made with quality natural cloth like silk, linen, cotton, or wool, and carefully tailored or even embroidered in fine stitching. Many of these garments had holes where the moths had eaten through the fabric, but these were considered a garment's badge of authenticity and no effort was made to repair or hide such damage. Their philosophy was one of continuing connection with physical objects in the face of constant novelty, impermanence, and change.

"I sort of remember some people called 'Menders'," Jenda mused. "Were the Vinties like that?"

"No, the Menders were different – into repairing, reusing, repurposing, rebuilding everything. They had a lot in common with Vinties, but where Vintagonists wanted to preserve and protect old things for their own sake, Menders wanted to fix things or find some way to make them useful again. They criticized Vintagonists for being overly attached to material things."

Jenda frowned, looking confused. "So who is this person in the photo, Luis? Zoom back out and let me see if it's anyone I can remember."

Luis placed his arm around Jenda's shoulders as he clicked the enlarge symbol several times in rapid succession and a face gradually formed on the screen.

Jenda's eyes widened and her hand came to her mouth. She glanced uncertainly from the photo to Luis and back again. There was no doubt. The face in the picture was her own.

Jenda grabbed Luis' arm with both hands. She couldn't breathe. Everything stopped stone still. Her tear-filled eyes stared fixedly at the photograph that claimed to be Jenda at the age of 15, a Jenda who looked like a normal teenager with short golden hair and too much makeup. But that was not her. She had been someone else, someone obscured by this very image, someone she couldn't remember. Jenda's body began to shake and everything broke into pieces.

Luis killed the offending picture and turned to hold Jenda as she began to sob. He led Jenda to the sofa. She whimpered like a lost puppy as he held her, gently stroking her hair, her shoulders, the nape of her neck. There was nothing left to talk about.

Luis insisted that Jenda take a few tabs of Duermata. "You need some rest, querida," he said. Jenda took it and slept.

She woke suddenly, just before dawn. Although Duermata usually blocked out dreams, Jenda had been dreaming. She struggled to retrieve the images. There had been a dark-skinned young man and laughter. It felt like a group of friends. The lady in blue was there, hidden in the shadows, filling Jenda with terror. In the dream, Jenda closed her eyes tight shut and willed herself to follow this woman, to break through whatever obscured her. It was no use. When Jenda opened her eyes, the dream was gone and she was awake.

It was exasperating. Why couldn't she make herself recall these things? Where were they hidden? She rose quietly and went into the bathroom where she splashed cold water on her swollen eyes. She stared at her reflection in the mirror, trying to imagine herself as a Vintie with sepia hair. She felt her anger resolving into a fierce determination. "I will find you, Jenda," she said to the woman in the mirror.

"Jenda?" Luis was standing in the doorway. "Are you okay?"

"Yeah. Yeah, I think I am," she said. "When can we order breakfast? I'm starving."

"How do you know so much about these Vinties?" Jenda asked, as they ate their omelets and toast. "If the corporate memory reconstructionists wanted us all to forget about them, how is it that you know so much?"

"I've never been subjected to memory restructuring," Luis reminded her. "That's probably the most important thing. But add to that the fact that I was one of them back in my youth. Yes, they were still active in the early 2040s when I was a teen. If anything, we had become more radical by then, although we were probably a somewhat smaller group."

"You never told me about that," Jenda said, feeling a bit hurt.

"Well, it never came up. Look, Jenda, at our ages we both have a lot of history behind us. And, no offense, but even though you may have a few more years, I have a lot more history, since my memories haven't been disrupted by photonic treatments. I'm not pretending I remember everything, nor can I claim to remember things exactly as they were. But at least nobody has been messing with my memories for their own ends. So, yes, there are probably still a lot more things you don't know about me. And probably a good deal of things I don't know about you, too."

"Considering there seem to be quite a lot of things I don't know about myself... Do we know where any of these Vinties have ended up today? Well, besides you, my love – you with the definitely non-sepia hair."

"Actually, yes. A lot of the people you find in Recall are old Vintagonists. Some Menders, too. And a fair number of Minimalists who were advocating overall reduced consumption of material goods." Luis chuckled softly. "We used to call them Simpletons because they were always going on about simplicity. And then they kind of embraced the term, claiming that 'any fool can see the wisdom of simplicity'." Luis grinned at Jenda. "You don't remember them either, I guess. I think the corporations hated them most of all. Most people who were once in one of these movements have had their memories and records redacted and rearranged to the extent that they don't identify with the movement anymore, nor even remember much about it. But yours is the most extreme case I've seen."

Jenda probed her broken mind for traces of memories about Vintagonists and Menders and Simpletons. A few vague images seemed to drift just below the surface, just behind the blank white screens that filled such a large part of her thinking mind whenever she tried to remember her youth. "This is going to take time, Luis," she said finally. "Can we talk about our project?"

Luis picked up her hand and gave it a quick kiss. "Of course we can. We'll have plenty of time ahead of us to investigate all kinds of things." So they spent the rest of the day looking at other people's files and discussing potential plans for their project. Since drawing down additional files was on hold for a while, Jenda offered to select a series of photos from among those she had already seen and propose them for her new YJ campaign. She would select photos that were absolutely perfect, except for some small detail that unfortunately marred the image. Then she would suggest that these be photographically altered. After that, they would see what happened.

11.

A week after her meeting with Luis in Houston, Jenda went to her supervisor with the set of photos she had selected for her campaign.

"Unfortunately," Jenda pointed out to him, "as you can see, a few of the photos contain elements that… Well, this picture would be absolutely perfect if we could get rid of that grumpy-looking child in the front here. Or block out that recycling barrel next to the table in this one. I tried cropping them out," Jenda continued, "but on some of them it's not enough. I know this is against everything we stand for as a company, but since this is for advertising and the pictures in people's files won't be changed, do you think… maybe… just this once?"

Jenda was wheedling. Her supervisor frowned. "It's nice that you understand you shouldn't even be asking to do this, Jenda." He studied the pictures. "But I see what you mean. And I love everything else about your proposed campaign. Let me take it up with my super. I know she's probably going to say 'no' but she's been pretty enthusiastic about your concept. So I guess we can try." He told Jenda he would get back to her.

"By the way," he added as Jenda turned to leave. "Your screen may be off for a while sometime this week. There have been some unusual usage patterns picked up, so they're doing a sweep of all the screens to make sure nothing has been irrupted – no infections or anything. Tech talk, I know. I'm sure it's nothing. I just didn't want you to worry."

Jenda thanked him and returned to her desk, grateful that she and Luis had decided to postpone further drawdowns of personal data.

Two days later, Jenda's supervisor called her into the office. She steeled herself for the possibility they had detected the drawdowns from her screen; she was fully resolved to deny knowing anything about it. That wasn't the topic.

101

"I'm sending you up to Ms. Landry's office to discuss your request about the photos. She's in suite G4 on the 25th floor." Jenda tried not to look startled. That was one of the restricted floors. She was being called to one of the restricted floors. Her appointment was in 20 minutes. She reviewed her proposal materials and then returned to her supervisor's office, where an escort was waiting for her.

The escort entered the elevator with her and quickly keyed in an access phrase. Then he exited, leaving her alone on the elevator as it ascended to the 25th floor. The elevator doors opened, sounding the same as they did on any other floor.

Jenda stepped out and looked around. It didn't look so strange. The signs letting you know which way to go for which suites were a different color, but otherwise looked the same as on other floors. "So what was I expecting?" Jenda asked herself. "A portal into a separate reality?" She took a deep breath, adjusted her grip on her portable screen, and headed off in the direction that the signs indicated for suites D1 through G7. There was no plexi around any of the rooms, so Jenda couldn't see what lay behind the closed doors. A man in a suit came out of suite D5. He acknowledged Jenda with a nod, while also giving her a look that made her feel like an intruder.

Other than that single encounter, the hallway was quiet and empty. Jenda hesitated at the door marked G4. Should she knock or just walk in? She knocked.

The door opened, and a smiling gentleman in casual attire motioned for her to enter. "You're Ms. Swain?" he asked.

"Yes. Jenda Swain." She tried to keep her curiosity reined in, resisting the temptation to stare at everything in the office. There seemed to be more machines than people. "Keep focused," she told herself.

"Ms. Landry is expecting you," the man said, as he led Jenda through a maze of equipment and opened a large plexi door at the far corner of the space.

Ms. Landry shook Jenda's hand. "Please. Have a seat."

Jenda sat. She could see that it had been unnecessary for her to bring her own digiscreen with the proposal materials, as

Ms. Landry had the whole thing spread out on her desktop screen. She enlarged a couple of the photos, rearranging them and studying them closely. Then she looked sternly over her glasses and directly into Jenda's eyes.

"You know this request goes against everything we stand for here at YJ," she said, reiterating the point Jenda's supervisor had made. "You of all people – the originator of 'Your lifeline to your life's story'. You should understand this."

Perhaps she had been sent upstairs to be scolded. And maybe fired. She and Luis hadn't considered that possibility.

Ms. Landry continued. "We're taking something of a risk here. But we're impressed with your campaign concept and we're hoping the people whose pictures are used will be so flattered that they won't even notice the slight alterations. Everybody always likes their pictures to look good, and these… Well, I have to say I think they will look fantastic." She gave Jenda a reassuring smile. Jenda thought she could almost guarantee that the subjects would be thrilled – after their next Chulel spa day, anyway.

Jenda was relieved. They were going to alter the photos. She was confused, however, by the genuine discomfort she sensed in Ms. Landry. If there was a sector at YJ that was engaged in systematic altering of files and memories, Ms. Landry didn't seem to be part of it. Was it possible that there was nothing going on within the restricted floors of the YJ building in Dallas other than diligent minding of the termini that guarded people's precious memories?

"It will take a few days to get the processing done and we'd like to send you to our office in Abilene where this will be handled. That way you can give them immediate feedback on the pictures and guarantee that they meet your standards." Jenda wanted to shout "Aha!" but instead tried to look compliant and grateful. "Your supervisor will give you some time off, but we'll make the arrangements from here and let you know the details by tomorrow afternoon."

Ms. Landry bid Jenda farewell with a smiling but still ominous sounding, "Let's hope this will all be worth it."

The remaining two hours of Jenda's work day dragged on intolerably. As soon as she was in the autocar for the drive home, she unfurled her digilet and pulsed Luis. "Good day at work. Check with you later." She hoped Luis would be waiting for her on Interloc by the time she got home.

Jenda flew through the doorway and grabbed a glass of Prosecco as she dashed through the kitchen to her home screen. She felt celebratory. She quickly screened up Recall and made her way to Interloc. There was a message waiting.

MURCIELAGO: Good day??

POLILLA: Pukka day!

Becoming "Polilla" always made Jenda smile; it meant she was talking with Luis. She quickly recounted all that had occurred – her visit to the restricted floor, her conversation with Ms. Landry, and most importantly, her impending business trip to Abilene.

POLILLA: I don't think Landry knows anything. She seemed genuinely concerned about my request somehow pushing the envelope. I'm thinking I may learn more in Abilene.

MURCIELAGO: You may be right. Let's hope!

POLILLA: By the way, you remember my ex-husband?

MURCIELAGO: Wait. What? You were married?

POLILLA: Oh. I'm sorry, Luis – I've been divorced from him for more than 75 years. I sometimes forget about it myself.

MURCIELAGO: Okay. What about him?

Jenda told him that Ben had been working for YJ in the Abilene office in 2045 when they met. She added a few details about how they had married after a brief courtship when Jenda was on sabbatical in Barcelona.

POLILLA: Sorry I never mentioned Ben before. It never seemed important.

MURCIELAGO: No problem. I know you had a life before me. Most of it, in fact.

POLILLA: As did you yourself, Señor. We've talked about this. Anyway. I think the ex may still be in my LifeBook loop. Do you think I should pulse him that I'm coming to Abilene?

MURCIELAGO: You think he may still be in your loop? And you're asking your partner if you should pulse your ex-husband. Pukka. Is he the only one?

POLILLA: Only one, my love. I swear. So what do you think?

Jenda figured the story of her unfortunately brief engagement to Sandra could wait for a more appropriate time.

MURCIELAGO: It probably makes sense. What department was he in?

POLILLA: That's the thing. He was never clear about that.

MURCIELAGO: Ah. Well then, maybe it's time to find out.

After Jenda and Luis had both signed out of Recall – after some ambiguous exchanges that may or may not have been loaded with sexual innuendo – Jenda screened up her LifeBook loop. There he was – Benjamin Cohen. She wasn't sure what to say. Finally she pulsed, "Hi there, old man! It's been a long time. I've got a business trip to Abilene soon – probably next week. Think maybe we can get together? If you're still around."

Jenda checked LifeBook before heading to work the next morning, thinking there might be a message from Ben. There was nothing. "Oh, well," she told herself. "It was worth a try."

When Jenda arrived at work, all the details for her trip to Abilene were already there on her desktop. The trip wasn't going to be next week; it was tomorrow. There were monorail and hotel reservations and the name and office number of the person she would be meeting with. All of this was in a digital folder marked "Private" and keyed to her access phrase. She went to her supervisor's office to let him know about her assignment. "I know, I know," he said with a wave of his hand as she appeared in the doorway. "No explanation necessary. Have a good trip and I'll see you next week. Feel free to leave early if you need time to pack."

Jenda left early. She stopped by a couple of shops on her way home to buy some new outfits for the trip. She felt guilty about not having anything for the recycles box, but promised herself she would bring extra next time. Shopping was feeling like a chore until she ran across a dress in that lovely bright blue that matched her eyes. Jenda bought it, along with a coordinating scarf. But then she seemed to vaguely remember that this particular color had been Ben's favorite on her. "What am I trying to do? Seduce my ex-husband? What craick!" She had a sudden desire to share the joke with Luis, and that amused her even more.

As soon as she got home she screened up Interloc to tell Luis about her plans, leaving a lengthy message. She didn't mention the blue dress. Before screening off, she thought she would check LifeBook again.

There was a message from Ben: "Well, hi, doll! It's been a while, hasn't it? Would love to get together with you when you hit town. Are you still with YJ? Let me know if you might be available for dinner next Tuesday. Ciao!"

"How about this Thursday instead?" Jenda responded. "Turns out I'm coming this week instead of next. Arriving tomorrow for meeting at YJ." Then she screened out and started packing. She'd share this development with Luis later.

Jenda did not own a small suitcase. She did own several large ones. Even for short trips, she habitually took more outfits than the number of days she would be away, with each outfit fully accessorized. Satisfied that she had packed clothes suitable for whatever occasions might arise on her brief business trip, and having laid out the outfit she intended to wear for the journey, Jenda prepared a quick supper, poured a glass of wine, and settled into her nook next to the home screen. She had a message from Luis on Interloc.

MURCIELAGO: That all sounds great. Just take it easy with those folks – don't want to arouse any suspicions. You won't be able to communicate with me on any of the local screens out there, only on the digilet. And watch what you say while you're in unfamiliar zones. If I don't catch you onscreen before you go – GOOD LUCK! I LOVE YOU!

POLILLA: Looks like you caught me!

Luis was still onscreen.

MURCIELAGO: Pukka! So… did you hear anything back from your ex?

POLILLA: I got a message this evening. We may have a dinner date tomorrow evening.

MURCIELAGO: That would be good.

MURCIELAGO: You see how much I trust you?

POLILLA: I'm fully worthy of your trust, you know. Don't know if he's still with YJ, although he did ask if I was. Why else would he still be in Abilene?

MURCIELAGO: I guess it's fortunate you guys are still on good terms.

MURCIELAGO: I'd love to see your pretty face.

So Jenda pulled up the visual communication facility called Chat² and they enjoyed a half hour of banter that cheerfully avoided even oblique references to their project.

Jenda's monorail journey to Abilene the next morning was uneventful. By noon she was checking in at a hotel near the Your Journal building. Her appointment was for 2:30 p.m., so she unpacked her outfits and went out to find lunch. Jenda wasn't particularly keen on going anywhere that would remind her of the places she and Ben had frequented during their long-distance marriage (the distance between Dallas and Abilene being longer than most people think). The names and décor of the restaurants had changed, of course, but Abilene's options hadn't improved much over the years. Jenda ended up in a salad and juice bar similar to the one she had always loved and Ben had hated.

As she settled into a window seat with her salad, Jenda caught an image reflected in the window that made her catch her breath: It was the woman from the monorail – the one she and Luis agreed must be corporate police. This woman was definitely following her. Jenda controlled her inclination to look at the woman directly, since that always seemed to trigger her disappearance. "If this is about YJ," Jenda thought, "why would she follow me here? YJ knows what I'm doing here. Don't they trust me? Who does she work for?" She knew she couldn't talk to Luis about this latest sighting until she returned to the more secure communication available from her habitat in Dallas. The next time Jenda glanced at the reflection in the window, the woman was gone.

After lunch and a quick shower and change of outfits, Jenda walked the two blocks to Your Journal, feeling vulnerable as she scanned the faces on the street for the suspicious policewoman. She noticed that the modular façade of YJ had been altered again and now incorporated panels of digital colloids showing episodes from YJ's latest advertising campaign. The YJ building was easily the tallest building in the city and to emphasize the point YJ had installed an awe-inspiring photonic 3-D image generator at the apex of the structure.

Jenda's meeting with her primary collaborator – a slightly pudgy man named George Putnam – was not as interesting as Jenda had hoped. She described exactly what she was going for with her campaign and pointed out what needed to be done with the pictures. George acted bored and asked hardly any questions. Jenda felt irritated, despite the fact that George seemed to grasp precisely what she wanted.

"I should have something for you to look at by 9:30 tomorrow morning," he said, screening off the images in a way that clearly indicated they were finished. The meeting had lasted barely half an hour.

Jenda thanked him for his time and walked out of the conference room, wondering what she was going to do for the rest of the afternoon and evening. Then she noticed the name on the door of the big office at the end of the hall: "Benjamin Cohen. Vice President for Customer Relations."

Without hesitation, she walked down the hall and through the doorway. The executive assistant was sitting at a desk that was easily twice as large as Jenda's desk in Dallas. He looked at Jenda blankly. "May I help you?"

"Is Mr. Cohen in?"

"Do you have an appointment?" The assistant looked doubtful.

"No. No I don't, but I just wanted to pop in and say hello. I'm in town from the Dallas office and I thought…"

"Oh, are you Ms. Swain? Mr. Cohen said you might come by. Let me check and see if he has a minute." The assistant disappeared into the inner office momentarily, then the big frosted plexi door slid open again. The assistant was smiling. "Please come in, Ms. Swain."

Jenda returned the smile and walked into the office, taking in at a glance the fact that Ben had definitely reached the upper echelons of the YJ hierarchy. Ben himself, of course, looked much the same as he had when they married in 2045.

"Jenda!" Ben's face broke into a broad grin as he rose from behind his immense desk to give her a quick hug. "How have you been? It's been a while, hasn't it!"

"A while, yes," Jenda said, responding to the apparently sincere warmth of Ben's smile. "And here we are, both still working for the same company."

They chatted about nothing in particular for a few minutes, standing in the center of the office. "I wish I had more time right now, but I've got a meeting coming up. Can we have dinner this evening?" It was quickly settled. He would pick her up at the hotel at seven.

Jenda was wearing the new bright blue outfit as she settled into the rightside seat of Ben's top of the line personal autocar. She knew the top of the line models weren't that different from the others, but they did have better advertising. Ben had made reservations at a steakhouse similar to the one that had been their go-to place for date nights. Jenda wasn't much into steaks these days, but she figured she could make an exception. It wasn't like steaks came from actual cows anymore.

Jenda was surprised that Ben remembered her favorite wine – a Spanish Tempranacha with a delightfully tangy cherry note. Jenda herself had forgotten about this particular wine, but the taste seemed familiar so she said she remembered.

"Keep your head, Jenda," she told herself. The wine was beginning to make her respond to Ben's attempts at humor with more laughter than they deserved. She excused herself between the salad and steak to go to the ladies' room and give herself a talking-to.

With squared shoulders and freshly applied lipstick, Jenda was ready to take the conversation in a potentially more interesting direction.

"By the way," she said, as she settled back into her chair, "I have a message to your people from my grandmother. She wants to thank you – and these are her words, mind you – for 'pruning her memories' and making them more manageable for a 165-year-old lady." She watched to see Ben's reaction.

Ben was watching her, too, and Jenda tried to appear as open and ingenuous as possible. He hesitated for a moment, looking down at his steak. Then he looked up at Jenda. "Well, at least some people appreciate what we do, right?"

Jenda was uncertain where to go with this new opening. Then she said, "Well, you know, some of us in YJ have been a bit naïve about all this. But I guess I can understand how important it is." It seemed like the right thing to say.

Maybe it was the Tempranacha or maybe it was the way Jenda's blue eyes picked up the blue of her outfit, but Ben opened up.

"There's no point in people having to be forever burdened with remembering things best forgotten," he told her. "When we know, for example, that a certain person has moved out of someone's LifeBook loop, we remove the memories as well. That person just won't be in the picture, anymore." He winked at Jenda. "It's a good thing we're still connected on LifeBook, right? Otherwise we probably wouldn't be sharing this excellent dinner." Jenda laughed politely, wondering how Ben would explain the disappearance of her brother from her LifeBook loop. Ben continued. "And then there are those genuinely unpleasant things that can happen through nobody's fault, and we know what those are and we can make them go away. Or at least carve away a lot of the messy details. And of course managing demand to conform to what we know is going to be available in the market – well, that's just efficiency, right?" He smiled and nodded, agreeing with his own assertion.

He paused then, as if debating whether to go on. "And sometimes people make unfortunate decisions – poor choices in companions, that sort of thing – and we can help them manage that, too."

His face took on a stern look, as if he was afraid he might have said too much. "It's important for all of us at YJ to understand that everything we do is for the good of our customers. Some employees – especially lower level ones – might not fully grasp the critical need we're filling by aiding our customers with memory management. I'm glad you get it, Jenda. And I know I can trust you to be discreet."

Jenda said something that she hoped sounded appropriate. It occurred to her that maybe the mysterious policewoman did in fact work for YJ and that all of this was a way of testing her. She should be careful. Ben offered to top up her wine glass and Jenda demurred. He poured a little anyway.

"God, you look beautiful tonight, Jenda! Thank you for wearing my favorite color. You know I always loved you in that color."

Jenda was jolted back into the moment, wary about where Ben might be heading. She was reassured by his next statement: "You know I'm married again." Then she reminded herself that marriage had never deterred him before.

"Carol and I are very solid," he said.

Jenda relaxed. She listened distractedly as Ben recounted the mundane activities in which he engaged with the beautiful Carol and the child they had produced back in 2062. Apparently they had been married a long time.

"Of course, part of what has kept us together this long is the fact that we sort of give one another the freedom we each need to move outside the relationship from time to time." Ben reached over and took Jenda's hand, gazing deeply into her eyes.

"Oh, Lord, here we go," Jenda thought. "You're such a cliché, Ben Cohen." But in the last ten minutes, while Ben had been droning on about his life with Carol, Jenda had figured out how she would have evaded his advances if it had become necessary.

"Oh, Ben," she said, doing her best to look pained. "I'm flattered, of course, but... well... I've finally come to terms with the fact that I'm really more attracted to women than to men. You understand, don't you?"

Ben released his grip on her hand and patted it with suddenly fraternal affection.

"So." he said. "I guess maybe... maybe I had wondered about that."

Jenda restrained her desire to laugh. She knew that if Ben checked into her Your Journal files – and he certainly could – he would find that the last person she had written about being seriously involved with was Sandra. After Sandra's death, which of course was not mentioned in YJ, Jenda had been so distraught that she had vowed never to enter names of any of her lovers in YJ again, refusing to give them personal power over her story. Now she was grateful for what she had often considered to be a childish impulse.

After a nice crème brulée and a decaf with coffee liqueur, Ben took Jenda back to her hotel. He explained politely that he would be busy all the next day in meetings and she said that if the photos came up to her liking, she would be headed back to Dallas on the midday monorail. They gave each other a peck on the cheek and said their fond, platonic farewells.

Jenda walked into the hotel lobby with a distinct sense of relief. Hers and Luis' suspicions about YJ were confirmed. But what about the policewoman? Jenda was eager to get back to Dallas and her own home screen with all of its maze-like capabilities that would connect her with Luis.

12.

Max and Emily Feldman attended the big opening at Galería Picaflor for the collection of recyclable decorative paintings that Isabel Hernandez considered to be shit. There was an enthusiastic crowd and Isabel made a lot of sales. The gallery was busy for the next two weeks of the exhibit, as May's pleasant autumn weather gave way to the southern hemisphere's more wintry early June temperatures. Isabel took scores of orders for the unlimited copies the featured artist was willing to print. She had learned to put digital counters next to each piece indicating how many copies had been sold, since the more popular a piece appeared to be, the more likely the next consumer was to want her own copy.

Emily Feldman pulsed Isabel, congratulating her on her success and inviting her out to lunch for the Sunday after the show's official closing reception on Saturday evening. Isabel pulsed back: "That sounds wonderful, but why don't you pick up something to bring over? Then we can have a quiet lunch here at the gallery. I have some things I want to show you."

Shortly after noon on Sunday, Max and Emily went to their favorite Pakistani restaurant to pick up food to take for their luncheon. When they arrived at the gallery, Isabel was at her desk. She rose to welcome them, tasking her digilet to lock the door and darken the windows. "That smells delicious," she remarked. "Come this way."

Down a side hall at the back of the gallery, Isabel unlocked what looked like the door to a janitor's closet. The door opened to reveal a second gallery space, beautifully if artificially lit, with a table set up in the center, laid with real china and silver and crystal and table linens. The walls were lined with real oil paintings. The table and chairs looked like authentic Art Deco. Max and Emily were speechless.

"Hand me those containers before you drop them," Isabel chuckled, looking pleased at the effect her secret gallery was having on her friends. "I've opened a bottle of wine. I think it should complement your curry nicely." Isabel set the food containers on a small side table and poured wine.

"So this is where you're keeping the real art." Max's face glowed with evident delight. "Look, Emily, she still has the Xul Solar."

"Ah, I remember how much you liked his 'Ña Diáfana'," Isabel said as she poured some of her best Argentine Malbec into the crystal wine glasses and handed one each to Max and Emily. "It is an exquisite piece. I was fortunate to acquire it when they sold off the inventory of his museum." Max and Emily murmured excitedly as they identified the work of one after another of their favorite artists.

"I don't recognize this one," Max said, standing in front of a vibrant retro-Expressionist oil.

"That one is by an artist currently working in Mexico," Isabel said.

"You mean there are still people painting like this?" Emily said. "I'm stunned. Who is the artist?"

"He's known as 'Charro Negro'. In Mexico, that means something like 'black cowboy'. He always paints a tiny bat somewhere in his paintings – you see right here?" Isabel was pointing to a dark area where the silhouette of a bat was barely visible. "We don't know much about this Charro Negro, but his work is getting some attention in the underground art world. I was pleased to be able to acquire one of his paintings. These kinds of acquisitions are always a bit risky for both collector and artist."

"I can well imagine," Emily responded. There was more to see – more paintings, as well as some sculptures in stone and bronze. Emily noticed a few shelves of books inside a polished wood cabinet with glass doors. "I see you collect books, too," she ventured.

"I guess I do," Isabel said. "To tell the truth, I can't remember where I got most of my books. But I do know that it's a rather good collection. Many of the best Latin American novelists and poets are there." She opened the doors to the cabinet.

"My goodness, this is a fine collection," Max remarked, as he scanned the titles on the spines.

"There are only a few that I remember acquiring," Isabel said, running a finger along one row of books. "They are the ones I got from what used to be the Bartolomé Mitre archives. However…" Isabel reached for a slim paperback with a light blue cover and pulled it out. "I've always felt this one holds some special significance for me."

"Ah, Silvina Ocampo." Max held the book in his hands like a delicate flower as Emily peered over his shoulder. "*Viaje Olvidado*. Her first publication, I believe."

"That's right," Isabel affirmed. "That's not an original edition, of course. But look inside."

There was an inscription in pencil on the first page: "Feliz cumpleaños a mi querida mami – ¡besos y abrazos! Juanita."

"You have a daughter?" Emily asked.

"So it would appear," Isabel replied. "That's one of those things I don't seem to remember. And perhaps that's the one that makes me the most sad." She took the book from Max's hands and replaced it lovingly in its slot on the shelf. She ran her fingers along the line of books until she came to a pair of books in glossy dustcovers. She took one of them out and held it up. "This is another book that mystifies me," she said. "All the rest of my books are in Spanish and are by Latin American authors, but this one – there are two of them, actually – is in English and is by an American author by the name of Martin Jameson. As best I can tell, he was a highly successful novelist back around the turn of the 21st century. My books are signed first editions and I have no idea where I got them." Isabel replaced the book and closed the glass doors. "Well. Shall we let that yummy smelling food sit there or shall we eat it?"

Lunch conversation was animated, revolving around art and artists and authors. As Isabel poured out the last of the second bottle of wine, Max decided it was time to broach a new subject.

"Isabel, would you be interested in trying to find your lost memories? Emily and I might be able to help."

"¿Será? How could you help with something like that? It's hard to find something when you don't even know where – or when – you lost it. Anyway, it's just the Chulel and it's my punishment for having been vain enough to continue taking the stuff."

"Chulel has not done this to you, Isabel," Emily said gently. "Max and I have been taking it even longer than you have, and our memories are remarkably intact."

"Ah, but you come from North America and you've had access to the memory restoration process," Isabel rejoined.

"No, Isabel. We've never used that procedure. Not even once," Emily said.

"I don't understand. What are you telling me? Isn't it true that Chulel after many years of use destroys the memory?"

"No, Isabel." Max's voice was soft but forceful. "It is not true. It's a lie. A useful one for some people, but an absolute lie."

"Why have I forgotten so much, then?" Isabel looked perplexed.

Gently, carefully, Max and Emily explained to her about photonic memory restructuring, a process that could both remove old memories and implant new ones. They had recently uncovered information in some old scientific journals that referenced research conducted in the late 2020s and early 2030s at an institute somewhere right here in Argentina. The cited sources were no longer available, but the work appeared to focus on exactly this photonic process, the same one that was now being used in the Chulel clinics and called "memory restoration". They were having difficulty ascertaining exactly where the institute might have been located, but they thought it might be near Buenos Aires.

"What we know about the process, though," Max said, "is that it can leave latent memories that can resurge. At first memories may come back spontaneously, as a vague sort of familiarity. With patience and a little help, these memories can sometimes be restored in more detail."

Isabel's expression was drawn and tense as she fought to retain her composure. "Like a sense of déjà vu? That thing that some of the Sanguinista people say is a memory of a past life?"

"Past life!" Max snorted. "Like last year."

That made Isabel smile. She took a deep breath. "So, what would you propose to do to go about this search?"

Speaking in turns, Emily and Max suggested that they would first put together as complete a life history as they could manage in order to see exactly where Isabel's memory gaps occurred. Then, she would need to tell them about anything that ever caused her to have that sense of familiarity – of déjà vu.

"We don't want to get your hopes up too much, Isabel," Emily said. "This may not work. And of course, we're assuming that the cause of your memory loss is in fact the photonic process, which we don't know for sure yet."

"I understand. As long as you won't be giving me drugs or anything that will make me forget even more." Isabel paused. "Just one more thing: Why? Why would you want to help an old woman like me with something like this?"

"Max and I have become increasingly distressed about the way our... the Chulel is being used in conjunction with memory restructuring. That was not the intention of the drug's makers," Emily said, giving Max a sidelong glance.

"Oh, tell her, Em." Max slapped the table with his open hand. "Tell her we're the culprits who came up with this devilish Chulel thing in the first place."

"So you are those Feldmans," Isabel said. "You know I often check out people who start coming to the gallery and inquiring about, you know, real paintings. And the only Max and Emily Feldman I could find in the LifeBook directory had been scientists at Pharmakon. I didn't know if that was you or not. And now you tell me this Chulel was your own invention? Well, then I guess I need to believe what you tell me about what it does and doesn't do. Yes. Yes I will work with you in whatever way you recommend to see if I can find what I have lost." Isabel's face was glowing. "When do we start?"

117

13.

When Jenda arrived home from Abilene and tried to screen up Interloc, she found herself locked out. "Well, zujo!" she thought. She screened up LifeBook instead and found a brief personal pulse from Luis: "Looking forward to seeing you next weekend. Until then."

Jenda didn't remember any plans to meet so soon. Their next meeting was supposed to be in El Paso in early July. Had Jenda missed something on Interloc? "Well, I can't check now," she told herself. Then she noticed some new pictures in her current LifeBook chapter. One was a photo of her and Luis in San Miguel – a very bad photo. You couldn't see either of their faces. "Oh," Jenda thought. "The Dark Knight is sending me a message." She examined the rest of the photographs more carefully. One of them was of a hotel, its name clearly visible. Jenda searched and found that there were several hotels with that name, but the one that matched this photograph was in San Antonio. In fact, this was the same photograph, drawn directly from the hotel mediazone. As she looked at the other photos again, she realized that they all seemed to be from San Antonio.

"So. I guess I'm going to San Antonio this weekend," Jenda said aloud, quickly glancing around as if looking for some kind of surveillance. The worries that had nagged her in Abilene after her latest sighting of the policewoman were now compounded by concerns about Luis.

Jenda reserved a room for Friday and Saturday nights at the hotel in the picture and bought a ticket for the hyperloop for Friday morning. Then she deleted all the photos Luis had posted.

Jenda's project at work was moving at hyperloop speed now that she had the photos she needed. Nevertheless, with no communication from Luis, the week seemed to drag on. She went to a couple of entertainments with friends. She went shopping for some outfits for the weekend. She even called up Granny El and took her to a new restaurant that had recently opened. It wasn't really a new restaurant, but it had been thoroughly rearranged and redecorated and had a revised menu. Wherever she went, she kept an anxious eye out for the corporate policewoman. Even when she didn't spot her, Jenda had the distinct feeling she was being watched.

Friday morning finally came and Jenda settled into her seat for the 40-minute hyperloop journey to San Antonio. She checked her digilet for messages and found a reply to the pulse she had sent weeks earlier to her brother. "Hi, Jen. I'm okay, although I'm not sure I'm someone you want to know at present. Here's an alt contact phrase in case you ever need it. Be well!" He had appended the phrase. She wondered what he meant and why it had taken so long for this message to come through.

Jenda considered taking a tab of Duermata and sleeping for half the journey, taking advantage of Duermata's guarantee of precisely 20 minutes of restful sleep per tablet. She decided against it, occupying herself instead with conjuring up explanations for why she was going to San Antonio to meet Luis, pondering what might be happening to her brother, and trying to fathom the motives of the mysterious policewoman.

Although she knew he wouldn't be there, Jenda scanned the crowd in the hyperloop station, hoping to glimpse Luis' familiar form and face. She didn't see the policewoman, either. She went to the autocar dock and selected a shiny blue vehicle. She tapped the trunk; it opened and the grabber snapped up her suitcase. Inside the car, she passed her digilet across the blinking blue light that both started the car and tasked her account. Then she spoke the address of the hotel and the autocar moved onto the street.

Jenda glanced into the rearview mirror just as a dark green autocar pulled onto the street behind her. The car had only one occupant: It was the policewoman. Jenda's mind went into overdrive. She couldn't lead the woman to the hotel where she and Luis would be staying. But where could she go? She didn't know San Antonio. Only one idea presented itself. "Redirect." Her voice was tense as she gave new instructions to the autocar.

"San Antonio Art Museum." The car confirmed and set in a course for the museum. All Jenda knew about the museum was that it was on the river walk. She thought if she could lose the policewoman somewhere in or around the museum, she would be able to walk the rest of the way to the hotel.

When the autocar pulled up in front of the museum, Jenda got out quickly and sent the car to park itself, unconcerned about the fate of her suitcase. Inside, Jenda paid her entry fee with her digilet and glanced at the map of exhibits that popped up. Her heart thumped wildly as she headed for a darkened gallery featuring holographic sculptures. It was a good place to hide, but offered no vantage point from which to see whether the policewoman had followed her into the museum. Through the gallery, she found stairs leading up to the next level. Obscured by some hanging textiles, she peered over the balcony. The policewoman had entered and was heading for the main staircase.

"Zujo! What now?" Jenda looked around the second floor. All the galleries seemed to open onto the main balcony. Desperate, she ducked into the bathrooms and locked herself inside a stall. "God, Jenda, is this all you can think of? You know she'll come look for you here!" Just then the bathroom door opened and through the slit at the edge of the stall door, Jenda saw the policewoman. She sat on the toilet and pulled her feet up on the seat. She would have to remain perfectly still so as not to trigger the automatic flush, but she was shivering from the chill air of the museum and her mounting fear only made it worse. It was just a matter of time now and Jenda wished desperately that she had chosen to take self-defense classes instead of dancing.

The bathroom door opened again and Jenda saw that the person entering was a man. He stood with his back against the closed door, facing the policewoman. "You need to let this go, Selena," he said.

"What are you doing here?" the policewoman replied testily. "You know this is my assignment. I've been tasked to find him and by god I'm going to find the comemierda, even if

I have to follow this bitch all over Texas and back! What business do you have interfering?"

"Let it go. You're on the wrong side here. Come with me and I'll explain."

"What the zujo? Are you fucking crazy? What's got into you, Nick? They've got to you, haven't they? You're on report, amigo, and right now."

Jenda saw the woman remove her digilet and then she heard the high-pitched zing of a laser shot, followed by a thud as Selena collapsed onto the floor. Jenda's eyes went tight shut. She heard the door to the bathrooms open and close. Then silence.

She opened her eyes and waited.

"I can't wait too long," she thought. "Someone else might come in." She got down cautiously from her perch and jumped as the automatic flush engaged. She opened the stall door and saw the woman – Selena – lying motionless. She was still breathing. On impulse, Jenda picked up Selena's digilet from where it had fallen on the floor and tucked it into her bag.

With the aid of her museum map, Jenda quickly located a back exit that opened onto the river walk. The sunshine and warm air began to calm her shivering. As she approached the cover of an overhead bridge, she took Selena's digilet out of her bag. Leaning against a support post, out of sight, she touched the screen and a photo of her own face emerged. She gasped as she recognized the emblem of Marvaworld in the corner of the screen. Was Selena searching for Luis? She touched the screen again and Jenda's picture was replaced by another – her brother's.

Jenda stared for a moment, not comprehending. "Is that what this is about?" She didn't understand, but she knew that as soon as Marvaworld knew something was amiss, they would be tracing Selena's digilet. She needed to get rid of it. She dropped the digilet onto a rock and stomped on it with the heel of her shoe, pleased at the crunching sound it made. Then she kicked the digilet out into the current, watching as it floated for a moment and then went under. She glanced around, desperately hoping no one had observed her action. There was no one in sight. Clutching her bag under her arm, she hurried away. The hotel she had booked – the one Luis had selected – should be about 1.5 kilometers downriver.

Arriving at the hotel at last, Jenda checked in and made her way empty-handed to her room. It had a big window overlooking the hotel's main entrance and she stationed herself there to watch for Luis. She wondered if one of the people she saw might be Nick, the man who had lasered Selena. She hadn't seen his face. The people she saw were uniformly youthful and energetic and appeared fully engrossed in one another, happily going about their own lives, oblivious to the fact that a corporate policewoman lay unconscious in the bathroom of the art museum.

Then she saw Luis. He had shaved off most of his beard, maintaining a small goatee and mustache. It made Jenda smile. She thought she would recognize him anywhere, no matter how his facial hair changed. She pulsed him the room number and waited, her need for his reassuring presence growing more intense with each passing second.

Finally there was a soft knock on the door. Jenda opened it and there he was, smiling broadly. He closed and latched the door behind him and Jenda flung herself into his arms. After a long kiss, Luis said, "God, I'm so glad you understood what to do. I was so afraid I might have been too cryptic. Why are you trembling, querida? It's not that bad."

"Yes it is, Luis. It's worse than you know."

As Jenda recounted her experiences of the day, Luis grew increasingly agitated. When she got to the part about the Marvaworld emblem on Selena's digilet, he was dumbfounded.

"Marvaworld? Good god, why would they be looking for you. Or your brother?"

"I think my brother worked with Marvaworld on his last flick. You knew he was a flickmaker, right? Of course, he used his Buddhist name, as well as our mother's maiden name. So professionally he was Jampel Jenkins."

"Wait. Jampel Jenkins is your brother Jonathan?" Luis placed both hands on his forehead, his eyes wide as he stared at Jenda. "And you told me his last flick had been withdrawn. What was the title of that flick?"

"I told you that, too, Luis – 'The Nagas and the Garuda'."

"Zujo! Why am I just now putting all of this together? That film was a huge hit in the Recall community. Why didn't I realize it was a Marvaworld production? Or know that your brother directed it? Damn Marvaworld! Is there no one a decent man can work for anymore?" Luis paced angrily. "Why did I convince myself that my contract with them was okay? 'They just do entertainment,' I thought. No, what they do is propaganda. That's it! I'm done with them. This can't go on. You know there's a plan in the works to bring an end to all this. I don't know the details, but I know it exists and the word going around Recall is that it will be happening soon. I'm glad you don't know where your brother is – my bet is that he's found a safe place and he's protecting you by not telling you where it is. It's obvious Marvaworld doesn't know where he is."

Jenda watched Luis' tirade in thoughtful silence, trying to make sense out of everything. "What about the woman – Selena?"

"Well, if she's still alive… Yes, she's probably still alive, but from your account, I'd say the setting on that laser pistol was likely high enough to have wiped a fair few neurotransmitters. She probably won't remember anything about that encounter, which is lucky for – what did she call him? Nick? Lucky for Nick, who is probably working with Recall. You didn't think you were the only spy in the corporate ranks did you Jenda?"

"Won't Marvaworld assign another officer to finish Selena's task?"

"They might. Or they might be so concerned about what happened to her that they'll let it drop for a while."

Jenda wasn't sure whether Luis truly believed that or was merely trying to placate her fears.

"In any event, you should be careful, Jenda. And we probably need to get your suitcase back, don't we? Hand me your digilet and I'll call in the autocar you were using."

Jenda handed him the digilet, relieved that he seemed to consider this a simple task. "So why were you being so secretive about this trip, Luis? I'm assuming it didn't have anything to do with my brother's flicks or Marvaworld."

"Recall's been irrupted. As soon as I knew about the irruption, I deleted your persona. We'll have to set you up again, once we're sure the zone is secure."

"Irrupted? Who…?"

"We're not sure yet," Luis replied. "Our people are still analyzing. But I've been dying to hear about your exciting trip to Abilene. Well, I guess not so exciting compared to today." He held up a hand as he picked up his digilet. "But wait just a minute while I order us some drinks. I think we could use drinks."

A short while later, as they settled onto the boxy sofa with glasses of 12-year-old Cuban rum with lots of ice, Jenda began her story, telling Luis about George, the photo specialist she had worked with and how bored he seemed to be with her project.

"But he was proficient," Jenda said. "He obviously had a lot of experience. It all seemed so simple and straightforward at the Abilene office. I don't understand why they wanted me to go there instead of doing it all through the atmo. It wasn't that complicated."

"Well, if you truly want something to be secure," Luis said, "it's best to keep it in-house. You know the history of the 'nets – something gets irrupted, new security protocols are initiated, then that gets irrupted, prompting more new security systems. And on it goes. There's no such thing as absolute security outside the supranet and maybe even there… Anyway. It's a challenge. But the thing is, if everybody working on a project is kept denned up together and disconnected from the digital world – well, that's pretty secure. Then you only have to worry about your location and your people."

"Yeah, I guess I get that. The most interesting information came from the Vice President for Customer Services."

"You got to meet with a vice president?"

"Yeah. Ben. My ex."

"Your ex is a vice president at YJ? Oh, please, tell me all about this." He took Jenda's hand and cradled it against his chest, relaxing into the uncomfortable little sofa as best he could. Jenda told him about her first encounter with Ben in his office, followed by their dinner date.

"Ben ended up telling me about their guidelines for revising people's memory files. Basically, we each have a set amount of file space on YJ and when we reach our limits, they have algorithms that start deleting files." Jenda described in detail his revelations about how this is done. "Anyway, Ben seems convinced that the file revisions are an important service, helping people feel happier with their lives, helping them adapt to change and especially to new technology. He kept emphasizing that this wasn't that different from the memory loss the elderly used to experience anyway, just more organized and beneficial."

"What a convenient misunderstanding. Yes, of course people have always had memory loss with old age, but mostly they'd lose their short-term memory. Long term memories – the very things that YJ is taking away – would be retained in often amazing detail right up to the day someone died. Old people's memories were the continuity of the whole culture and society. That used to make them special."

Jenda was thinking, formulating a question. "So, if Granny El hadn't been going in for Chulel – well, for the memory restructuring – for all these years, she'd have a lot more information about what her life was like back in, say, the 1970s and 1980s? More information about my mother's life? More information about me?"

"Without a doubt," Luis said. "Now, exactly what she'd remember and how she'd tell the stories... Well, that would be somewhat unpredictable. Human memory is hardly infallible. But at least they'd be her memories and her stories and not some set of memories deemed socially or economically beneficial and cobbled together by algorithms at Your Journal."

Jenda continued her story. "After Ben and I finished dinner, he started telling me about his wife – yes, he's been married to her for the past 75 years and counting – and how important it has been to their relationship that each one has had the freedom to experience other relationships along the way." Jenda watched Luis to see his reaction.

"No! So he tried to seduce you?"

"Yes." Jenda said calmly. "So I told him I had finally come to terms with being lesbian."

Luis laughed and pulled Jenda closer to him on the sofa. "You'll never get away with it. You don't seem like a lesbian to me," he said.

"I guess I never told you about Sandra." So Jenda told him, and for the first time she understood how important Sandra's vibrant femininity had been to her after Ben's arrogant alpha male displays had left her lonely and desolate. As this understanding dawned, it reinforced another feeling that had been emerging into her awareness over the past several months – the conviction that she did know what true love is and that she had experienced it somewhere, sometime, maybe more than once, even before Luis.

The next morning as Jenda lay on her side, facing away from Luis, he started stroking the small of her back, seeming to trace a pattern over and over.

"When are you going to tell me about this tattoo?" he asked.

"What? I don't have any tattoos." Jenda turned to face him. "You old Joker!"

"No, really, Jen. There used to be a tattoo here." He gently turned her back on her side and traced the pattern again.

"How can you tell? It's probably... maybe where I was lying on the crumpled up sheets."

"I noticed it a long time ago. In San Miguel in fact, one day when we'd been to the pool and you were a little sunburned.

I could see where the ink was removed. Those areas never quite blend in with the surrounding skin when it changes color."

"Okay," Jenda said. "If there's something there, show me."

Luis got up, pulled on his undershorts, retrieved his digilet, and took a photograph.

"You just wanted to take some nude photographs of my backside," Jenda grumbled as she got up and pulled on the hotel robe, which was skimpy but adequate.

Luis had already linked his digilet to Jenda's traveling digiscreen and was processing the photograph, enhancing the contrast.

"Wayee, it does look like … something," she conceded. "Can you get any more detail?"

"Not without a better equipped screen," he said. "But at least you know I wasn't making this up. Does the shape or anything look familiar at all?" Luis zoomed out to show the entire figure. It was about 12 centimeters high by 8 centimeters across, narrowing at the top.

"No, I don't think so," she said, then suddenly added, "Can you make it blue?"

"What? Blue? Why?"

"I don't know. Just do it. Blue."

Luis complied.

"No, not my whole back," she complained. "Just the image. Or maybe only part of it."

Luis did his best. It still didn't look like anything, but Jenda continued staring.

"It reminds me of something," she murmured, her brow knitted into a frown.

"Well, let's wait and see what a better giz can do," Luis said. "You know, you're not the only one who had a tattoo. Can you see mine?" He raised his left shoulder toward Jenda.

"You, too?" she said, examining the shoulder he presented. "Hmmm. I don't see anything. Maybe you need some sun. What was it?"

"Nothing interesting. Just Batman." Luis grinned.

"You're craicking me. You had a tattoo of Batman?"

128

"Well, I got it when I was 18 and I thought it was terrific. Maybe yours is something like that, too."

"Why did you have your tattoo removed, Luis?"

He leaned back in the chair and folded his arms, glancing again at the shoulder where the tattoo had been. "Not my choice," he said. "I got picked up at a protest back when I was… oh, maybe 22? And that had become standard procedure. Tattoos weren't against any law, but if you passed through the hands of the corporate police you were going to come out the other side with no tattoo. I've thought about having it redone, but there are so few good tattoo artists anymore. And they mostly make those temp-tats that can be erased whenever you want or that fade away on their own after a year or so."

"Why do you think I would have gotten a tattoo? Why did you get yours?"

"I think Vintagonists were drawn to anything that felt permanent. Making images in ink on your own skin felt like a statement, regardless of what the image was."

Jenda walked over to the window and stared out at the street, wondering if anybody out there also had tattoos, old or otherwise. "Do you think we could risk a walk by the river, Luis? I need to do something with all this nervous energy. We could get lunch."

They left questions of tattoos and corporate intrigue behind, then, and went for a stroll along the river. It was one of those summer days when the cool moist air along the stone-lined banks of the river gave way only grudgingly to the heat of the sun. They watched the ducks and the grackles and listened to the cooing of doves, all of which had escaped Jenda's notice as she fled her morning encounter with Selena. They admired the new sculptures, the ones with digital skins that beamed back versions of whatever the oscillating hidden camera was perceiving. They even laughed a bit as their own faces showed up on the faces of one sculpture.

Suddenly Jenda stopped. "Oh, look, Luis!" She pointed to the edge of the pathway. "Poor thing." She was looking at a young dove – a dead young dove.

Luis stared at the bird for a moment. "This reminds me of something – something I haven't thought about in years. There was a flick I watched back in graduate school. It was an old flick – in fact one of the first ethnographic flicks ever made. Can't remember the guy who made it, but it was about a group of people on a Pacific island. They had this legend about how at the origins of humanity there had been a contest between a bird and a snake, to determine whether human beings would be like snakes – shedding their skins and living forever – or like birds, who have to die. They say the bird won. I wonder if maybe they were wrong."

Jenda was feeling more fragile than she wished to admit and the dead bird brought her close to tears. Luis took her hand and pulled her away onto a little bridge so they could cross over to the other side of the river.

After stopping for enormous ice cream sundaes that they figured would hold them until dinner, Jenda and Luis made their way back to the hotel.

"What's next?" Jenda asked, settling down on the sofa next to Luis.

"Well, there will be dinner. Maybe some heterosexual sex," he responded.

"That's good." She nestled closer. "But you know what I mean. What's next for our project? And can we talk about exactly what that project is now?"

A major part of the project, Luis acknowledged, had been accomplished in that they had solid information on where and how YJ managed people's files. Much that had only been suspected was now confirmed.

"Personally, I'd like to find out more about what happened to my grandmother in Argentina," he said. "And of course I want to help you find more of the missing pieces of your own past." There was a bitterness in his voice as he added, "Now that I'm finished with Marvaworld, I should have plenty of time." He folded his arms across his chest. "I'm sure higher level plans will be on hold until they figure out who irrupted Recall and recreate a secure means of operation. So why don't

130

we take the opportunity to concentrate on our personal concerns – finding out what happened to my abuela and finding out why you don't remember having been a crazy Vintagonist?"

"Pukka," Jenda said. "I've been kind of wanting to see if Granny El can remember anything that might help me piece things together. Her memories may be full of holes, but at least she has some. It would be great if she had something like the little book you found in your mother's things, but you should see how vanguard Gran's habitat is. I can't imagine she would have kept anything old. But she might remember something."

"That would definitely be worth a shot," Luis said. "And as for me, I've been thinking maybe I should take another trip to Argentina."

Realizing that it might be difficult to communicate for a while, they made a date to meet again at this same hotel in two weeks. Most of Sunday they spent in bed.

14.

Back in Dallas, Jenda sorted through the oldest photos she could find in her personal YJ files. She was dismayed at how few there were. She indexed some of them to ask Granny El about. One of them was the altered photo she and Luis had examined from her Vintie days. Another showed her as a child with what appeared to be a white cat in the background. A third showed her as a serious looking teenager in front of an easel, with a paintbrush in her hand. This one also had been altered to obscure her Vintagonist traits. Now all Jenda had to do was convince Granny El that instead of tennis this Friday, they should get together at Jenda's place for dinner and a flick.

"Why don't we go out to that new dinner theater?" Granny El countered.

"I'd rather you come to my place, Gran." Jenda hesitated. "Sometimes it seems so empty and I like having people over." There was no response so she took a new tack. "I redecorated my front room and I want to know what you think of it."

"Ah, well then. Okay, we'll do it. Shall I bring the dinner or are you cooking?"

Jenda thought she heard Granny El snicker. She knew Jenda didn't cook. Most people didn't cook these days. Kitchens were designed strictly for entertaining and convenient preparation of pre-cooked meals.

"You can bring the dinner. I'll pick out a flick," Jenda responded, quickly calculating when she'd have time to go to 3Dec and buy some new items to redo her front room. She wouldn't have time to order anything custom made on the 3-D printers they were known for. She'd have to settle for something pre-scripted.

On Friday, Granny El showed up three minutes early at Jenda's door, bearing containers filled with barbequed beef product, mashed potatoes, fried okra, and coleslaw. "You are so old-fashioned," Jenda chided her, but she had to admit the spicy fragrance of the sauce was making her mouth water.

Jenda modestly accepted Granny El's effusive praise for her redecorating job. In fact, Jenda hated the bright oranges and yellows in the floral patterned window treatments and sofa pillows, but she knew her grandmother favored this color range and she hoped to put her in a good mood. She had also selected one of Granny El's favorite musical comedies for their entertainment.

"I love that show," Granny El sighed, after the final big number left her once more with happy tears.

"So do I!" Jenda tried to sound enthusiastic, despite the fact that she had found the story thin and meaningless this time around. Why had she never noticed that the song lyrics were one long sequence of clichés?

She served up ice cream with chocolate mint syrup, and as she and her grandmother scraped the bottom of their plastimold dishes, Jenda said, "How about looking at some old pictures?" as if the thought had just occurred to her.

"Oh, Jen, why would you want to do that?" Granny El demurred.

"No, no, I think it will be fun," Jenda said, hastily opening her YJ folder on the home screen. "Let's see what I can find." She pulled up the indexed photos. They had a good laugh over a picture of Jenda as a young child wearing what they agreed was a ridiculous swimsuit. Jenda moved on to the picture with the cat.

"Do you see that little white cat in the back of this one? Do you suppose I ever had any pets, Gran?"

"Pets. Such a foolish indulgence, only designed to make you cry or make you sick," Granny El replied. Then she squinted at the screen, studying the photograph. "Maybe you did have a pet. That little cat does look… familiar." Jenda could see that her grandmother's mind was taking a detour. Her head tilted to one side as she murmured something that sounded like, "Sweet Milly…" Then she turned abruptly to Jenda and said, "No, I don't remember any pets."

Jenda moved on through another few pictures and then to the one of herself as an altered teenager. "Do you know how old I was in this picture, Gran?" Jenda asked. "The tag says it's from 2028, but I look… I don't know, older than 15, don't you think?"

Granny El studied the screen. "If the YJ tag says 2028, then 2028 must be right."

"Do you remember my crazy friends from back then?" Jenda laughed, trying to imply that she herself remembered them only too well.

"Oh, yes. I don't know how you ever fell in with that crowd, but I'm so glad that gap year trip got you over it."

"Yeah…" Jenda's mind was racing. "Gosh, where all did I go that year?"

"Oh, I don't remember – South America, I think. Yes, maybe South America, but I don't know exactly where. The important thing, of course, is that you came back refreshed and ready to tackle your coursework at Perry University." She sounded almost like she was quoting from a brochure for gap year trips.

"You made some beautiful paintings that summer," she continued softly. "I put them in the closet after your mother died. My beautiful Tessa…" Granny El suddenly looked sad and old, in spite of her good skin and hair.

"What closet?" Jenda almost whispered.

"Closet?" Granny El came out of her reverie abruptly. "Oh, there are several closets at my place that I don't use anymore. Who knows what's in there? Feel free to use them if you want, if you need to store anything for a while."

After Granny El left, Jenda wished she could talk to Luis. Instead, she picked up one of her little paper books and wrote her thoughts there:

Your Journal thinks they're doing such a fine job of pruning and reorganizing people's memories, when what they're doing is condemning people to live with broken memories and lives that don't make sense anymore, fragmented memories that don't fit together, lives that don't link up with the lives of the people they love.

135

Part III:
Pieces of the Puzzle

15.

Dr. Emily Feldman took on the task of piecing together Isabel Hernandez' life story while Max continued his search for more information about the clandestine institute that had engaged in photonic memory experimentation back in the 2020s and 2030s.

Emily preferred interviewing Isabel inside her secret gallery, hoping the proximity of the artworks and books would be conducive to remembering. It quickly became evident that most of Isabel's life before about 2080 was a grab-bag of scraps and fragments. Whatever had scrambled her memories had done a thorough job.

Isabel did remember a small apartment where she used to live in Buenos Aires, and Max had examined residential records and determined that she had moved into that apartment in November of 2080. Isabel had lived there for about ten years. She didn't remember moving in. One of her earliest memories of that apartment was of a man arriving at her door with several large boxes with her name on them. He claimed to be someone she knew. They had gone out to dinner that day and he had come back to visit a few more times. The boxes were filled with books and small works of art.

"Who was this man?" Emily asked. "How did he know you?"

"He said his name was Silvestre Ocampo. He claimed that I'd worked for a while in his home village, near one of the old estancias up-river," Isabel said.

"What kind of work?" Emily prompted.

Isabel laughed quietly and looked away. "Well, it sounds kind of crazy, but he seemed to be implying that I'd been involved in some kind of … I don't know, spying activity? He would never say much about it. And once he realized that I had no memory of him or his village, he didn't come back anymore. He seemed a simple fellow. Not like someone who'd know about spies and such. Maybe it was just a story he made up."

"Did he say how he'd ended up with the boxes?"

"He claimed I'd left them with his family and made them promise to find me and return them to me afterward," Isabel said, looking thoughtful.

"After what?"

"I don't know. He never said. But I must have been expecting to go away somewhere for quite a while. Otherwise, why would I have packed up my precious books and paintings so carefully? They were all wrapped in paper and then the boxes were wrapped in Defense-Coat to protect them from moisture. It was quite well done. That's why my books are in such good condition."

They sat in silence for a few moments as Emily scribbled some notes in her paper notebook.

"I have so enjoyed reading – or I guess re-reading – all of those books," Isabel continued, glancing toward the corner where the books were shelved behind their glass doors. "Some of the passages seem so familiar and the characters feel like old friends."

Guided by her books and artworks, Isabel said, she had constructed a life for herself in Buenos Aires. She had found a job working at a commercial gallery, where she met a couple of people in the underground art network who seemed to appreciate her apparently intuitive knowledge of literature and art. Through them she had secured a position at Galería Picaflor, which she eventually took over.

"And you were taking Chulel all the time?" Emily wanted to know.

"I can't say about the time before 2080. But when Sr. Ocampo delivered the boxes, he also gave me a small packet containing several doses of Chulel." Isabel paused. "It took me a while to figure out what it was, but it seemed like it wasn't going to do me any harm, so I learned what the proper dosage and time interval was and I went ahead and took it. And by the time that ran out, I'd found out how to get it for myself." Isabel gave Emily a sly look. "Are you trying to figure out how old I am? I've done some work on that, too. Not that it seems to matter so much anymore – thanks to you and Max – but a person does want to know how old she is."

Emily agreed.

"Some of my books seem like they were used as textbooks for university classes and the latest publication date on one of those is 1996. So I figure if I was in college in the late 1990s I would have been maybe 20? So maybe I was born in the late 1970s. Unless, of course, those books were from a post-graduate course, in which case I could be a little older. But not much."

Emily nodded appreciatively. "Good sleuthing. If you weren't a spy, maybe you should've been. What about the publication date on the book that's signed by your daughter – the one by Silvina Ocampo?"

"The date on that one – it's a reprint, of course – is 2010. And the handwriting looks like a younger child. I have only a few books with publication dates past 2000."

"I also noticed that particular book – the Ocampo – is from a California publisher: Zuckerberg University Press."

"True. Most of my earlier books are from Mexican presses. The few I have after 2004 are all California. So maybe I was in California, like you thought based on my accent. The two Jameson volumes are from a California press, too. I think the publication dates on them are 2002 and 2006. Did you see how they were signed?" Isabel went over to the polished wood bookcase and opened one of the glass doors. She retrieved the volumes in question and returned to the table, placing the books in front of Emily. Emily picked up the first one and opened it. The inscription read, "To the keeper of my treasure. Fondly, Martin." This was the one from 2002. The second book was inscribed simply, "With undying gratitude," and signed.

"These look very personal, Isabel," Emily said, closing the second book and stacking the two books neatly. "This Martin Jameson must have been someone you knew well. Yes, I think you must have spent quite some time in the Republic of California."

Emily glanced back through her notes. "So, did this Mr. Ocampo... That's interesting that he has the same surname as the author. Do you think you remembered that correctly?"

"I've asked myself that question. But I'm pretty sure that's what he said his name was. It didn't mean anything to me at the time, only after I started re-reading my books."

"Hmm. So did he tell you the name of his village, or of the old estancia you said it was near?"

Isabel closed her eyes to think. "It was... San... San something." She opened her eyes and grinned at Emily. "That doesn't help much, does it? Everything is named after some saint or another." Isabel put her hand over her eyes. "San... San Román? That could be it. San Román."

They ended their session with a couple of glasses of Malbec and a free ranging discussion of art. Emily made only a few additional notes.

Later that evening Emily told Max about her visit with Isabel. "I get the distinct feeling that her mental state must be something like the visual field of someone with macular degeneration. You know, where you see things in your peripheral vision, but as soon as you turn to look directly at them, they go all out of focus and you lose them."

"But of course that's only when she's trying to look at things from the distant past, right? Her more recent past – since about 2080 – seems remarkably clear. Her case is far worse than what's caused in patrons of the Chulel spas. My god, if this was the work of that research institute, I wonder how many people they did this to?"

Emily nodded in sympathy. "I asked her about the name of the village where the man came from with the boxes of her things, and she said it might have been San Román. She didn't seem entirely convinced."

"San Román? Well, let's see what a map can tell us." He screened up a map of the Buenos Aires region and searched.

"By the way," Max remarked as he scanned the map. "Have you seen some of the reports coming out of East China about a blood disease they're calling 'idiopathic hemolytic anemia'? It seems to be affecting mostly Gen1 and Gen2 people."

"Idiopathic?" Emily snorted. "That just means they don't know what causes it. I'll look for the reports, Max – sounds interesting. Do you think it might be related to the changes in the beta chains of hemoglobin we've been monitoring?"

Max reached up and patted Emily's hand, which was resting on his shoulder. "Exactly what I've been wondering myself, my dear. In fact, you can help me finish a message I've been drafting up to send to a couple of our colleagues, suggesting that they look into it."

"Max, you know I think Isabel must have had more or less continuous access to Chulel from an early point. As best I can figure, she must be at least 145 or so and…well, you know what she looks like."

"At least those scoundrels who were experimenting with her mind were offering her something of modest benefit as well. At least I suppose it's a benefit."

 Max pointed to a spot on the digiscreen he had spread out on the desk. "There's a locality fairly near here called San Román. But it's to the south and near the coast. Didn't she say the village and estancia were 'up river'?"

"She did," Emily replied. "And she seemed pretty sure of herself when she said it."

"So let's loosen up our search parameters."

Max and Emily watched as several new tags popped up on the map. One of them was alongside the name "San Ramon." This locality was up river.

"Would you like to take a little day trip tomorrow?" Max asked Emily.

16.

On the plane to Argentina, Luis reviewed his plan. His main goal was to meet again with Silvestre Ocampo and possibly talk with some of the other people in the village of San Ramon where Silvestre lived. Maybe he could find out more about this mysterious estate his grandmother visited. Luis' first journey had been hurried and he had only gone to San Ramon at the end of it. This time he planned to spend a full week in the village, which would leave him a few days in Buenos Aires at the end of his journey before flying back to Texas to meet Jenda in San Antonio.

Luis was impatient to get to the village and stayed only one night in Buenos Aires before accessing an autocar for the short journey. He used a device supplied by one of his friends in the underground that would effectively scramble the data on the autocar's navigation recorder so that there would be no accurate records of where he went. Luis wasn't sure why he wanted to do this, but on this particular day he enjoyed doing it simply because he could.

He left the autocar near what passed for the San Ramon town plaza and walked the few hundred meters to Silvestre Ocampo's house. The weather was cool and clear – a perfect late June winter day. The door opened, and Silvestre's wife Rosalí, after a moment's pause, gave him a smile of recognition and a hug.

"And your husband?" Luis inquired.

"Yes, he's here," Rosalí said. "But he's ill – more so than the last time you came. I can't promise he'll remember you. Please, come in." She gestured toward the doorway of Silvestre's room.

Silvestre was propped up in the bed. Luis thought he looked fragile, perishable.

"Do you remember this man?" Rosalí said in a loud voice. "He's Isabel's grandson. Isabel Hernandez' grandson. He visited us once before."

Silvestre squinted at Luis for a moment and then held out a trembling hand in greeting. "Oh, yes, I remember him," he said. His voice was thin, but his eyes glowed with genuine recognition.

Luis was surprised by Silvestre's rapid decline into old age. He chided himself for not having been prepared for this. But when was the last time he had seen an old person?

Luis let Silvestre talk about whatever he wanted to, listening as he again told about the many flowers and birds and insects he and Isabel had enjoyed viewing together. "Did I show you our flower book?" he asked. He told Luis that he and Isabel had made a book of pressed flowers. Rosalí pulled it down from a shelf and dusted it off. Luis watched while Silvestre told him about each of the flowers, many of which were now disintegrating in the pages of the album. Silvestre's impaired vision still perceived each blossom to be as fresh and colorful as the day he had picked it.

"I should have given this to her with the other things," he mused.

"Other things? What things did you give her?" Luis asked.

"Her boxes. The ones she left with us. She made us promise to get them back to her after she was released." Silvestre was still holding the book of flowers.

"Released?" Luis didn't wish to interrupt Silvestre's thoughts, but he did want to direct them.

"Oh yes, they put her in prison, you know," Silvestre murmured. "Those hijos de puta put pretty Isabela in prison." Luis knew that Isabel had been in prison, but Silvestre had not talked about it before.

"And you gave her some boxes?" Luis spoke softly. "After she was released?"

"Her things. We had promised her. And I kept the promise. I found her in the city and I gave her the boxes. But she didn't remember." Silvestre started to cough. Rosalí coaxed him to drink a little bit of water through a straw. He lay back on the pillows.

"That's probably enough for now," Rosalí told Luis as she gently stroked Silvestre's forehead.

"I understand." Luis took Silvestre's hand and told him how happy he was to see him again. Silvestre thanked Luis for visiting, but his eyes had lost the spark of recognition.

Rosalí invited Luis to stay for supper and he readily accepted. "Do you remember when or where Silvestre delivered those boxes he talked about?" Luis wanted to know. He had always believed his grandmother had died in prison, but this sounded like she may have been released. Perhaps Silvestre had been one of the last to see her alive.

"You know, I had forgotten that those boxes were Isabel's," Rosalí said. "They were here for so long – they became like part of the furniture. Let me think. I believe Silvestre took the boxes away about the same time that the old estancia was razed, and that was in about 2080."

Luis was stunned. How could this be? According to the story he knew, Isabel had died in the early 2030s, when Luis himself was only six or seven years old. "Are you sure?" Luis asked.

"Well, it could have been a little earlier or later, but about 2080. I'm sure of that," she said.

Luis struggled to grasp this new information that called into question the one solid fact he had always had about his grandmother. Was it possible that she had been alive for 50 years or more after his mother was told of her supposed death?

"Do you think you might still have the address where Silvestre delivered my abuela's boxes?"

"I think so. I still have a lot of old record books stored in the back room. I can look for it this evening. Will you come back tomorrow?"

"That would be great," Luis said. "Yes, I'll come back tomorrow."

"For breakfast?" Rosalí asked.

"I could be persuaded to do that." Luis smiled. "Also, do you remember Silvestre talking about an old estate that he used to frequent with Isabel? Do you know where it was?"

"Yes, of course," Rosalí replied. "That's the one I was talking about that they destroyed back in 2080. Would you like me to take you there tomorrow?" Luis' eager expression indicated that he would indeed like that. "You know, it's kind of odd, you showing up like this. There were some other people here earlier this week asking about the old estate and I took them out there, too."

17.

Jenda packed up a box with bedroom curtains, a bedspread, and a couple of throw pillows to take to Granny El's. "I only took these down last week, but I'm not sure I like the new ones, Gran. Can I put the box in one of your closets until I make up my mind?" That's what she told Granny El as an excuse to look inside her closets and see what was already stored there.

"Seems kind of silly, Jenda," Granny El scolded. "Just take them to recycle and if you decide you don't like the new stuff, recycle that too. Recycling makes the world go 'round, sweetie." But she invited Jenda in and pointed her to a hall closet. "There may be room in there, but if not you can check the closet in the spare bedroom. I don't know why I still have such a big place." Granny El busied herself opening some bottles of lemonade and a packet of ginger cookies.

Jenda opened the door to the hall closet. It was stacked to the ceiling with boxes and things wrapped in brown paper. Then she checked the bedroom closet. It was full, too. There were a few out-of-season clothes hanging to one side and Jenda quickly realized they were also long out of style. Both closets looked like they hadn't been opened in years.

"Gran!" Jenda called out. "These closets are both pretty much at capacity. Why don't you let me help you clear them?"

Granny El appeared in the doorway to the spare bedroom and peered into the open closet. "Oh, Jen, it seems like such a waste of time. I don't need the space and I'm sure you have better things to do."

"No, really, I wouldn't mind. I'd even volunteer to take some of this away for recycling. I bet we could get some great credits at the shops for some of this. Think what fun we'd have spending those credits."

"You're sure you wouldn't mind? You want to start with this one? I'll bring your lemonade."

Jenda pulled out one of the boxes and opened it. What she found was a jumble of old papers, greeting cards, brochures, gift bags, notebooks, and something wrapped in an old, badly mended shirt. She knew she would take this one home with her, so she set it aside and pulled down another.

Granny El sat on the edge of the bed, sipping lemonade as she watched Jenda opening boxes, one after another. "Look at all that junk!" she laughed. "Why did I ever hang onto such trash?"

"Gran." Jenda looked at her sternly but spoke quietly. "Gran, were these my mother's things?"

Granny El looked confused. Then her eyes fell on the object wrapped in the old shirt that Jenda had found in the first box. "Let me see that," she said.

"This?" Jenda asked. Granny El nodded. Jenda picked up the object and removed the wrappings. What she held in her hands was a graceful bronze sculpture of a child dancing. Jenda recognized the posture; it was almost identical to the painting she had made in San Miguel.

"Oh, Jenda... I... why?" Granny El closed her eyes tightly. "I can't... I don't remember." And then she let go a huge sob that seemed to overwhelm her like a tidal wave. Her eyes opened wide, as if fixed on something in the distance. "I do remember. I remember you, Tessa. My beautiful Tessa." Jenda reached to take Granny El's lemonade, which was teetering precariously in her trembling hand. She set it on the floor and took both of Granny El's hands in hers and knelt as she laid her head in her grandmother's lap.

"I'm sorry, Gran," Jenda whispered. She stroked Granny El's hand and wiped her own tears away on the sleeve of her blouse. "Has all this been here ever since... ever since Mom died?"

"I guess so," Granny El replied. "I never use this closet. Never even use this room. I should move to a smaller place."

"Look, Gran. If you won't mind, I'd like to take most of this stuff back to my place to sort out. It's going to take some time, but I'm beginning to think I need to remember Mom, to remember my own childhood, you know? I think this could help me."

"Please. Take it all if you like. I may not remember everything, but I remember enough. Sometimes I think I remember too much. But yes, take whatever you want." Granny El's tears had stopped. Her hands were steady and her voice firm.

It required three trips with a tiny autocar packed full for Jenda to transfer all of the boxes and wrapped items to her apartment. At both ends, the neighbors looked at her like she was some kind of sociopathic hoarder, but Jenda didn't care.

By evening the task was done and Jenda was physically exhausted from the unaccustomed exertion of carrying all those heavy boxes in the summer heat. Her curious mind, however, was still crackling with energy. "One box," she told herself. "I'll pilfer through one box. And I'll unwrap a couple of the packages, just to see what's inside. And then I'll take some Duermata and get some sleep."

She opened a pack of Nutrichips, poured a glass of wine, and reached for the nearest box. This was a heavy one. She opened it and found it was full of books. She took them out one by one, leafing through pages, looking for something, though she didn't know what. They were mostly books on art. A few of them she knew were her own college textbooks. Others clearly had been her mother's. Near the bottom were some children's books, including a few by authors Jenda thought she might remember – Beatrix Potter, James Herriot, Nikki Loftin, Ty Weaver. And there was *The Wonderful Wizard of Oz*. These were good memories, gentle memories. Jenda thought she might be able to get some sleep after all, even without the meds.

She reached for the nearest of the wrapped items. The encircling tape was resistant and she had to use scissors. Finally the corner of a painted canvas emerged. The opposite corner revealed the artist's signature – Jenda Swain.

Half an hour later, Jenda sat in the center of the floor, surrounded by fourteen paintings, each one produced by someone calling herself Jenda Swain. She held her head in her hands and wept. Her memories were all around her and they made no sense at all.

Jenda fell asleep on the floor, curled in a fetal position. She awoke after only a brief sleep, feeling stiff and old. Her hip and shoulder hurt. The sight of the paintings was less of a shock now, and she sat up to look at them. Each one evoked a wave of emotion from some forgotten place. She got up and found her digilet and carefully photographed each painting, as if she were afraid they might go away again if she had no digital record.

One painting, dated April 2031, kept drawing her back for another look. It showed a crowned female figure draped in billowing embroidered blue robes, surrounded by spikes of light. Jenda was sure it was the lady in blue, the one that hid in the shadows of her dreams. Seeing her face-to-face like this frightened Jenda, grabbing at her belly and throwing up a dense cloud in her mind. She took another photo and turned the painting around to face the wall.

After an early breakfast, Jenda called her office and told them she was not feeling well and would be working from home today. By noon, her front room looked like an old fashioned yard sale. She had devised a sorting process for the materials.

Her mother's things were assembled on one side of the room, her own on the other; shared things were kept on Jenda's side.

Her mother's side included books, sketch books, assorted papers, and a couple of small sculptures. There was one more sculpture to unwrap. Even before Jenda had finished unwinding the tattered cloth that had protected it, she knew what it was. It was the bronze of the little girl reading a book – the same one she had bought for Luis in San Miguel as a Christmas present. She turned it over to look at the base, and there was the artist's signature: Setha Tica. Tessa Jenkins Swain and Setha Tica were one and the same. Jenda didn't know whether to laugh or cry. She and Luis both loved her mother's work.

The collection of things on Jenda's side of the room was more diverse, including pieces of clothing from her childhood and youth, a neck chain with a small clock pendant, mementos from various events, some school papers. There were printed photographs on both sides. One pile on Jenda's side kept getting larger and was rapidly reaching critical mass in terms of her ability to resist delving into it. This was the pile of little paper journals that apparently she had kept ever since she learned to write. The earliest ones were all dated in her mother's clear hand. Jenda tried to put them in order.

She spent much of the afternoon reading these notebooks, alternately laughing and crying as she read. She found out that she had indeed had a pet – a white cat named Milly, who had been a close companion and who was the subject of many of Jenda's childhood journal entries. The notes she wrote shortly after her tenth birthday told of Milly's death.

My dear, dear Milly is no more. They wouldn't let me see her at first, but I cried so hard they finally let me. She had her eyes closed. She didn't look comfortable with her paws the way they were. I tried to move them but she was so stiff. And cold. Not warm and soft like always. Well, her fur was still soft. Her fur was always the softest! It was so strange seeing her dead. Daddy and Paloma dug a hole in the ground in the back garden and put her inside and covered her up with the dirt. I've been saying some of Mommy's prayers to the Buddha, because she says the Buddha can bring people and animals back again for another life. Paloma says she's in heaven with Jesus. I want Milly to come back. I miss her so much. OM MANY PEMMY HUM.

"The cat in the photograph was Milly," Jenda thought, as she wiped away a stray tear for her long forgotten pet. She had even forgotten Paloma, the woman who had been her nanny from infancy until she was a teenager, although by that time she was more of a cross between a personal maid and a best friend.

Jenda found a gap in the sequence of notebooks between the start of 2030 and the summer of 2031, just before she began her studies at Perry University in Austin. Some of the other books had pages missing. Even so, Jenda found a few references to friends who must have been Vintagonists, and remarks that clearly showed her own sympathy with the Vinties. In a 2031 book, she found remarks such as "when Paloma and I were in Chile" and "after Paloma took me to visit the museum in Buenos Aires."

As she rummaged through one final box, she found – at the very bottom – an old paper passport. Her passport. And it showed clearly her travels from May 2030 through March 2031 through Ecuador, Bolivia, Peru, Chile and Argentina.

Luis had notified Jenda that Recall was partially restored, although the burdensome encryption this required meant that real time messaging was still impossible. Jenda decided it was time to post a message to Luis:

POLILLA: I can't handle this on my own. I need you.

Jenda went to the kitchen to pour a glass of tea. She checked Recall's Interloc again. There was nothing from Luis. But Jenda knew what she was going to do.

POLILLA: Fuck YJ. I'm coming to you.

Then Jenda screened out of Recall and closed down her screen. Taking the tools she had been using to assist in opening boxes, she broke through the back cover of the screen's housing and began prying apart everything she could lay a hand on. She was amazed at the array of intricate, tiny pieces. Leaving it all

154

in a pile on the table, she hurriedly packed a suitcase, spending almost no time selecting clothing and taking great care in choosing notebooks, photos, and papers from the recently opened boxes. She tucked her current plastiflex digital passport into her handbag. Then she secured a couple of small notebooks and the old paper passport in an inner pocket, snapped her digilet around her wrist, and headed for the airport. She would find a flight once she got there.

18.

Luis spent a sleepless night at the San Ramon inn. The bed was uncomfortable and his mind was bedeviled by the idea that Abuela Isabel had still been alive for 50 years after they had given her up as dead. He was grateful for the steaming mug of coffee Rosalí offered him as she prepared a breakfast of eggs, ham, and rolls. As they were finishing their meal, a neighbor arrived who would keep an eye on Silvestre while Rosalí and Luis went out to the old estancia.

The drive didn't take long. "We could have walked, I guess," Rosalí said. "There used to be a path on the back side of the village that led out here. The workers used to take it. Nobody had a vehicle back then, much less an autocar."

They got as far as they could inside the property with the car. Luis parked where the road became a path, and they continued on foot. The weather had grown colder overnight but the sun kept playing with the edges of the clouds, promising a warmer afternoon.

"Tell me about the couple who came to visit. Earlier this week you said?"

"They were a delightful couple, probably Gen1. A little bit old, you know?"

"Why did they want to come here?" Luis asked.

"They said they were scientists and that this might have been an important research institute of some kind. They found something under the rubble in one of the rooms and took it with them. I'm not sure what it was." Rosalí motioned to Luis and they stopped next to the remains of what once must have been an elaborate gateway. "This was the main entrance to the grounds. And up there was the entrance to the central building. Such a beautiful place. It's a shame they destroyed it."

"The entries were decorated with those tiles," Rosalí continued, responding to Luis' obvious interest. "They all had the same design, just different colors."

Luis recognized the medical professions emblem – the Rod of Asclepius – but this particular rendition was distinctive with its little fan-shaped leaf at the crest of the staff. Luis took a couple of photographs of one of the unbroken tiles before placing it in his pocket.

"So this place was a medical research institute?"

"We always thought it was a clinic," Rosalí said, kicking some rubble out of her path. "But for rich people only. Patients used to come and go by air shuttle. People say the villagers who got jobs here were well paid."

"What do they tell about their experiences here?"

"That's a funny thing," she replied, shading her eyes and looking toward the trees on the periphery of the grounds. "Nobody seems to remember much about working here. They all say it was a wonderful place to work and that they were treated well."

Luis asked Rosalí to show him where the previous visitors had found the items they took away. He poked around through the rubble there, but found nothing remarkable. In fact, he found the whole place to be a rather unexceptional knocked-down building. Nothing but stones and broken concrete. It must have been cleaned out long before the wrecking equipment arrived. He wondered if even an experienced archaeologist would be able to learn much from the jumble.

"What about that little house over there?" he asked, as they headed back to the autocar, gesturing toward a cottage off near the crumbling fence. "Why was it left standing?"

"I don't know," Rosalí responded. "It wasn't part of the clinic. Just the caretaker's house. Maybe they ran out of time."

"Why would anyone want to destroy this place anyway?"

Rosalí shook her head and shrugged her shoulders. "I can't even guess. By the time they came, there was nothing going on here at all. It had been empty for years. But they came one day with all these big machines and by the time they finished, this was all that was left."

Over the next couple of days, Luis spoke with at least a dozen people who had once worked at the old clinic – or research institute or whatever it was. They all said the same thing, "It was a wonderful place to work and we were treated well." And they all said it in exactly the same words. None of them remembered anyone named Isabel Hernandez. No one remembered the names of anyone who had worked at the clinic other than their closest kin or neighbors. One man did show Luis where the path used to be that they would take to go to work. Luis had thought he might try going back to the estancia the way the workers had gone – the way his grandmother and Silvestre Ocampo would have gone – but the path was so overgrown now, he felt it would be pointless.

On his way back to Rosalí and Silvestre's house, Luis stopped by the village church, the chapel of San Ramon No Nacido. It was cold inside and dark, except for the patterns of afternoon light slanting through the colored windows and the flickering of a few candles. The stone floor was worn smooth from the footsteps of generations of worshipers. At one side there was a niche with a statue of San Ramon and on the other side a similar niche for Nuestra Señora de Lujan, the patron saint of Argentina. Luis sat on one of the wooden benches to review his situation.

It was clear there was little more to learn in San Ramon. Luis was still trying to comprehend the possibility that his grandmother had been alive so long after his mother was told she had died. Could she still be alive? That seemed unlikely. He should go back to Buenos Aires. Rosalí had given him the address where Silvestre delivered the boxes. He would try to

159

find that apartment and see if anyone was still around who might remember Isabel Hernandez, anyone who might know what happened to her in those missing 50 years. As he rose to leave the chapel and continue on to Silvestre and Rosalí's house, he found his feet nearly numb from the cold stone floor. He walked toward the niche dedicated to Nuestra Señora de Lujan, drawn by the warm glow of the candles. He looked at the lady with her crown and her billowing embroidered blue robe, surrounded by beams of golden light – her potencias. The candles emitted more glow than warmth. As Luis turned to go, he instinctively crossed himself. "God," he thought, "I haven't done that in ages."

Luis left his contact phrase with Rosalí, with the request that she let him know how Silvestre was doing. Also, he wanted to be notified if, by chance, she or Silvestre or anyone else might remember any additional information about Isabel Hernandez.

When Luis went in to bid Silvestre farewell, the old man insisted that he take the book of pressed flowers. "When you see your grandmother, you can give it to her," he said. Luis didn't know how to refuse, so he reluctantly accepted the fragile book.

"Thank you. I'll do that," he said.

Luis had one last question for Rosalí. "Those people you took to the estancia last week – what were their names?"

"I believe they said their name was 'Field'," Rosalí said. "Something like that. I know the woman's name was Emily, but I don't remember his. I never expected to see them again, so I guess I wasn't bothering to remember."

As Luis packed up his small suitcase to check out of the San Ramon inn, he wrapped the book of pressed flowers carefully inside one of his shirts. He had the fleeting thought that maybe Silvestre had just given him a talisman that would lead him to new information about his grandmother.

Back in Buenos Aires, Luis felt less optimistic. The next morning he left his hotel early, thinking he would let the various aromas of fresh coffee and pastries and fried foods help him choose where to have breakfast. He was also remembering that there was an underground gallery somewhere in Buenos Aires that had acquired one of his paintings. Maybe he would seek out that gallery. The quest for information about his grandmother could wait one more day. He needed time to formulate a plan.

As he drank his café cortado and devoured his simple tostada de jamón y queso, Luis searched through data files on his digilet for some reminder that might help him locate the gallery that had his painting. Connecting underground transactions with real world people and places was intentionally difficult, even for those on the inside. It was supposed to be impossible for those on the outside, and Luis now found himself mostly on the outside. He finally found what he was looking for – the address where he had shipped the painting. He was surprised to see also the name of his contact – Elena Troika. He figured the address would probably lead him to a place that didn't exist, but he thought it was worth a try.

Luis' NaviGiz placed the address on the Plaza Wanxiang, about three kilometers away from the café where he was sitting. Plazas in Buenos Aires, as in so much of the world, had come to be known only by the name of their corporate sponsors and old commemorative statues had been replaced by vanguard sculptures in plastimold that could be switched out every few months like old-time billboards. The Plaza Wanxiang appeared to be in the old San Telmo neighborhood, once famous for its art and antiques.

The route to Plaza Wanxiang led through a couple of other plazas and a small park. Down a small alley, Luis noticed a shop with a display of what looked to be real silk scarves printed with watercolor flowers. He selected one of these scarves for Jenda. Beside the shop was a small café, where he ate a piping hot empanada and drank a mug of sweet mate. Warmed and reinvigorated, he continued his trek.

At last Luis found his destination, and was surprised to see that it was indeed an art gallery, with a sign reading "Galería Picaflor". He pushed open the door, and found himself surrounded by the usual inventory of commercially viable recyclable paintings and small sculptures in plexiform and plastimold, the same kinds of things sold in most of the galleries in San Miguel.

"May I help you?" the woman behind the small desk asked as she rose to her feet. "They are lovely paintings, don't you think? Which one would you like to take home today?" She smiled engagingly as she delivered her sales pitch.

"Oh, yes, lovely," Luis responded, with an obvious lack of fervor. "Actually, I'm looking for someone. Her name is Elena Troika. Is she by any chance someone you know?" Luis was examining the paintings, trying to discern which of the successful commercial artists of the day had produced them. Everything looked so similar. The woman who had spoken to him was silent. He looked over at her and saw that she was studying him intently.

"The name sounds maybe a little familiar," she said. "Why do you ask?" Now it was Luis' turn to engage in that intense visual scanning that attempts to ascertain how far to trust a stranger you have just encountered with sensitive information.

"Well…" Luis decided to be cautious, despite an almost overwhelming urge to fully disclose his intent. "A friend of mine… I think he may have sold her a painting once." He paused. "An oil painting."

"Ah," the woman said. "We don't have any of those in this gallery."

They were studying each other again. Luis looked away and took a deep breath. "Of course," he said. "I didn't mean…"

The woman interrupted. "What is your friend's name?" she asked.

"He calls himself…" Luis took a deep breath. ("Here we go," he thought.) "He calls himself 'Charro Negro'."

The woman seemed to stand a bit taller. Her eyes narrowed and her brow furrowed; then she appeared to make a decision. She passed her digilet over a pad on the desk and Luis heard the front door lock click. "Follow me," she said.

He felt uneasy, but the small woman hardly seemed threatening, so he followed her down the hallway. She unlocked a door that looked like the door to a janitor's closet. The woman swung the door open and tasked on the lights. In front of him, Luis saw a second gallery and this one was full of real paintings and real sculptures. And there in the center of one wall was his own painting.

"So," the woman said, crossing her arms and giving him a mischievous look. "You say you know this Charro Negro fellow?"

Luis was overwhelmed. Without consciously deciding to do so he said simply, "That would be me. I am el Charro Negro. But my real name is Luis-Martín Zenobia."

"And I am Elena Troika," the woman said, holding out her hand and grasping Luis' proffered hand. "But my real name is Isabel Hernandez."

Luis felt the room suddenly flooded with bright light and the ground slipping out from under his feet.

"My hand," the woman was saying. "You're hurting me."

Luis released his grip on Isabel's hand, his thoughts still incapable of forming sentences.

"Would you like to sit down?" Isabel said kindly. "I'll get you a glass of water. You don't look well." Isabel led Luis to one of the chairs next to the table and went to fetch some water. She glanced toward the door anxiously, as if wondering how she would get this strange and rather large man out of her secret gallery if he passed out and required medical attention.

When Isabel returned with the water, Luis was still staring at her, but now his face was contorted into a crazy grin and tears overflowed from his eyes. She set the glass down and backed away. Luis reached out and caught her hand again, more gently this time.

"You don't know me, do you?" he said softly.

"Should I?"

"I'm your grandson. I'm Juanita's son."

Isabel pulled her hand back. There was fear and confusion in her eyes. It struck Luis that maybe this was only someone who happened to have the same name as his grandmother. The room became solid again.

"I'm sorry," he said. "Perhaps I've made a mistake. My grandmother's name is Isabel Hernandez, like you. I lost her a long time ago, after she was in prison here in Argentina. I thought…"

"Your grandmother was in prison? Here in Argentina? How do you know?" Isabel asked, a bit less fearfully.

"My mother Juanita kept a little book when she came here to look after my grandmother. And there are people in San Ramon who remember, too."

Isabel's eyes widened. "That was it. San Ramon," she whispered to herself. "What people?" she asked Luis.

"Well, there is an old man there named Silvestre Ocampo. I just came from visiting with him, and he told me he brought my grandmother some boxes here in Buenos Aires after she was released from prison."

Isabel's eyes were closed. Tears were forming, and one ran down her cheek.

"I believe," she said, sitting down in the chair across from Luis and leaning slightly toward him, "I believe I may be that same Isabel Hernandez. I believe I may be your grandmother."

Luis reached over and took Isabel's hand in his.

19.

The first flight to Buenos Aires from the Dallas airport wasn't until early the following morning, but Jenda bought a ticket anyway and checked her suitcase, paying extra to have it stored until flight time. She hoped it and its precious contents would travel safely. She purchased a full eight hours in a sleep pod, not caring whether she slept or not but craving the privacy. After a couple of hours looking over the two notebooks and old passport she had hidden in the inner pocket of her handbag as well as the photos of the paintings on her digilet, her anticipated sense of privacy felt more like claustrophobia. She took 12 tabs of Duermata and accessed the sleep pod's audio options, selecting the lakeside sounds of lapping water and gentle breezes...

She awoke exactly four hours later. She was hungry and decided to sacrifice her last two hours of prepaid sleep pod claustrophobia in favor of food and exercise. The transit way of the airport seemed vast after her stay in the pod. Jenda made a quick mental inventory of the cuisine on offer, finally selecting the Americana Café. She found a seat in a secluded corner and ordered the burger with fried broccoli and a NutriQuaff shake. She finished off the meal and then dawdled over the last of the shake, mentally trying to organize what she had learned from her recently un-closeted artifacts.

She now knew that almost a full year between the summer of 2030 and summer of 2031 was missing from her records. She knew the names of a few of her friends from the period in question. One of them was Leticia Poole, the woman she had been taking dancing lessons from, the woman who sold pendants with watches and lockets in her boutique. Of course they hadn't been able to remember one another.

Jenda also knew she had traveled to various South American countries, including Argentina, during her missing year. She had been accompanied by her old nanny, Paloma. Jenda still found that part a bit odd and wondered whether in fact her companion might have been a school friend who happened to have the same first name. She had not been able to find Paloma's last name in any of the notebooks or records. "I should have asked Granny El about that," she thought. Jenda also suspected that there was a lot to be deciphered from her paintings, with their oddly juxtaposed figures and objects. And then there was that one haunting image of the lady in blue.

She hoped Luis had received her message before his intended departure for their rendezvous in San Antonio, Texas. They were supposed to be meeting there – Jenda checked the calendar on her digilet – day after tomorrow. She let out a slight groan. What if he didn't get her message in time? Maybe she should cancel the Buenos Aires ticket and go to San Antonio on the hyperloop instead.

"Shut up!" Jenda told herself. "There you go, second-guessing yourself again. This time go with it, Jenda, okay?" But she did allow herself to take a moment to send off a quick pulse to her supervisor at YJ: "Family emergency. I am requesting a week off. Please task this against my next scheduled sabbatical." Then she went back and made it "two weeks", and transmitted. She screened up LifeBook to see if she might have a message from Luis. There was nothing. Checking Recall was still impossible. She waved her digilet at the pay point and left the café, heading for her departure area. She stopped briefly at a kiosk to draw down a trashy novel into her digilet. She was tired of thinking.

The novel lasted until two hours before the plane was due to arrive in Buenos Aires. Jenda shut off her digilet and curled it around her wrist as she settled down, hoping she could manage a short nap. But as soon as she started to think about her situation again, she panicked. How was she going to locate Luis? What if he hadn't gotten her message and had already left for Texas?

She unwrapped her digilet again and tapped the LifeBook symbol. There were a few entries from friends. And then she saw the photo of a hotel. In Buenos Aires. Jenda felt a wave of relief. She made a note of the name and address of the hotel. It was going to be okay. Luis knew she was coming. He would be waiting for her at the hotel.

And there he was. Feeling no need for discretion, they embraced right there in the lobby, and in that imbricating kind of not-quite-conversation told each other, "I'm so glad you're here" and "I have so much to tell you." Then they stole a quick kiss and, leaning heavily on one another, headed for the elevator.

"Have you found out anything useful?" Jenda asked Luis.

"Yes, quite a lot. But you go first. You're the one fleeing Your Journal to come here to Argentina."

She hardly knew where to begin. "Well, it turns out Granny El did keep things after all – a lot of things. I had forgotten about all the little notebooks I kept as a child. Some of my mother's sculptures, too. Her art name was Setha Tica, Luis. She made the bronze I gave you. And there were photos – not so many as I might have hoped, but still – real printed photos. And my paintings – Luis, Granny El kept more than a dozen of the paintings I made in high school and college. I couldn't bring those, of course, but I took pictures. God, Luis, I'm babbling!" She had flung her suitcase into the middle of the bed and was opening it to show Luis her collection.

"Take it easy, querida. Come sit here next to me and tell me one thing at a time."

So Jenda sat on the edge of the bed beside Luis, leaning lightly against his solid frame, her folded hands between her knees, and told him about the things she had found and about what she thought some of it might mean.

"One of the best things," she said, grabbing for her handbag, which had fallen to the floor, "is this." She pulled out her old passport and handed it to Luis. "I may not remember what I was doing, but now we know where I was."

He leafed through the passport. "So do you think we should take a trip and try to track you down?"

"Oh, do you think we could? When?" Jenda's mind was already on board with its seat belt fastened. "But first, you have some things to tell me, too, I think."

"Mmm," he responded, still holding Jenda's passport as if it were a signed first edition. "Yes. Well, the most important is – I found my grandmother."

"Oh my god, Luis!" Jenda felt as if her chest would burst open. "She's alive? Where? Here? Oh, tell me." She huddled up closer to Luis to listen to his story, savoring every syllable as he told about his visit to San Ramon and then finding the Galería Picaflor.

"So you'd sold one of your paintings to your grandmother?"

"Another thing I've found... Wait, let me show you." He led Jenda to the desk where his packable digiscreen was laid out, attached to a couple of odd-looking devices. He pulled up Recall and then an advert within its deeper recesses:

ARE YOUR ANNUAL ADJUSTMENTS NOT DOING JUSTICE TO YOUR CHERISHED MEMORIES? WE HAVE UNIQUE ACCESS TO NON-YJ RECORDS OF PEOPLE WHO SPENT TIME IN ARGENTINA ROUGHLY 2025-2035.

There was a contact phrase listed.

"What do you think? Is it worth a try?" he asked.

"Sure, why not? This person might know something about me and maybe even about your grandmother. But of course, now you can ask her about things."

"Not really. She has bigger memory gaps than you do. But I'm glad you agree we should talk to the person who's running this ad, because I've already contacted him and made an appointment for tomorrow morning. And then in the afternoon we're meeting up with my grandmother. I can't wait for you two to meet. She's also invited her friends, who turn out to be the couple that visited San Ramon the week before I did."

"Pukka!" Jenda's eyes grew large with excitement. "Oh, Luis, this is all so amazing. Scary, but amazing!" Jenda felt she had left much of the scariness back in Dallas. If not for her nagging concern over her brother, she would have been more than ready to celebrate. She hugged Luis and planted a big kiss on his cheek, which was again becoming shrouded in a beard. "Shall I show you the pictures of my paintings?"

Jenda took off her digilet and transferred the pictures to Luis' screen. As the pictures came up, Luis remarked, "Wayee, Jen. You painted these in high school? They're beautiful."

"Tell me what you think of this one. It seems to be the first one I painted after I got back home from my South American travels," Jenda said, as she screened up the image of the lady in blue.

"You painted Our Lady of Lujan?"

"Is that what it is? It's like the statue in the chapel in San Miguel, right?"

"Well, that was the Virgin of Guadalupe, but they're both the Holy Virgin Mary. The one in your painting, though, is definitely Our Lady of Lujan. Your image is odd, though. You see what she's holding there? Most paintings of Nuestra Señora de Lujan show her with hands joined in prayer." He zoomed in on the center of Jenda's image. "Very odd."

"What is it?" Jenda was examining the picture more closely. What she saw the beautiful lady holding looked like a tall thin tree with a snake curled around it.

"Basically, it's the Staff of Asclepius – the symbol of the medical professions," Luis said. "But usually it doesn't have that little tree-top, or gingko leaf or whatever it is. However…" He screened up a photo from his own files.

"It's the same symbol," Jenda said. "Where did you find that?"

"At the old estancia, or rather clinic or maybe research institute. The whole place was decorated with this symbol. I've never seen it represented exactly like this anywhere else. Also…" He screened up one more photo from his files. "I think the Virgin of Lujan may be the image that was tattooed on your back."

The next morning, Jenda and Luis met with the man from the Recall advertisement, who handed them a business card, introducing himself as Dr. Maurice Winfield. He told them he was once employed at a research institute north of Buenos Aires that had been doing some early experimentation with what had become known as photonic memory reconstruction. Their early methods had been crude, he claimed, and many people had lost significant portions of their memories. But apparently Dr. Winfield, whose business card touted a Ph.D. in clinical psychology, had – out of his deep humanitarian compassion for the unfortunate patients – salvaged most of the institute's old records. He had also, he claimed, developed methods that over time would assist people in restoring their memories.

He seemed a bit shady, but Jenda and Luis agreed Dr. Winfield might very well have some legitimate information. They were interested to learn more and invited him to join them later in the afternoon at Isabel's. They hoped they might entice him into giving them a discount on the information he was offering to reveal to them in exchange for a shockingly large sum of money. Dr. Winfield agreed to the meeting, assuring them that they were lucky he had that time slot open, as his calendar was generally kept quite full attending to so many satisfied clients

Jenda was eager to meet Isabel, this woman who Luis barely remembered and who apparently remembered him not at all. Luis reminded Jenda that he had been only six years old when his mother Juana left him with his father in Merida and went to Argentina to care for Isabel. Luis said his mother had never been quite the same after her return, apparently blaming herself or maybe her husband as somehow culpable for Isabel's presumed death.

After a light lunch at a café, Luis and Jenda walked to Galería Picaflor. Luis held the door for Jenda to enter.

"Here we are, Abuelita," he announced. "Here is my lovely Jenda, come to meet you."

Isabel was smaller than Jenda had imagined, but as she rose from the desk, her smile seemed to give her a presence much grander than her diminutive body. She was dressed in a simple dark skirt, golden yellow blouse, and sensible shoes. Her dark hair with its gray streaks was drawn up in a twist and fastened with a gold ornament.

She greeted Jenda, embracing her warmly and offering the little pecks on the cheeks that people of her generation still occasionally practiced. Then Isabel hugged Luis, clinging to the big man with shy affection. "Come," she said. "Let's go into the private gallery where we can be together, just us three." She tasked the front door to lock and a sign lit up, informing subsequent arrivals about ringing for attention.

Jenda was breathless in her admiration of Isabel's private gallery, heading immediately for Luis' painting. She looked at Luis and said simply, "It looks so right here – so at home." Isabel gave Jenda a quick tour, ending at the polished wood bookcase with the glass doors. She offered tea and they went upstairs to her apartment, leaving further exploration of the secret gallery for another day. As they sipped tea, they exchanged disjointed vignettes about their lives. Watching Luis and Isabel, Jenda thought how odd it must feel to be with someone who, by all rights, ought to know so much about your life but who in fact knew almost nothing. At least Granny El had a few selected memories about Jenda.

The bell rang and Isabel excused herself to go admit her callers, Max and Emily Feldman. "I haven't seen them since they got back from visiting San Ramon," Isabel said.

"She's so different from my own grandmother, Luis. You know, they both have lost memories in one way or another, but Granny El doesn't even seem to mind about that. She never tries to remember anything. Your abuela, on the other hand – such a passion for life, in spite of all that's happened to her. I like her, Luis." She gave his hand a squeeze.

As Isabel and the Feldmans came back up the stairs, Jenda could tell by their easy banter that these were people who trusted one another. When they entered the room, Jenda was surprised at how old the Feldmans looked. She would have been even more surprised to know that Luis – who knew from Isabel that the Feldmans were early Gen1 – was thinking how young they looked compared to Silvestre Ocampo in his sickbed in San Ramon.

After the requisite introductions and greetings and congratulatory remarks about Isabel and Luis' reunion and Jenda's unexpected arrival, the conversation quickly turned to their shared research interest.

"I understand you were in San Ramon just a week before I went there," Luis said to Max. "And you met Silvestre Ocampo and his wife Rosalí?"

"All roads seem to lead to San Ramon on this quest," Max replied. "Yes, we met Silvestre and Rosalí, but she didn't seem to have a lot of information and he was so ill he wasn't able to tell us much. But Rosalí took us out to the old institute grounds. Interesting place."

"Rosalí said you found something."

Max accepted a cup of tea from Isabel. "Nothing of great importance," he said. "That place was rumored back in the 21st century to be conducting experiments with photonic memory restructuring. Well, under some of the rubble I found some broken goggles that looked like the kind that were used by laboratory workers to shield themselves from photon bursts. Turns out that is indeed what they are. That's not a lot of evidence, but it does lend credence to the rumors."

"We may be able to help you on that," Luis said, and he told Max and Emily about meeting with Dr. Winfield. "We hope you don't mind, but we invited him to come over later this afternoon. If you'd rather not talk to him, we can leave him at the front door and Jenda and I can explain to him later."

Max waved his hand. "No, no. We'd be interested to meet with this fellow. Winfield you said his name is? Nothing to lose, you know." Then the Feldmans began telling Luis and Jenda about their mounting concerns over reports of a deadly blood disorder that was attacking primarily Gen1 and Gen2 people, but also some from Gen3. It had originally been confined to East China, but was now cropping up in Indonesia, the Philippines, and Maha Pradesh as well, with a few cases reported in Germany. It produced acute anemia and was not responding to treatment. An alarming number of people had died.

172

The buzzer indicating the arrival of another visitor interrupted their conversation and they all turned to look at Isabel. "Yes, go let him in," she said. Luis volunteered to go down and fetch the expected guest.

Luis let Dr. Winfield in, switched off the sign about bell ringing, and locked the door. He led Dr. Winfield down the hallway, past the little door that looked like the entrance to a janitor's closet, and up the stairs to Isabel's apartment. They went inside and Luis closed the door behind them.

"I would like to introduce..." Luis began, then stopped as he looked toward Maurice Winfield.

The man's face was drained of color, frozen into a look of stunned terror. He cast a desperate glance back toward the door and saw Luis standing directly in front of it. Max Feldman had risen to his feet and Emily's eyes flashed daggers.

"Winslow... Morris..!" Max spat out the words like a mouthful of poison.

20.

Winslow Morris had encountered more trouble than he anticipated getting his millions in Fontana profits out of China. As he bided his time in Mexico waiting for things to work out, most of his stash of Fontana was stolen. When your inventory is all black market anyway, you can't just go to the authorities and report a theft, so Winslow had taken it into his own hands to track down the culprits.

He had finally found them in Argentina and, because he was still short on cash and because there were more of them than there were of him, he joined up with their thieving and smuggling ring. They weren't a big operation nor were they terribly sophisticated, so Winslow had also put together a convincing résumé and secured a job as a research assistant at a private institute outside Buenos Aires.

Winslow, who was always quick to suspect the worst of almost everyone, readily ascertained that the institute was in fact engaging in some pretty nefarious business. Seeing an opportunity for profit, Winslow began copying and smuggling out records from the institute. He did not share these with his pharmaceutical thieving colleagues. This was something he wanted for himself. He thought of it as an investment in his future.

Now, face to face with the very people from whom he had stolen the original formula for Chulel back in 2021, Winslow found himself questioning some of his career decisions. He guessed he was probably not going to make a lot of money from Luis-Martín Zenobia or his partner and grandmother.

Winslow Morris held up both hands in a gesture of surrender. He looked at Isabel, almost as if he were appealing to her for help, but Isabel didn't seem to notice.

~~~

Luis stood dumbfounded as Max explained who this man he and Jenda knew as Maurice Winfield really was and exactly how he and Emily knew him. Luis' effort to restrain his laughter out of respect for the Feldmans' justifiable outrage was only partially successful. Jenda was saying something about karma.

"My god, man!" Max said, now that it was clear Winslow was not going anywhere. "How did a scoundrel like you get involved in this institute's work?"

Luis was less interested in hearing about Winslow's circuitous career track than he was with ascertaining what the man might know about Jenda or Isabel. He got the distinct feeling that this would be their one and only opportunity to interrogate Winslow Morris.

Here is what Winslow told them: For one thing, most of the institute's experimental subjects were being recruited under the auspices of an international cult deprogramming business. For another, the clinic end of the operations purported to provide abortion services, but instead ran a brisk business providing babies to plutocrats around the world. And, yes, he had records. It was obvious that he had brought his packable digiscreen with him and his interrogators insisted that he show them records immediately. Winslow feebly agreed to do as they demanded.

With a pitiful sigh and a defeated look, Winslow unfolded his digiscreen. Luis stationed himself at Winslow's elbow so he could monitor his every keystroke. "So. What am I looking for exactly?" Winslow asked.

"Search 'Isabel Hernandez'," Luis said.

No one noticed when Winslow glanced toward Isabel again, looking as though he were about to say something. Then he turned toward his screen and entered the query. "Nothing," Winslow said after a few seconds. "She's not mentioned in any of the records." He seemed relieved and perhaps slightly defiant.

Luis had another idea. "Can you check to see if there are any records of dealings with the Argentine criminal justice system – penitentiaries in particular?"

Winslow paused for a moment, and then tapped some syllables into the screen. "Oh," he said, looking surprised.

"Actually, yes. They had a standing contract as medical consultants with several prison facilities."

Luis glanced at Isabel. She was wide-eyed. Emily Feldman was holding her hand. So this was where Isabel had lost her memories. He had hoped for some evidence regarding why she ended up in jail in the first place, but at least this was something.

"Now search, 'Jenda Swain'," Luis instructed, spelling the name out for Winslow. Luis turned and sent Jenda a reassuring look. Isabel rose from where she had been sitting and went to stand next to Jenda.

"Hmm." Winslow stared at the screen. "Yes... Jenda... Jenda Swain. Entered the clinic on 31 May of 2030 for both deprogramming and abortion. I guess she got the package deal," he joked. But as he looked at Luis looking at Jenda, his smile vanished.

"What?" Jenda cried. "No! My mother... Oh my god..." She covered her face with her hands and turned away. Luis saw Isabel put an arm around Jenda's shoulders. "It's okay, hija," Isabel said. "Tienes tu gente aquí contigo." There were tears on Jenda's face.

"Stay here, Max," Luis said. He strode across the room to take Jenda in his arms. Jenda clung to him for a moment and then said, "Go, Luis. Go find out more. I'll be here with Abuela Isabel. Make him tell you what happened to me." Her face was a prayer and a plea and Luis did as she asked.

"Hers is an odd case." Winslow turned toward Luis and explained what he meant without looking back at the screen. "I have the admission record, and a few months of treatment records. And then nothing. No release record." Once more he glanced toward Isabel, then looked back at the screen and shrugged.

Luis pulled out a storage device like the one Jenda had used at Your Journal. "Give us what you have," he said. "In fact, let's draw down all of your data on the institute." Luis and the Feldmans gathered around Winslow, examining records and interrogating him for some minutes more. By the time they finally agreed to let him go, all of his stolen data were duplicated in Luis' storage unit. Just before Winslow screened out, Luis reached over and entered a few syllables of his own. Winslow stared at the screen as if he expected to see all of his data disintegrate before his eyes. When nothing happened he looked puzzled. Luis patted him on the shoulder.

Luis walked him back down the stairs and out through the gallery to the front door without speaking. As the door closed behind Winslow, Luis headed back upstairs. "What a stroke of luck for us," he thought. "Although not so lucky for that poor rascal." He took the stairs two at a time returning to his grandmother's apartment. More than anything, he wanted to hold Jenda in his arms and tell her everything was going to be okay. He hoped that would be the truth.

21.

Jenda was still clinging to Isabel. As Luis put his arms around the two of them, she felt momentarily reassured and safe. She wanted desperately to hang onto that. The news that she had in fact been pregnant as her mother said ricocheted through her mind, finding no lodging place. The entire contents of her heart were spilled. Jenda gave Isabel a kiss on the cheek as Luis said their farewells. They walked downstairs in silence. Luis offered to summon an autocar.

"I think I need to walk," she said. "It might help clear my head."

They walked in silence, Jenda clutching tightly to Luis' arm. Halfway back to the hotel, they passed through a tiny park and she insisted they stop. They sat down on a bench, which felt warm from the late afternoon sun.

"This has got to be pretty overwhelming," Luis said to Jenda, folding her left hand gently between both of his strong hands.

"You might say that." Jenda stared absently at a small child dipping his fingers into the icy waters of a fountain a short distance away. The fountain was clogged with dead leaves and the child seemed to be trying to retrieve something. "I keep thinking I should remember this – at least remember something about it. But there's nothing there. I find nothing but a big aching hole where the memories should be. My poor mother. Why didn't we believe her? And don't ask what I feel about all this, Luis. I don't even know. Shocked. Angry. Sad. I think mostly angry. How could they have done this to me?" Jenda's palms went to her temples and her fingers cradled the top of her head. "How can someone just decide they're going to alter your life and obliterate your memories without your permission? Without you even knowing what's happening?" As soon as she said this, she heard an annoying inner voice saying, "Isn't that what you've been doing for a living?" She looked at Luis, but if he thought anything like this, he wasn't saying it.

"Well, you're the one in charge now," he said. "What do you want to do? This is your story. Where we go with it is your call."

They sat in silence for a while as Jenda battled for control of her jumbled thoughts and feelings. "I have no time for tears," she thought. "I've lost too much time already."

Finally she spoke. "We should compare the dates on the clinic records with the dates on my passport," she said. "And I think I'd like to go see this San Ramon place and meet your old man and his wife." Jenda shivered in the evening twilight. She got up from the bench and held out her hand for Luis.

By the time they reached the hotel, Jenda was cold and tired. She welcomed that coldness and tiredness; this was something she could name, something normal. She handed her passport to Luis. "Here," she said. "If you don't mind, you can check on those dates while I go take a hot soak in the tub."

Emerging from the bath with wet hair and no makeup, Jenda felt revived but still disoriented. She thought she wasn't going to have a headache after all and she didn't mention to Luis that she had thrown up. She rubbed her hair with one of the soft white hotel towels, remembering how she had always loved hotel towels in foreign countries where they were still made of cotton and meant to last.

"Did you find anything?" Jenda asked.

"Yes," Luis said. "Look at this." She peered over his shoulder at the screen while he explained what she was seeing. The dates did not match up at all. According to clinic records, she was admitted on a date when her passport said she was in Ecuador and receiving daily treatments while her passport tracked her through Bolivia and Peru. Her passport put her in Argentina only after the clinic records abruptly ended.

"So what do you think? Is it possible someone else used my name at the clinic while I was traveling elsewhere?" Jenda knew she was grasping at straws.

Luis flipped through the pages of her passport again. "That's odd," he said, looking at a page near the front of the book. He held the book in front of the digiscreen camera and snapped two photos.

"What are you looking at?" Jenda asked, as the photos came up on the screen. All she saw was the page showing traveler's contact information at home and address of destination abroad. It had her parents' contact and the address of a hotel in Ecuador. The second photo was the back of that page, which contained general information about travel protocols. Luis put the second photo through some changes and then pulled it up side-by-side with the contact page. "You see that?" he said.

"I see what looks like a bunch of backwards writing."

"Oh, sorry. I can fix that." He flipped the page horizontally.

"Wait. These are not the same. Something different was written on the contact page first."

"Exactly," Luis said. "What we see on the second page – with enhancement, of course – is the original information. Look what it says."

The contact information was the same, but the destination address read: "Instituto Nueva Vida, San Ramon, Buenos Aires, Argentina."

"So the clinic records are probably right. I must have gone there first. And my famous gap year traveling around South America was an utter fiction." Jenda was standing behind Luis and she put her arms around him. He felt like the most real and solid thing she had in her confused life.

On their drive out to San Ramon the following morning, Jenda was pensive. "Luis," she said finally, "since I was apparently at the clinic for nearly three months, and since there's no record of an abortion... do you think? Do I have a child out there somewhere?" Then, with an ironic smile, she added, "Of course he wouldn't be a child would he? He'd be – what? – 95 years old now. That's insane. What if he didn't get Chulel? He'd be older than me!"

"We can paint all sorts of possible scenarios, querida. But let's not do that. Let's just wait and see where this takes us, okay? There's still so much we don't know." He put his arm around Jenda and, when she turned to look at him, he gave her a long reassuring kiss. It was still a long drive before the turn for San Ramon. They would let the autocar navigate on its own.

By the time they reached San Ramon, they agreed it would probably be a good idea to go ahead and check in at the inn before going to visit Silvestre and Rosalí. They didn't emerge from their room until mid-afternoon.

Rosalí met them at the door. "This must be your partner," she said, releasing Luis from her warm abrazo and turning to embrace Jenda. "Silvestre is having a pretty good day," she said. "I think he'll be happy to see you."

He was. "Ah, Luis-Martín!" His voice was fragile, but his eyes sparkled behind their drooping lids. "Did you give the flower book to your abuela?"

"Oh, yes," Luis said. "She said to tell you 'thank you'." Jenda sent him a questioning look and he quickly gestured her into silence.

"I knew she'd be pleased," Silvestre said, stroking the bedcovers with his gnarled hands. "Who is this pretty señorita with you?"

"This is Jenda Swain," Luis said. "She visited San Ramon a very long time ago."

"Jenda? Swain you said?" Silvestre was thoughtful. "No, I don't remember that name."

"Maybe you remember my friend," Jenda said. "Her name was Paloma."

"Oh, yes. Paloma – the sweet dove," Silvestre replied. "She was so kind. She was Isabel's friend." He was getting that distant look.

Jenda's eyes widened as she looked first at Luis and then back at Silvestre.

"Do you know Paloma's last name?" Luis asked.

"No. No, I don't recall. Just Paloma – the sweet dove." Silvestre was drifting. Then suddenly he looked at Rosalí. "But I think we were sending her the medicine. After she left. Wasn't she on our list, Rosalí?"

Rosalí looked embarrassed and muttered something into Silvestre's ear in Spanish that made him laugh. "Oh, they won't mind about that." Turning to Luis, he said, "Rosalí doesn't want you to know that our families used to be Chulel thieves." He was grinning like a schoolboy. "I'm pretty sure we sent it to Paloma for a while."

Luis was looking at Rosalí now. "Do you remember Paloma, Rosalí?" he asked.

"I'm not sure," she said, looking chagrined. "It must have been a long time ago. But I may have a record of the address where we sent her the… the medicine. Come with me." She motioned to Luis and Jenda. Silvestre's eyes had closed and his jaw had gone slack, but there was a faint smile at the corners of his mouth. His hands continued gently stroking the bedcovers.

"So, did you really find your grandmother, Luis?" Rosalí wanted to know, "or were you humoring the old man."

"Oh, yes, I found my grandmother – strong and well. She's been running a little art gallery in Buenos Aires for decades now. I lied about the book, though. I promise I'll remember it next time I go to visit her."

"Well, that is exciting news," Rosalí responded. "Tell me about it while we look for the address."

Luis began his story as he and Jenda followed Rosalí down the hallway to a back room. The room held only a bed, a small table, and a couple of old wooden cupboards against a wall.

Jenda found the room suffocating, as if it were filled with a dense fog. She looked at Luis, but he and Rosalí didn't seem to notice anything. The fog was oppressive and frightening. She sat down on the end of the bed to catch her breath. As she looked up at the wall, at the painting on the wall, she gasped. She inhaled the fog and the room began to clear.

Rosalí opened one of the cupboards and took down a cardboard box. It was filled with old paper notebooks. "Do you know what years we're looking for?" she looked at Luis for guidance, interrupting his tale just as he was getting to the part about seeing his own painting in Isabel's gallery.

"Let's try 2030," he said. "No, try maybe 2031 or even 32."

Luis glanced over his shoulder at Jenda. She was sitting on the end of the bed.

"Jenda?" Luis called to her.

Jenda was motionless. Tears streamed down her cheeks. She was staring at a wall on which someone had painted an image of Nuestra Señora de Lujan. The painting was old and faded, but it was identical to the one in Jenda's own painting, except that the hands of this lady held only a prayer.

Luis walked over and sat down next to Jenda. He reached for her hand, but she pulled away. She was trembling.

"Jenda?" Luis said again. "You remember this picture, don't you? Do you think you remember this room?" His voice was gentle and he looked as if his heart would burst with wanting to care for this woman he loved.

"I don't know," Jenda whispered. She heard her own voice coming from somewhere far away. There was a quiet hum of other voices. She closed her eyes to listen. "Milly, Milly," she murmured, rocking slightly as she drew her knees up and grasped them in front of her.

"What did she say?" Rosalí asked, looking suddenly pale. "Milly?"

Rosalí went to a different cupboard and opened another box, pulling out an old and tattered stuffed animal. It looked like a cat and had probably once been white. She brought it over and held it out to Jenda. "Is this Milly?" she asked.

Jenda opened her eyes. She saw her precious cat. She saw her friend Rosalí. "Gracias, hermanita," she said. Then suddenly she doubled over, screaming in pain. She fell back onto the bed, clutching her belly, her eyes wide. "What's happening to me?" she thought. She looked desperately around the room, searching for someone who could make this stop. The only one she saw was Rosalí, who knelt beside her, placing the stuffed cat onto Jenda's stomach.

Rosalí looked at Luis. Through her own tears, she said, "I know this woman. I know your Paloma. And I know Jenda's child."

Luis lifted Jenda from the bed. "We need to get her out of here," he said. Rosalí led them to the sitting room where he placed Jenda on the sofa. She continued trembling, moaning, and convulsing painfully every few minutes. Luis sat on the floor next to her, stroking her arm and talking to her softly. Gradually, the intensity subsided.

"Rosalí grows beautiful flowers, doesn't she?" Luis remarked, as Jenda's blank stare came to rest for a moment on a small pot of purple chrysanthemums. Jenda turned her face toward him and gave him a faint smile.

"I'm thirsty," she whispered hoarsely.

An instant later Rosalí was offering her a glass of cool water. Jenda struggled to sit up. She took a small sip and then a huge mouthful, which made her cough and spit water all over herself and Luis. She began to laugh. "Oh, I'm sorry, Luis," she said, setting the glass on the table and brushing Luis' shirt with her hand.

"It's okay, querida," Luis said. "It's all okay." He handed the glass of water back to her and this time she sipped it slowly and carefully.

"How about some cookies?" Rosalí said. "Have I shown you our little garden? The sun has come out. Let's take a walk in the garden and then have some cookies and tea."

Luis helped Jenda put on her coat.

The garden was exactly what Jenda needed to settle her disturbed mind. It was spacious and open at the center, with a clear view of the bright blue sky with small clouds scudding across. The garden was surrounded reassuringly with a hedge of what Jenda knew was fuchsia and flowering jacarandas, along with a few fruit trees. She remembered the taste of fresh plums.

"This was Silvestre's pride and joy," Rosalí said. "He and his father planted everything here and looked after all the plants with such love. They even built the little stone wall with the fountain there at the end of the path. It used to work, but the pipes rusted through some years ago and nobody fixed it."

They went back indoors and sat around the table in Rosalí's warm kitchen. They drank hot spiced tea and ate cookies, complimenting Rosalí on her baking skills. They could see the garden through a big window and Jenda wanted to know about the plants. She knew the names of many of them, although Rosalí had to remind her. There weren't any flowers at this time of year other than the carefully tended pots of chrysanthemums by the back steps, but Jenda could see the garden overrun with a riot of colorful blossoms.

"What is the blue butterfly, the one that loves the little yellow amancay flowers?" Jenda asked, gesturing toward an insect only she could see in the brown winter garden. Rosalí named it and told Jenda a bit about its habits.

Jenda reached across the table and placed her hand over Rosalí's. "You said you remember me. Can you tell me about that?"

Luis intervened. "Jenda, we don't have to go there today. We can wait. We can give you a little more time. You've been through so much already."

"No, Luis," she said. "I don't think I can deal with these strange fragments of memory until I know what they mean." She didn't know how to explain to him that the memories seemed to be arising from deep within her body rather than from her mind and that her mind was longing to link up with them.

"Well, here is what I remember," Rosalí began. "I was only a little girl back then, so my memories won't be the whole story. You know Silvestre and I were childhood friends, so I used to come over here to play. I remember when Paloma brought you here to the house. Your hair was a different color then – kind of a grayish tan. I think you didn't wear makeup. You looked so different from the way you look now. And they never told us your name. We called you 'hermana,' 'older sister.' You seemed so sad. I kept wanting to bring you my toys to play with. You know, to cheer you up. I probably came over more while you were here than I had before. Maybe that's when Silvestre and I became so close. Isabel was here, too, now that I think of it. She seemed to be friends with Paloma and both of them were looking after you."

"How long was I here?" Jenda asked.

"A long while. It seemed like that to me, anyway. You kept getting fatter and they told me you were going to have a baby. You never talked about it. Not with me. Then one day they told me you had become ill and I was not to go into your room. I heard you screaming, so I sneaked in and brought you my stuffed cat, the one I showed you earlier. You took it and you were stroking it and calling it Milly." Rosalí stopped and looked out the window, brushing some cookie crumbs from the tablecloth. "I had forgotten why I named it that. Anyway, the stuffed toy seemed to calm you, so they let you keep it, but they shooed me out of the room and I went to play out in the yard with Silvestre. A while later, we heard a baby crying."

Luis was watching Jenda carefully; she was fully absorbed in Rosalí's story.

"You and the baby – it was a little girl – stayed here with us for a while longer. Then you and Paloma went away and left the baby with Isabel. I think it was with Isabel. And that… that is all I know. I'm sorry I can't tell you more."

"Thank you, Rosalí." Jenda's voice was quiet, calm. "You've told me a lot, and I'm grateful for your memories. I think you were a good friend."

"Would you like me to take you out to the old estancia?" Rosalí asked, looking at Luis.

Jenda answered. "No. Maybe another time, Rosalí. I don't think I have anything more to learn right now from going there. Were you able to find Paloma's address?"

"Maybe so. I think I found the right book. Let me go get it. Would you like to move back into the sitting room? It's so warm and sunny this time of day." Jenda and Luis got up from the table and went back to the sitting room, settling onto the sofa while Rosalí went into the room with the Holy Virgin on the wall. She returned with two notebooks. She lay the books in her lap and opened the first one, scanning its pages carefully.

187

"Here it is," she said finally. "Paloma Suarez – and an address in Costa Rica. Shall I record it for you?" Luis unfurled his digilet and handed it to Rosalí to enter the address.

"You know," Rosalí said as she tapped the syllables into the screen, "they came around a couple of years ago collecting up old paper for the recycling and I almost gave them all these boxes. Now I'm glad I kept them." She handed the digilet back to Luis and he coiled it around his wrist, giving it a pat as if instructing it to guard this information.

Jenda thanked Rosalí again and then looked over at Luis. "One more thing," she said. "Is it okay if Luis takes some pictures of the room – especially of the painting?"

"Of course," Rosalí said. While Luis went into the little room to photograph the Holy Virgin, Jenda and Rosalí sat by the window in the sunshine, like two old friends. Rosalí was in the easy chair and Jenda sat with her feet drawn up under her on the end of the sofa. Between them was the little table with the pot of purple mums.

Luis and Jenda said their farewells and went back to the hotel to collect their belongings. Although they hadn't stayed the night, they felt they had made good use of the room.

Luis guided the vehicle back to the main road. Then he put the car on auto and turned in his seat to face Jenda.

She was looking out the window, but she knew she had his attention. "You know," she said, "at first I thought I just wanted to know what happened during my missing year." She turned and reached for Luis' hand. "Talk about your gap year…" She chuckled softly and began again.

"At first I only wanted the story – you know? The sequence of events. But now I'm finding that the story itself seems to be about a different person. And yet, that person was me. Is me. Was I really such a committed Vintie, Luis? Was I foolish enough to get pregnant in high school? I thought I was just an ordinary, sensible, reasonably successful mid-level professional and obedient 22nd-century consumer. Now I find someone completely different claiming to be me – a crazy girl with sepia-colored hair, a baby born in a back room in an

Argentine village, and a tattoo of the Virgin Mary on her backside." Jenda looked out the window again and sighed. "Maybe we can track me down in Costa Rica, Luis. Is that where we go next?"

22.

Jenda and Luis awoke the next morning to a tentative winter sun shining through lace curtains in Isabel's spare bedroom, which she had insisted they occupy. As they snuggled under the mound of quilts, Luis stroked Jenda's tousled hair. "Maybe you should go sepia again, querida," he said.

"Only if you will. And we both have to get our tattoos restored." Jenda caught a sudden fragment of memory: She was peering over her shoulder into a mirror at a colorful tattoo on her back of the Virgin of Lujan. The image stung.

After a quick shower, they got dressed to join Isabel for breakfast, trying not to trip over one another as they sidestepped their bags. It was a small room, but a pleasing one, with real wood furniture and what looked like a handmade wool rug.

"How are you feeling this morning, mi amor?"

Jenda thought for a minute. "You know, I think I'm feeling okay. It's like I've stopped looking away every time I almost remember something. Yesterday shook loose some things in my mind, Luis, and it will take time to figure out what it all is, how things fit in. I don't know what I'd do without you, my love."

Luis looked at her, standing there only half dressed. Jenda felt his gaze. She had such desire for this man, but without urgency. She knew her desire would not go unfulfilled.

"This is my last outfit," Jenda said, pulling a soft purple knit top over her head. "I'll have to go shopping today." The prospect was not pleasing. She arranged the colorful silk scarf Luis had bought for her around her neck.

"You could try washing some things," Luis said. "I think it used to be called 'doing laundry'." It had become customary to buy new things and almost never bother with washing clothes. It kept the recycling process moving along at a nice clip.

"Hmm. Maybe I'll try that." Jenda picked up a couple of items from her jumbled suitcase and shook out the wrinkles. "I think the old Jenda probably did laundry."

By the time they entered the kitchen, Isabel was adding the last pancake to a delicious looking stack.

"Wayee." Jenda inhaled the sweet aroma. "You made those yourself? They smell wonderful." She was also noting the fragrance of freshly brewed coffee. It smelled as good as the stuff Luis made for her in San Miguel.

As they sat around the table, exchanging pleasantries, Jenda thought about how different this felt from her breakfasts at the beverage shop in Dallas with Granny El. Dallas felt very far away.

They finished the pancakes along with some fresh oranges and grapes. Isabel poured them each a second cup of coffee. "So how did it go yesterday?" she asked.

"Amazing," Jenda answered. "Rosalí remembered me. And my companion Paloma. She gave us the last address they had for Paloma – in Costa Rica. Rosalí also said that you and Paloma were friends. Do you remember her at all? Her last name is Suarez. She even said you kept my baby while Paloma took me back home to Texas."

"Your what? So it's true then. But you had the baby? And they didn't… "

"Oh, I'm sorry, Isabel. All of this is still such a jumble. So, yes, Rosalí said I had the baby there at their little house in San Ramon, in the room with the Virgin of Lujan on the wall. Like my tattoo."

"Your what?" Isabel said again.

"Oh, Luis, I'm going to make a muddle of this," Jenda groaned. "You tell her." She knew her own telling would be filled with feelings she couldn't name and images that kept slipping away even as she sought to describe them. So Luis took over, telling what they had learned as best he could.

"I wish I could recall something that would help." Isabel looked at Jenda. "It seems like I may have as much shared history with you as I do with my own grandson." She reached across the table, placing one hand over Jenda's and the other over Luis'.

"I have something to give you," Luis said suddenly. "Wait a moment." He went back to the bedroom and came back with the flower album.

He laid the book on the table, opened it, and pushed it over in front of Isabel. "Silvestre wanted you to have this," he said. "He told me you and he made it together, back when he was a child and you were in San Ramon."

Isabel stared at the book. "Oh," she said. As she began carefully turning the pages, her eyes took on a faraway look. "From the garden…" She turned another page. "And from the meadow behind…" She looked up at Luis. "Maybe I do remember, just a little bit. Or maybe I know these flowers. It's a beautiful album, but some of the flowers have almost turned to dust. We shouldn't be handling it. I know someone who might be able to encase what remains in polyplex to preserve it. Thank you for bringing this, Luis. One day soon, I think I need to go visit this Silvestre and his wife."

Luis got up and started collecting the dishes to take to the kitchen. "We had something we wanted to ask you," he said, pointing his chin at Jenda, "about doing laundry."

"Oh, yes, I still have one of those old-fashioned laundering devices," Isabel said. "It was here when I moved in and it still works. I use it myself from time to time." They collected up some of their used clothing and, with Isabel's advice, put it into the machine.

Jenda suggested that, in light of the new information they now had, it might be a good idea to take another look at the things she had brought from the boxes at Granny El's. Jenda's suitcase was nearly full of the stuff, which accounted for her clothing shortage. They pulled the case into the middle of the floor in Isabel's sitting room and sat next to it. The items were in a jumble. Luis went for the bundles of photographs and papers.

"Luis," Jenda said, staring at the chaos in her suitcase, "if Silvestre and Rosalí are the same generation, why does he look so much older?"

"Rosalí told me that whenever Chulel was in short supply – and given the way they were accessing it, that happened a lot – whenever there wasn't enough for both of them, he insisted that she take it and he would do without. And then after a while he stopped taking it altogether. I think she's stopped taking it now, too, although I'm not sure Silvestre knows."

Jenda turned her attention to her digilet. "Here's something I wanted you to see, Luis. I couldn't bring it with me; all I have is a photo." She handed the digilet to Luis.

"Wayee," he said. "Is this what I think it is?" He looked at Jenda and then back at the photo.

"It's one of my mother's sculptures. And, yes, it's the same figure I put in the painting I did at your studio in San Miguel, the one you said was a self-portrait. And of course this picture is the same sculpture I gave you for Christmas in San Miguel. You know I thought I'd forgotten what my mother's work looked like. This tells me I still remembered it – somewhere, somehow." Jenda paused, looking over Luis' shoulder at the photo of the little dancer. "Did I tell you I was taking a dance class?"

Luis and Jenda started at a sudden loud buzzing noise.

Isabel laughed, "Calm down, it's only the washing device telling us it's finished its job. You keep on with what you're doing. I'll go put your things in the dryer."

Jenda looked relieved. "So you have a drying machine, too. I was wondering what we were going to do with all those wet clothes. Thank you, Isabel." If devices such as washers and dryers had ever been part of Jenda's experience, she had no recollection of it. Paloma might remember, Jenda thought. She hoped Paloma might remember a lot.

"By the way," Isabel said as she moved toward the closet that housed the washing and drying machines, "I've invited the Feldmans over for supper. I hope you don't mind."

"Oh, no," Jenda said. "We'd love to see them again before we go to Costa Rica."

Luis had collected several of Jenda's printed photographs and arrayed them in a line. "Look at these," he said to Jenda.

She scooted over next to him and peered at the pictures, trying to see what had caught his interest. The photographs showed groups of obviously Vintie young people, one of whom was Jenda. Some other individuals seemed to repeat in the various pictures, too. In particular, a number of the photos showed a well-built young man with dark hair and a dark complexion, and in all of them he and Jenda were hand-in-hand or had their arms around one another.

"Do you think that was my boyfriend?" Jenda asked, realizing at once that this was not a particularly insightful inference.

"What I find interesting is who your boyfriend is."

"You know him?"

"Well, unless I'm seriously mistaken, your boyfriend is Montagne Williams, who is still a committed political activist. He got his start as a leader in the Vintagonist movement. And – given the time frame of the photographs here and what we know about your trip to San Ramon – he could very well be the father of your child." Luis looked up from the photos to see Jenda's face.

Jenda stared at the images. The Jenda in the photos looked so happy. Her boyfriend – Montagne? He looked happy, too. Jenda's heart warmed as her observation morphed into a fragment of memory. "Why hadn't I even thought about the fact that the baby – my daughter – would have had to have a father?" she said softly. "My mind is such a mess. So you know this Montagne?"

"Not well. We worked together on a project once. But everybody in Recall knows who Montagne Williams is. You may have run across some of his writings," Luis continued. "He goes by the name of HillBill."

"Zujo! Are you craicking me?" Jenda rocked backward, her hands on her knees. "I've been following him ever since San Miguel. He makes a lot of sense. A bit extreme sometimes." She was trying to comprehend that the faceless scribe she had been following might be the father of her child, the 95-year-old child she had not been sure even existed until yesterday.

As Luis went to reclaim their freshly washed and dried clothing, he found himself wondering if Jenda could be the girlfriend Montagne had told him about, the one he had adored for her fierce loyalty to Vintagonist principles and her whimsical creativity in devising acts of rebellion and disobedience. Could she be the girl who had created that incredible web-like installation of broken chairs, old clocks, discarded books, and ropes plaited from torn clothing that had mysteriously appeared on the steps of 3Dec headquarters one morning? Montagne said it was his girlfriend who made it. The installation itself was legendary.

~~~

The Feldmans arrived right on time and Jenda went downstairs to let them in. After a glass of the wonderful Malbec that Isabel favored, they sat down to a home cooked meal. "I could get used to this," Jenda thought, looking around the table at the group of friends and family.

"We've bought the old estancia, the old institute property out by San Ramon," Max Feldman announced, as they were finishing the soup and moving on to the main course. "While we were checking into the records, we found out that it was available for the price of back taxes and so we bought it."

"And what exactly do you propose to do with such a ruin?" Luis wanted to know. "It would cost much more than the price of back taxes to set it up as a research institute again."

"Oh, no," Max said, "our research days are over. We've done all the damage we intend to do on that front. No. We're going to turn it into an old folks' home. And we have people coming out next week to clean up the old caretaker's cottage and repair it so we can move out there right away." He gave Emily a triumphant look. They raised their wine glasses and tapped them together with a musical clink.

"An old folks' home?" Luis laughed. "And where do you expect to find the old people to populate it?"

Max raised his eyebrows and looked suddenly serious. "I guess I shouldn't joke about it," he said. "You remember that blood disorder we were telling you about that was breaking out among Gen1 and Gen2 people in several different parts of the world? Well, it's now clear that it affects Gen3 and even Gen4 people and has been most recently documented in Kurdistan and Cataluña and even a couple of cases in southern California and northwestern Mexico. The doctors are scrambling to figure out how to deal with it, but their best line of attack so far is to tell people to lay off Chulel. The current hypothesis is that it's a virus, but they haven't isolated it. So, you see? An old folks' home may not be so far-fetched. Besides," he added, "Emily and I will be there and we're both finished with Chulel."

After the Feldmans left, Luis went back to the digiscreen to confirm his and Jenda's tickets to Costa Rica and select a return schedule.

"How long can we stay in Costa Rica, Jenda?" Luis asked. "Are you planning to go back to YJ?"

"I don't think so. But maybe we should get one-way tickets. Who knows where we might want to go if we don't find Paloma at the address Rosalí gave us."

Jenda had told her work supervisor she would be gone for two weeks. One week of that was already gone. They would have to move quickly if they hoped to find Paloma.

23.

It rained a little that evening, and then shortly before midnight the sky exploded in a spectacular thunderstorm. Isabel hated thunderstorms. She found something deeply disturbing about the flashes of lightning. She had learned to pull the extra set of darkening curtains over the only window in her room and to put on her sleep mask whenever storms were threatening. This one caught her by surprise.

By the time she awoke to an unusually loud clap of thunder, she was in a cold sweat. She had been dreaming. In her dream, she was packing up boxes of books. A young man was helping her and he called her "Mama". They were frightened. And then she was in a little garden. The garden was beautifully planted. It was spacious and open at the center, and surrounded by a hedge of fuchsia, a few fruit trees, and flowering jacarandas. Isabel found the spaciousness threatening. She was cowering behind a little stone wall at one end of the garden, clutching an infant and quaking with fear that the baby would awaken and reveal their hiding place.

Isabel got up and, with trembling hands, closed the extra curtains. She found her sleep mask, but she didn't put it on. For a while she just lay there on her damp pillow, letting her tears flow as she remembered that little garden, remembered the beautiful brown baby, and as she tried to remember what it was that terrified her so.

24.

Parts of Costa Rica were fully as vanguard as Dallas or Buenos Aires. The part that Jenda and Luis found themselves in was not one of those. The address Rosalí had given them led from an international airport near Liberia, Guanacaste, to a small town near an old sugar plantation on the Tempisque River.

The town itself was pleasant enough, with a clean plaza surrounded by small shops and an old church, but the address Rosalí had given them seemed to confuse their NaviGiz. Most of the intersections had no street signs. They parked the autocar and went into a shop to ask for directions.

The Gen1 shop assistant made it sound like their destination should be within walking distance, so they left the car where it was. Twenty minutes later, they were questioning this decision. They went inside another shop to get out of the sun and to see if they could figure out where they had gone wrong.

"Traveler's tip, Luis," Jenda said, rolling the sleeves of her blouse down to protect her arms, "when you're in a new place, always ask at least two people for directions before you set out."

"Now you tell me. But who would have thought we could get lost in a small town like this?"

Luis told the youthful shopkeeper the address they were looking for and waited. "I'm pretty sure that place was knocked down maybe 80 years ago," she said at last. "I think it was where the technical college is now. They renamed the street after the college was built."

Luis and Jenda exchanged a defeated look. They were afraid this might happen, but they had been hopeful nonetheless. What now? They bought a couple of bottles of fortified water.

"Gosh, you'd think we were still in Buenos Aires," Luis complained, describing to Jenda that city's reputation for constantly changing names of streets, and thereafter having them called differently by members of different generations.

"Why are you looking for this address?" the shopkeeper asked. "Do you know someone who lived there?"

"Yes," Luis responded. "We're looking for an old friend. Her name is Paloma Suarez."

The shopkeeper looked down, shuffling some papers behind the desk. "Paloma?" she asked. "Suarez you say?"

"That's right," Jenda replied. "I knew her back in Texas. And in Argentina." The shopkeeper was giving Jenda a hard look, as if trying to decide if it was worth spending any more time on these strangers.

"Well, I will tell you where you can ask. Where they might know something." She wrote another address on a slip of paper. "This place is across the street from the college," she said, explaining how to get to the renamed street. "Good luck," she added, as Luis and Jenda left the shop.

"Well, this looks promising," Luis said, showing Jenda the address written in block letters on the slip of paper. It read: "NO. 27, AVE SUAREZ".

This time they found the address with no trouble, although they began to wonder how they would remember their way back to the car. As they walked up to the door, checking the number on the paper one more time, they looked at each other and Luis said, "Well, here goes." He knocked firmly on the wooden door.

They waited, squinting at each other in the bright sunlight reflecting off the brilliantly blue door. Luis knocked a second time, and at last the door opened.

"Yes? May I help you?" asked the woman peering from the shadow of the half-opened door. Then the door opened fully. "Luis? Luis-Martín?"

"Meli?" Luis responded, as he recognized the woman in the shadow as one of his friends from San Miguel.

"¡Adelante!" she said. "Please come in."

They entered the cool breezeway. "Whatever brings you here to the margins of the civilized world?" Meli laughed, closing the door behind them.

"I might ask you the same question," Luis responded. "This is surprising, to say the least."

"Well, I'm here because this is my home," Meli replied. "Please, come let me introduce you." Luis and Jenda followed Meli into the patio, where a dark-skinned man sat talking with an old woman with wrinkled fair skin.

"No introduction necessary for us," Luis said, as the man rose from his seat and strode forward to grasp his hand. "Meli," Luis said, "Why did I never know that you were kin to Montagne Williams?" Luis abruptly turned to look at Jenda, who still stood at the edge of the patio, staring. He quickly moved back toward her.

"Well," Meli said, in answer to Luis' question, "I've only known it myself for the past few months. It turns out he's my father."

Luis reached Jenda just in time. She had taken a step back as her knees weakened. She stared first at Montagne and then at Meli. Montagne had taken a few steps in her direction, his hand extended for an introduction. Then he stopped, looking suddenly serious. "No," he said. "It can't be. Jenda?"

Luis grabbed Jenda as she swayed uncertainly. "Okay, can we all back off a minute?" he said sternly, taking Jenda in his arms and leading her to the sofa.

Jenda sat silently, looking from one to the other of the people in the room. She felt all of their eyes on her and heard them speaking to one another, although she could not make out what they were saying. She was caught somewhere between abject tears, hysterical laughter, and an impulse to bid all of these people a polite farewell and run away. And yet, she could almost feel a clarity dawning. Wasn't this what she'd come to Costa Rica to find? She was pretty sure she was looking at her own daughter, the man who had impregnated her at the age of 17, and the dear old nanny who had accompanied her during her missing year in Argentina.

25.

The little group spent the next several hours arranging and rearranging the pieces of a story that involved all of them in one way or another, but which none of them had fully known until now. Paloma's pieces were the most encompassing and Jenda hung on every syllable she uttered. Despite her visibly advanced age and quavering voice, Paloma's memories painted a vivid picture of Jenda's infamous gap year.

Shortly before her 65th birthday in 2029, Paloma Suarez had retired from her many years of service – first as nanny and then as more of a personal maid – to Tessa and James Swain's daughter Jenda and younger son Jonathan. As a parting gift, she had received her first Chulel treatment and a generous amount of cash and investments, which the Swains thought would provide her with a nice pension.

"I was grateful, of course," Paloma said, "and happy to be back in Costa Rica with my husband. But I was lonely for Jenda and Jonathan. I was never able to have children of my own." Less than a year later, the Swains contacted Paloma, pleading with her to come back to Texas to accompany Jenda on a trip to South America. They made it sound like Jenda was in trouble and so Paloma said goodbye once again to her husband and set out to care for the girl she had loved for so many years as her own.

Jenda was pregnant and threatening to run away with her Vintagonist friends, which included Montagne Williams, the father of her child. Tessa and Jim were beside themselves. Their son, Jonathan, had left home the previous year to follow a Buddhist guru of questionable lineage. They couldn't bear to lose their daughter as well. Besides, Jenda had earned a prestigious art scholarship to Perry University in Austin and was due to start college the next fall.

The family was torn by the issue of an abortion. They were perfectly legal and readily available in Texas. "But you know your mother was a sensitive Buddhist and your dad was a bit of an old-fashioned Catholic, so this distressed them terribly," Paloma said. Then they had found out about a clinic in Argentina that offered both abortion and a new form of cult deprogramming. They were eager to get Jenda over what they saw as her ridiculous Vintagonist ideas before she started college, and so finally agreed to send her to Argentina. "They knew you would never go willingly," Paloma said, "so they told you it was going to be a wonderful vacation for the summer between high school and university. You still weren't too excited about the trip, but you agreed to go, even though I think you were a little embarrassed about going with your old nanny instead of your school friends."

Paloma said she remembered arriving at the clinic and seeing Jenda's horror as it dawned on her what was happening. She screamed for Paloma to take her away, but Paloma turned her back.

"I think that is the most painful memory of my entire life," Paloma said. "I let my loyalty to Tessa and Jim override my love for you, Jenda. I had no idea what that place intended to do to you. How can you ever forgive me?"

"It wasn't your fault, Paloma." Jenda was fighting back tears. "You weren't the one who sent me there."

For the next several weeks, Paloma said, she was barred from the clinic and told varying stories about complications with Jenda's abortion and treatment. When they finally agreed to let her see Jenda, they put her in a room where they told her she must wait. Paloma remembered that there was a strange flick that seemed to be on all the walls at once. And there were bright flashing lights and a loud monotonous noise. Paloma became upset and – convinced she was still not going to be allowed to see Jenda anyway – she sneaked out of the room and fled.

"The next part I don't remember myself, but I trust I've been told truthfully what happened," Paloma said. A kind woman had found Paloma, wandering distressed and disoriented along one of the side streets in San Ramon. The woman was Isabel Hernandez. Paloma could not explain why she was in San Ramon or even how she came to be in Argentina. Isabel took her in. Going through the items in Paloma's bag, they found a small notebook that included contact information for the clinic. There were also two passports – Paloma's and Jenda's. Isabel knew about the clinic and its activities, so she and Paloma began making a plan to rescue Jenda.

"Isabel knew someone inside the clinic, and he helped us get you out. I know now that he was part of a ring that was stealing medicine to give to the poor, but I was unaware at the time."

"I don't suppose you remember that person's name, Doña Paloma," Luis said.

Paloma paused to reflect, staring at the melting ice in her drink. "Winston? Something like that. I think that's what Isabel called him. I never met him myself." Luis looked at Jenda, who was staring at him wide-eyed. They both knew she was talking about Winslow Morris. Perhaps he was not the total thug and scoundrel they had thought him to be.

By the time they got Jenda away from the clinic, Paloma said, her pregnancy was well advanced and they knew abortion was out of the question. Furthermore, she had been extracted from the clinic in the midst of the deprogramming treatments.

"Experiments, more likely," Luis interrupted. "Those people had no idea what they were doing. I'm sorry, go ahead, Doña Paloma."

Paloma described how Jenda had been left in a daze and could not even comprehend that she was pregnant. They cared for her as best they could. She took walks in the garden with the little boy who lived in the house where they stayed. His best friend was a little girl who came by frequently and spent time with Jenda, bringing her toys and paper and colored pencils. Jenda had become like a child herself, and seemed to enjoy the company of this young friend.

It was in this house that Jenda gave birth. It was hard to watch, Paloma said. Jenda did not understand what was happening, but was comforted by the little girl's plush cat toy, which reminded her of the pet she had when she was a little girl.

After the baby came, Paloma and Isabel were left with looking after not only a still confused and needy Jenda, but a newborn infant as well. They needed a name for the baby girl, and Isabel suggested Ermelinda. Paloma agreed, but insisted on calling her Meli for short, as a nod to her mother's beloved feline companion.

"You said Isabel is your grandmother, Luis? I'm so glad to know she's well." Paloma picked up her iced tea glass from the table and took another sip. "When I met her, she was in Argentina with her son, Julian, who was not one of the Vinties, like Montagne and Jenda, but also a dissident. Many of their friends were Menders, but the political group Julian sided with often went by the name of 'Unpreoccupied' – 'Despreocupado'. I never knew exactly what that meant until Montagne explained it to me recently. They talked a lot about how critical medicines were being kept in short supply by corporations like Pharmakon. They used to say they were liberating supplies of medicines to be used in treating the poor. Isabel was sympathetic, I guess. I suppose that's why she had gone with her son to Argentina."

"I didn't know at first what they were doing," Paloma continued, "so I didn't understand the risk I was taking in leaving little Meli with Isabel while I took Jenda back to her parents in Texas. Jenda was still in a confused state, so we took a little time, going back. You know, to give her some fresh memories and stories to tell when she got back home. Her parents had been okay with extending Jenda's trip on into the new year, since I wrote and told them she was doing well and that we were in this country or that one. Julian's friends knew how to fix up our passports so that her parents would never know."

The Swains had been distressed by Jenda's state of mind upon her return, but deeply grateful for Paloma's service. They had given her the gift of additional doses of Chulel and another generous payment and investments.

"After getting you safely back home, Jenda. I went back to collect your baby daughter from Isabel. I was horrified to find

Isabel was in hiding and it took me a while to track her and Meli down. Isabel told me the corporate police were after her and her son because of the stolen medicine, so she was happy to hand Meli back over to me. I brought Meli here to Costa Rica and this is where I raised her – here in Ortega, here in my hometown. I took the Chulel the Swains gave me and then what I received later from the Ocampo family in Argentina," Paloma continued. "I didn't want to look too old to have a daughter Meli's age. But after she was an adult and gone away, and after my husband died... Well, as you can see I stopped taking it."

"Please understand," Paloma said, looking at Jenda, "I never told Meli your name. I was trying to protect both of you."

"That's true," Meli said. "I begged her for years to tell me my mother's name. At first she told me she didn't know, and I believed her. Then she told me…"

Paloma interrupted. "What I told her was that the names of people with whom we have no shared stories are not so important. Only the stories we share are important. Meli and I shared stories. Jenda and I also shared many stories. But for Meli, Jenda was such a minor character in her story, the name was not important and would only make her mother seem more real than she was." Paloma paused for a moment, her eyes on a tiny yellow butterfly that had alighted on the edge of her tea glass. "Memories are as short-lived as butterflies, you know, unless they form stories. And stories must be shared."

"How did you and Montagne find each other?" Luis asked Meli.

"He's the one who found me." Meli replied.

Montagne scowled at the empty glass in his hands. "I can't believe it took me so long," he said, sounding apologetic. "I had always assumed that Jenda had the abortion. She hardly seemed to remember me after she got back, so we parted ways. I always wondered what had happened to her in South America. I had no idea." He paused and looked over at Meli. "But I never forgot. And then several months ago I ran across this advertisement on Recall from a guy who claimed he had access to records from a clinic in Argentina."

Luis stifled a laugh and even Jenda was smiling. "What?" Montagne said. "You know Dr. Winfield?"

"Oh, you might say that," Luis replied. "He's out of business now, you know. But that's for later. Please continue."

Maurice Winfield told Montagne about Jenda's abrupt disappearance from the clinic, with no record of an abortion being performed. "That's when I knew I needed to try and track you down, Jenda, you and our child. I thought maybe Paloma could help me, since she never seemed to dislike me nearly as much as your parents did."

"How did you find Paloma?" Jenda asked.

"It took a while. I knew her last name and I was pretty sure she was from Costa Rica. So I searched every area of the medianets and the infranet and finally found a small reference on Recall to a Paloma Suarez who had founded a technical college in rural Costa Rica in 2045. It turned out to be her and...well, here I am," he said. "Of course, it did take a while for me to convince Paloma to let me tell Meli who I am. She had never told her my name either, Jenda."

"So the college is yours, Doña Paloma?" Luis asked.

"Well, I built it, yes, but it belongs to the people. Jenda's parents had been so generous to me and I wanted to do something useful with their gifts."

"Some of the best trained 'net scripters in the world are coming out of this little college," Montagne added. "And not a one of them is owned by a corporation. They're doing great work for Recall."

Luis had one more question for Paloma. "Do you know what happened to Isabel?"

"I was told," Paloma said. "That the corporate police finally caught her and put her in jail. I believe her son Julian was killed."

Meli and Paloma insisted that Luis and Jenda stay at their house. It was a big house by 22nd century criteria and a vanguard one for rural Costa Rica. After receiving directions from Montagne, Luis headed back to the plaza to fetch the autocar containing their bags, leaving Jenda with Meli and Paloma and Montagne.

~~~

As Luis walked back toward the plaza, he chided himself for the twinges of jealousy he was feeling. "She and Montagne were lovers, yes," he told himself, "but that was nearly a century ago. Why should I not feel only joy for them to find each other again, and especially to find their daughter?" But he knew that Jenda was finally reconnecting with some pieces of her past and that Meli and Montagne were easily the most important of those pieces.

Despite these vague trepidations, Luis was pleased to see Montagne again. Montagne had been aligned with the branch of Vintagonists that had persistently called for direct political action. As the movement evolved over time, his commitment and dedication had never wavered. The fact that he had managed to evade the corporate police was a tribute to his ingenuity. Luis had always been more inclined toward symbolic resistance.

After dinner that evening, Luis and Montagne discussed recent developments in the Recall community. The zone on the infranet had finally been restored and re-secured after the irrupting incident, which had galvanized the more radical participants into putting into motion a plan they had been working on for many years, a plan designed to bring down all the medianets and with them the supranet.

"Zujo!" Luis said. "That will have disastrous consequences for everything. It will disrupt food supplies, banking, energy – everything."

"Well, that's kind of the point. But you know we have a widespread network of sufficiency communities that are equipped to survive whatever happens. The ones we used to call Simpletons led the charge on that, thank goodness. And we should have a new and independent 'net up and running to unite those communities within a few weeks of the collapse."

Luis looked doubtful. "Can you share any details with me? I've been aching to know exactly what's in the works."

"It's a new and fiendishly clever type of digital infection – one that should remain undetected for just long enough to become unstoppable. But it requires that we introduce it simultaneously in all of the key sectors. We have recruits ready within the energy distribution network, in the transportation net, media – pretty much every major sector. The only thing we're missing is someone to introduce the infection into screens at one of the LifeBook or Your Journal centers." Luis guessed that Montagne didn't know yet where Jenda worked, and he quickly decided it was not his place to offer up this information.

~~~

While the men talked, Jenda was left with Meli and Paloma and after a few minutes, Paloma excused herself. "I'm an old woman and I need my rest," she said, offering each of the younger women a peck on the cheek as she retired to her bedroom.

Jenda and Meli – mother and daughter – sat looking at one another in awkward silence.

"When I first met you in San Miguel, I felt there was something familiar about you," Jenda offered at last.

"I wish I could say the same," Meli replied. "But I had never seen a picture of you and of course I'd never known your name."

"I'm not sure how we're supposed to do this, Meli. I never knew my own mother that well – she was always so troubled. And I've never been around children. But of course," she added, "you're hardly a child."

"This has kind of taken both of us by surprise."

"I guess I just don't know how to be your mother."

"Paloma was my mother," Meli said softly. "She is my mother. And since she was kind of like your mother too… Maybe you and I are really more like sisters. Do you have sisters or brothers?"

"I have a brother. We were always close as children."

"Well, then maybe we could start with that."

Jenda smiled and nodded. She reached over and took Meli's hand in hers, their fingers intertwining. By the time Luis

212

and Montagne rejoined them, they were engaged in lively conversation. The topics may not have been as portentous as the ones that had occupied the men, but the simple exchange of small facts about their lives felt monumental to Jenda.

They all said goodnight reluctantly and Jenda and Luis retreated behind the closed door of their little bedroom off the main courtyard. When Luis returned from showering in the shared facility across the yard, Jenda was sitting cross-legged in the middle of the bed, staring at the calendar on her digilet.

"You know, YJ is expecting me to report for work on Monday. To make that, I'd have to start back day after tomorrow." She laid the digilet on the bedside cabinet and leaned back on the pillows. "I can't go back, Luis. I'm so sick of what YJ does. I don't see how I can continue to be part of that." She turned to face Luis and folded her arms. "If I went back, I'd probably end up planting a bomb in the building or something."

Luis studied her face. "Maybe you should talk with Montagne."

"What? So now Meli's daddy knows about bombs? You know I'm just kidding about that. You know I'm not a violent person, Luis."

"Well, Montagne isn't a violent person either. But he knows much more than I do about the plans being formulated in the Recall community, and part of that may involve bringing down YJ. More or less peacefully."

"More or less? What are you talking about, Luis?"

"It's not for me to say. Talk to Montagne." Luis lay down and Jenda rolled over toward him. She wanted to feel the strength of his body next to hers. Luis reached over and pulled her closer.

After breakfast the next day, Jenda and Luis and Montagne gathered under the banana trees in the courtyard.

"One of our old Vintie friends from high school got in touch with me a year or so back to say she had run into you in a café in Dallas," Montagne said.

Jenda's eyes grew big and she exchanged a quick glance with Luis. "Who was she anyway?" Jenda asked.

"Her name is Malia Poole. She was a couple of years behind us in school, but she idolized you. As I recall, you thought she was a pest." Montagne laughed. "She had a twin sister Sophia. I think they must have been in your brother's year. Their older sister, Leticia, was in our year. Surely you remember her."

"No. I don't," Jenda said, "or at least I didn't until I saw her name in one of my old journals." She still felt angry, knowing that the woman she'd been taking dance classes from was an old high school friend and that neither of them remembered the other. Her bitterness toward Your Journal intensified.

"Luis says you know about a plan. Something to do with putting an end to what Your Journal has been doing with memory restructuring. Is that true, Montagne?" Jenda asked.

"Well, yeah I've heard... Why do you ask?" Montagne hesitated, looking toward Luis, who seemed suddenly engrossed in studying the design printed on the throw pillows.

Jenda laughed. "So Luis didn't tell you? YJ is where I work, Montagne. I've been there for 90 years now. And over this past year I've become, let's say, disenchanted with our work."

"Ah," Montagne said. "In that case." And he explained as succinctly as he could exactly what the plan was.

"So what would someone at YJ need to do?" Jenda was intrigued.

"It's simple, really. We'd give this person…" Montagne paused and glanced from Jenda to Luis and back to Jenda. "Whoever this person might be, we would give them a digital reservoir – a simple 2XV insert – containing the infection, which they would introduce into one of the work screens connected to their corporate medianet."

"Why can't this be done atmospherically?" Jenda asked. "Why does it have to be done on site?"

"There are too many layers of anti-infection when you come in through the atmo. And with a corporation like YJ, there's the problem of supranet protection as well. We're pretty confident our infection is unique enough to slide through most of these things undetected, but even a minor drag could prevent the whole scheme from unfolding according to plan. It needs to be done internally, on schedule, by all of our operatives at once."

"What if I got caught?" Jenda asked, dropping all pretense.

"It won't be detectable – we hope, anyway – for at least six hours after it's introduced. And it won't be traceable to the point of introduction at all, because by that time everything will be falling apart."

"You hope?"

"I'm only being honest. You can never be 100 percent on these things, Jenda, but we're confident enough to be ready to go ahead as soon as we have this one additional person in place. And if that person were to be you… Well, it can be done in such a way that by the time things start coming apart, you'd be safely back here in Costa Rica with us."

Jenda knew she wanted to do this. All the confusion and shifting realities had left her with a burning need to take charge of her life, to do something that mattered. The more she remembered, the more she knew she couldn't go back. Doing this would be an unequivocal, irrevocable commitment to her newly claimed reality, a pledge of faith between the girl with the sepia hair and the woman Jenda intended to be going forward, the woman she might have been if not for Argentina.

Jenda leaned closer to Luis and slipped her hand inside the crook of his elbow. "Okay, then," she said. "I'll do it."

Part IV:
Coming Together,
Falling Apart

26.

They found her a flight back to Dallas departing Liberia airport shortly after noon on the following day, which was Sunday. They also booked a return flight on Monday evening under the name given on a passport Montagne provided. Jenda borrowed a small suitcase from Meli, knowing she wouldn't really need anything, but figuring she shouldn't travel without some kind of baggage. Montagne spent the afternoon notifying all of the project operatives that they were a go for 4:50 p.m. Texas time on Monday. He gave the data insert containing the infection to Jenda, who stored it in her bag along with her other 2XV camera inserts. It was the one with the diagonal scratch across it.

Despite the early hour of their departure from Paloma's house, everyone was up to bid Jenda farewell and wish her good luck with her mission. Montagne treated her like some kind of superhero. Paloma was more subdued, not fully understanding what was happening, but sensing that Jenda was about to put herself in serious danger. Hugs were exchanged all around.

Jenda lingered as she embraced Meli. Both women had tears in their eyes. As they released one another, Meli reached up to give Jenda a kiss. "Make sure you come back," she said. "We have so much more to talk about."

"Don't worry, hija," Jenda reassured her. "I'm only leaving for a couple of days." And she returned the kiss.

On the drive to the airport, Jenda and Luis talked mostly about what they were going to do when Jenda returned. "We could stay here in Costa Rica," Luis said. "Montagne has collected all the materials to set up a sufficiency community here and life should go on pretty smoothly. Or we could go to Argentina and live with Isabel in Max and Emily's old folks' home at the old estancia. It sounded like they were going to set that up as a kind of sufficiency community, too."

"We should probably stay here at least for a while and see how things go. Would Abuela Isabel come here? Can you get in touch with her and the Feldmans to tell them what to expect? And what about Granny El? What can I tell her? Could we bring her here, too?"

"We'll figure this out. I wish we could tell all of them exactly what's happening, but we can't jeopardize the project. Isabel is the only one on Recall so far and I did send her a message, but you know she doesn't check very often. And I was pretty cryptic. I should have set Max and Emily up on Recall before we left. As for your grandmother – as soon as we know all the operations have been completed we can send information to her. I'll talk to Montagne about it as soon as I get back and let you know."

Jenda inhaled deeply. "I hope we're doing the right thing." She knew she had to do something and she fervently hoped this was the thing.

"Well, we both know we can't go on forever as if it's all okay," Luis reassured her. "We've tried for years – decades – to fight off the plutocracy, and they keep getting stronger, richer, and more controlling. It has to stop."

She leaned closer and lay her head on his shoulder.

"I'm glad you agreed to do this, Jenda, even though, selfishly, I wish you hadn't. You know I won't rest until you get back and I have my arms around you again."

Arriving at the airport, they looked like just another pair of lovers saying their goodbyes. On her own, as she boarded the plane, Jenda felt frightened. She decided to re-read one of her favorite novels on her digilet. About twenty screens in, she realized how trivial and boring its story was next to the real-life one she was involved in and she put it away.

The plane arrived on schedule at the Dallas airport and Jenda was surprised to see how crowded the international terminal was. "I wonder what the holdup is?" she asked herself. And then she almost panicked. What if the international corporate police had caught wind of their plan and were searching bags? "It's okay," she told herself, "as long as you stay calm and don't attract attention." As she got nearer the gateways, Jenda saw that they were not inspecting bags, but rather scanning people with an infrared device. She felt relieved, relaxed enough to speak to one of her companions in the slow moving queue. "Do you know what's going on?"

"It's the IHA – that blood disease. Well, I think they're calling it VHA now that they know it's a virus. It's been spreading like wildfire. How long have you been out of the country anyway?"

"I didn't think it was contagious," Jenda said. "Why are they screening us?"

"I'm telling you, now they know it is contagious," the man replied testily, "although they're still a long way from understanding how to deal with the virus that's causing it. Lots of cases reported in Mexico and Guatemala this week, so it looks like all passengers from Central America are getting screened."

Jenda thanked her fellow traveler for the information. "Well, here's something else I could worry about," she said to herself, "but let's say I choose not to."

When Jenda finally passed through the screening device, she saw that several people had been pulled aside and equipped with face masks. A gloved and masked physician wearing a Pharmakon uniform was speaking with them. "I'm not going to worry about this." Jenda told herself again.

On the drive to her habitat, Jenda gave Granny El a call.

"Oh, I'm so glad to hear your voice. I've been worried about you, what with this VHA thing beginning to get all out of hand. At least I was glad you were in Argentina rather than Central America – it's getting pretty bad there." Not worrying about viral hemolytic anemia was becoming harder for Jenda.

"Are you back at work tomorrow?" Granny El asked. "How about we get together for lunch and you can tell me about your trip. I have no idea what possessed you to suddenly take off to Argentina."

Jenda knew she couldn't do that. The temptation to tell Granny El everything would be too strong and she had sworn to Montagne that she wouldn't speak to anyone about the plan until afterward – after she had successfully planted the infection via her screen at Your Journal.

"I can't make it tomorrow, Gran," Jenda said. "How about Tuesday? Yes, I promise." Jenda knew she would be back in Costa Rica on Tuesday. In her mind, the promise to meet for lunch morphed into a promise to let Granny El know where she could go for safety as soon as the deed was done on Monday evening.

The autocar stationed itself next to the entryway at Jenda's habitat, popped the trunk, and deposited her bag on the walkway. Upstairs, Jenda heard the lock for her unit click open as she approached. She walked inside and stared at the chaos. She had forgotten how she had left the place, forgotten how she had felt when she left.

Her paintings were still arranged in a semi-circle, propped against the empty boxes and piles of books and mementos. Jenda understood so much more now about what all of this meant, about who the girl was who had made these paintings and composed all these journals. What she was getting ready to do at Your Journal was something that girl would understand. She could almost hear that girl cheering her on. She walked over to the painting that faced the wall – the one of the lady in blue – and turned it around.

Jenda stared at the disassembled screen on her desk. "Whatever did I think that would accomplish?" she thought. But she had felt such perverse pleasure at the time. She wondered if she would feel that way again as the whole system of 'nets began to come apart on Monday evening.

Jenda and Luis had promised one another they would make no contact other than the confirmation of her arrival. So Jenda sat down at one end of the sofa. She uncoiled her digilet, screened up Recall, and navigated to Interloc. "Back home," she said, watching as the syllables came up on the screen. "See you soon." Then she deleted the second part. "He knows," she said to herself as she snapped the digilet back onto her wrist.

Jenda spent the next several hours going through hers and her mother's things one last time, selecting what she would take with her and what she would have to leave behind. She decided she would be able to fit maybe one or two of her smaller paintings into her large suitcases. She had already decided she would pay the extra fee to take two bags. And when she finally finished packing, she threw a few outfits of clothes into the cases, almost as an afterthought. She removed the baggage tags that read "Jenda Swain" and replaced them with the tags Montagne had given her that bore the same name as her forged passport – Andrea Nelson.

In only four hours Jenda would have to be at work. She considered taking some tabs of Duermata, but instead made a cup of manzanilla tea and sat down on the sofa to read one of her old journals…

Jenda's dreams during her brief sleep that night were a medley of unlikely scenarios. Her mother Tessa was pushing an adult Meli on a beautifully sculpted swing in the garden of the house where Jenda grew up. Meli was cradling a white cat and both of them were laughing and singing a simple children's song. Paloma and Isabel were planting bombs at Your Journal, bombs hidden inside pots of purple chrysanthemums. Luis and Montagne were running a footrace along the road that led from Buenos Aires to San Ramon, while Jenda and her brother cheered them on. Luis was winning. Granny El sat at a little table with the Feldmans, drinking wine. Even Winslow Morris was there; he was trying to sell them something, although Jenda couldn't tell what it was. She thought it might be a picture of her father.

27.

Arriving at Your Journal the next morning, Jenda found her co-workers sympathetic but curious. "We were so sorry to hear. What was your family emergency?" Weldon wanted to know. His expression and tone of voice were redolent with compassion.

Jenda had almost forgotten about her excuse for being absent. "My brother," Jenda replied, looking away. "But I'd rather not talk about it yet." Weldon nodded and went away to share this small bit of new gossip with their workmates.

Jenda unfolded her digiscreen and consulted her calendar. There was a "New Assignment" indicated for the day. She tapped it and was grateful that it was one of those simple transitional assignments. It would keep her occupied during what she knew was going to be a very long day. It would also keep her engaged with her screen, while presenting little risk of distracting her from her primary task. Jenda noted that she had an appointment with the corporate psychiatrist scheduled for first thing Tuesday morning. She confirmed it.

Jenda's mind was racing and she had to deliberately slow herself down on her simple assignment in order to avoid completing it before lunch. She went to the ladies' room more than usual. She rearranged the few physical items in her work area several times as well.

When her colleagues came by to invite her for lunch, Jenda lied and said she was meeting her grandmother. Then she went to the modest little lunchroom down a side street, the café where the old woman – Malia Poole – had accosted her over a year ago. She ordered the grilled cheese sandwich with fries and a sweet tea. The sandwich contained natural cheese and the fries were made from fresh potatoes. She thought this might be her favorite café in all of Dallas. She ate slowly, glancing up occasionally at the row of stools by the counter, half expecting to see Malia Poole there. She wondered what life over the next few weeks and months was going to be like for all these people in the lunchroom. She wondered what would happen to Malia Poole.

The afternoon stretched on as if it would never end while Jenda fought back rising waves of anxiety. She wanted to tell her supervisor she was leaving early, but she knew she couldn't introduce the contents of the 2XV insert until the appointed time of 4:50 p.m. Her digilet buzzed, indicating she had a message. She glanced at it and didn't recognize the source, so she ignored it. She could tend to personal matters later.

At 4:50 Jenda placed the insert into the appropriate receptacle of her desk screen and continued working on her assignment, watching the clock. Montagne's instructions were to leave the insert in place for at least five minutes, but no more than ten. Jenda took a deep breath and waited. A few seconds later, her screen beeped, indicating that she had an urgent message. She touched the message symbol and heard her supervisor's voice: "Hi, Jenda. Glad to see you made it back OK. Could you step into my office for a couple of minutes before you leave for the day? It's important."

"A couple of minutes?" Jenda thought, wondering whether anything her supervisor could tell her could possibly be important in light of what she was now setting in motion. The clock ticked over 4:52. Should she get up and leave the screen unattended with the insert in place? What if the supervisor kept her for more than a "couple of minutes"? There was no time for indecision. Jenda got up from her desk and headed toward her supervisor's office. It was a long 10 meters away. She leaned inside the open door.

"You wanted to see me?" Jenda tried to sound casual.

"Yes, Jenda. Hang on one second while I finish this memo. Gosh, the screens seem even slower than usual for this time of day." He laughed.

Jenda felt perspiration breaking out in her armpits as she strained against the urge to look back at her own desk. She waited, glancing down at her digilet: 4:54... No, 4:55.

"There, that's got it. Yes. Well, I wanted to tell you how sorry we were about your family emergency. No, I won't pry.

You can share with the psych office tomorrow. I also wanted to tell you…" He paused and smiled mysteriously. "I want to say, first of all, that your new campaign looks to be your most successful yet. The hierarchy loves it. So much so, in fact…" He stopped and shuffled some images on his desktop as Jenda stole a glimpse of the time again: 4:56. "Well, I guess I could have just sent this right to your own desktop, but I wanted to tell you myself first." His digilet beeped and he paused to check it. "Anyway, what I wanted to tell you is this: You've been promoted! Let me be the first to congratulate you! The details are on your desktop now. What do you think of that?" He grinned expectantly.

Jenda had no idea what to think. She knew she should act surprised and she certainly was that. ("Zujo! 4:57…") She knew she should also look pleased and excited, which she wasn't.

"Well," Jenda said finally, "I'm speechless." There, that was true. "I'm overwhelmed. Thank you. I guess I'm eager to go back to my desktop and get a look at the details." She knew this was a feeble attempt to get away, but she didn't care. She hoped her forced smile was convincing.

"Well, I can certainly understand that. Let me just say, I think you'll be pleased with both your new title and your new pay level." Her supervisor rose from his chair. "Let me shake your hand anyway," he said. He walked over to Jenda and shook her hand. Jenda hoped he didn't notice how cold and clammy it was. "Now, go on and we'll talk more tomorrow." Jenda thanked him again. She looked over his shoulder and saw the clock on his screen tick to 4:58. She reined in her desire to run.

She saw Weldon standing at her desk, staring at the screen, and her heart skipped a beat.

"Weldon…what?" Jenda said as she came up behind him.

"Oh, there you are, Jenda," Weldon laughed. "I thought you had left without screening off and I was about to do it for you."

"Nope, I'm still here, Weldon. Thanks anyway." Jenda pushed him aside as she sat down, her hand reaching for the insert.

"Just trying to be helpful," Weldon sniffed as he walked back toward his own desk.

Jenda extracted the insert just as the clock ticked over 4:59. She exhaled. She saw the message that she knew contained the details of her promotion, a message destined to melt into oblivion in a matter of hours, if not minutes. She felt like laughing. She left the message unopened and screened out, tucking the insert into a front pocket of her handbag. She hoped all the other entry points had been equally successful. Then she picked up her bag and headed out of the building for the last time. And because it was what she always did, she called "See you tomorrow!" to Weldon and her other office mates as they parted.

On the street, Jenda passed a trash bin and dropped the 2XV insert into it, concealed in a wad of tissues from her handbag. Then she headed for an autocar.

Jenda had plenty of time to fetch her suitcases from her habitat and make it to the airport for her return flight to Costa Rica. In fact, she had more than enough time. She loaded her bags into the autocar and then went back inside and sat on the sofa to drink the last bottle of fizzy fruit drink from the fridge and check for messages on her digilet. Once she left her habitat, she would stop being Jenda Swain for a while and become Andrea Nelson. She wanted desperately to tell Luis about Jenda Swain's promotion; she knew he would enjoy the irony of it all.

There was a message on the digilet, but it was not for Jenda; it was for Andrea Nelson, and it was marked "URGENT". Jenda tapped the symbol and, as she read the message, her heart sank.

ALL FLIGHTS TO AND FROM CENTRAL AMERICA CANCELLED DUE TO HEALTH CONCERNS. PLEASE CONTACT YOUR AIRLINE FOR INSTRUCTIONS.

What now? Contacting the airline was probably not a good idea, due to the relatively thin cover Andrea Nelson provided. Montagne had cautioned Jenda that she needed to minimize her interaction as Andrea, because at some point face recognition would kick in or a fingerprint or iris scan would be required.

Although they had done their best, they hadn't been able to provide her with all the bells and whistles that would have made all of these things consistently read as "Andrea Nelson". Eventually something would come up "Jenda Swain".

Maybe she could make a reservation to go somewhere else under her own name. No, probably not. Jenda Swain's passport indicated that she had recently returned from Central America and that would raise a red flag. They might even place her in quarantine. In fact, Pharmakon might be looking for her now.

Jenda navigated to Recall on her digilet and pulled up Interloc. There was a pulse from Luis:

MURCIELAGO: I heard. Go here. Tell your grandmother.

And there was a list of syllables that Jenda recognized as an EarthSat location phrase. It was good to know Luis had her back. But where was he sending her? As much as Jenda wanted to ask, as much as she wanted to have a good long talk with Luis, he and Montagne had been adamant about minimizing communication during what they were calling "the interim".

POLILLA: Got it.

Jenda paused for a moment as tears welled up in her eyes. She suddenly felt very small and alone.

POLILLA: I love you.

MURCIELAGO: I love you too. Now go.

Jenda fought back the tears and sat down on the sofa to think exactly what she could say to Granny El. She didn't trust herself to have a conversation, so she dictated a pulse: "Hi, Gran. I have to go out of town again. Please meet me here as soon as you can." She added the EarthSat syllables. "If you know where Dad is, please invite him, too." Then she looked up the last pulse she had received from her brother and sent the location phrase to him, as well.

She snapped the digilet back around her wrist and walked out, listening for the lock to click as she walked away. Her bags were waiting in the autocar. She entered the EarthSat syllables into the control panel and sat back. She was glad to be leaving, but anxious about where she might be going. Knowing she was not going to Luis broke her heart.

28.

Luis and Montagne monitored developments as best they could from their outpost in Ortega, Costa Rica, growing anxious about the spread of what was now called viral hemolytic anemia in the region. The latest reports indicated that the disease had been identified as a highly contagious and exceptionally virulent form of human parvovirus. Urgent research was ongoing, but with no promising leads as yet for either cure or prevention other than abstaining from Chulel and from contact with sick individuals. Costa Rica was still unaffected, but Mexico and Guatemala reported massive numbers of cases. There were also a few cases in Honduras and Panama.

"Are you sure we need to do this?" Luis asked, as they both examined the statistics on VHA on the Monday afternoon, less than an hour before the digital infection was scheduled to be introduced. "I mean, it looks to me like this disease might decimate humanity pretty thoroughly anyway. Why make it worse?"

Montagne stared out the window and said nothing, his fists shoved deep into his pockets. When he spoke, his voice was heavy with sadness. "I know," he said. "It seems like a lot of people are going to die of this blood disease no matter what else happens. Except maybe for the plutocrats who are rich enough to isolate themselves. Or those who have already stopped using Chulel, like many of the people in the sufficiency communities. I stopped using it several years ago."

Luis confirmed that he had done the same. "But once the disease passes," Montagne continued, "what then? If we did nothing, the plutocrats would be able to go back in and start up again, fabricating a new series of lies about what happened. We have to stop them. And especially with so many people dying."

Luis rubbed his forehead with the heel of his hand and sighed.

Montagne looked at him with narrowed eyes and a hard expression. "Our little digital infection has what is essentially a self-destruct element for the machines as well as the scripts. No one will ever use those termini, those digiscreens – any of those machines ever again. Their world will no longer exist. Ever. Their power base will be gone." Montagne's expression softened. "But don't ask me what comes next. That's entirely in the hands of the people who make it through. The one thing I'm sure of is, with so many people dying, it wouldn't be right for the plutocracy to survive." He paused. "When we were working together, you and I had quite a few discussions about the basic nature of humanity, Luis. Do you remember?"

A faint smile flickered across Luis' face. "As I recall, I was always the more optimistic, the one arguing for the inherent creativity and adaptability of human beings and for our natural drive to look after one another."

"Well, I think you must have convinced me at some point, hermano. I don't think I could have gone through with this if I believed it would turn out worse than what we have now."

Around 4:30 p.m. a message came in on Interloc about the cancellation of flights between Texas and Central America.

"Fuck!" Montagne banged the desk surface with his fist, almost disconnecting the screen.

"Zujo! What do we tell Jenda?" Luis felt an unaccustomed sense of powerlessness. How could they cut him off like this from the woman he loved? "What about the sufficiency community that we were going to send her grandmother to?" Luis asked.

"Right," Montagne said. "It's in New Mexico." He moved over to let Luis send the message to Jenda on Interloc.

Carefully, Luis entered the syllables, along with a brief message. "Done," he said, wanting desperately to do more.

"What about Granny El. Do we have her contact phrase?" Montagne asked.

Luis shook his head, realizing that Montagne actually knew Granny El and that he didn't. "Sorry. No. But Jenda will pass the location on to her."

They sat back to wait for a response from Jenda. Luis tried to imagine what Jenda was going through as she introduced the virus at YJ. Montagne kept checking his sources, focusing on the bigger picture in which Jenda played one vital part. They scanned a few more stories about VHA.

"I'm beginning to think maybe all of us would be better off in Argentina than here, and the sooner the better," Montagne said. "This disease is looking pretty bad and getting closer to our doorstep all the time. You're the most mobile, Luis, so maybe you should go on back and look after your grandmother and her friends in Buenos Aires. We'll plan to join you as soon as we can. And we'll hope to get Jenda out quickly and send her to Argentina, too." Luis nodded in agreement.

Montagne and Luis knew when each of the operatives – including Jenda – had fulfilled his or her task. If it hadn't been for the predicament Jenda was in, they might have celebrated. They continued monitoring Recall. Montagne was one of only a few designated "reporters" being allowed to use Recall. It was a precaution they had taken to avoid crashing the entire zone with people eager to contribute their pieces to the picture of a collapsing society.

Luis began to breathe again when he knew Jenda had received the location. His heart swelled painfully when he received her affirmation of love. He knew she was feeling lonely and a little scared, although she hadn't said anything about it. Luis knew that because he knew Jenda. Montagne, who only knew the old Jenda – the one with sepia-colored hair and badly mended old clothes – assured him that she could handle the situation. Luis hoped he was right.

Luis and Montagne watched as the transport network began to fail and as power outages began to spread in the expected locations. They smiled with satisfaction when Your Journal and LifeBook went dark, followed almost immediately by FlixNews. When the banking network and then the EarthSat system began to fail sooner than expected, both Luis and Montagne became more anxious about Jenda.

29.

The autocar left Dallas heading west on a primary artery. Not many people took autocars on long journeys, preferring instead the comfort and speed of the hyperloops. Jenda didn't know if this was going to be a long journey, but she was pretty sure the hyperloop didn't go wherever it was she was headed. The car breezed along though the continuous inosculation of endurbs that, at some undefined point along the way, became Fort Worth. It occurred to Jenda to be thankful that whatever was beginning to happen out there would find most people at home rather than at work.

By 6:30 the car had entered the suburbs, with their sprawling mansions, each surrounded by its own little world of miniature lakes and forests. Jenda checked the charge meter on the car and realized that, with the overcast skies, the autocar was going to need a recharge. Jenda figured she could use a pit stop, too, and an opportunity to look at a map to figure out where she was going before the medianets started to fail.

At Jenda's request, the autocar pulled into a recharge station in the center of Weatherford, across from an entertainment complex called The Old Courthouse. She connected the car's cable and went inside the café. She bought two sandwiches and a large NutriQuaff and sat down at one of the tables.

Setting the sandwiches aside, Jenda unfurled her digilet and was relieved when NaviGiz screened up with no problem. The location phrase from Luis tagged a destination well off even secondary arteries near nothing in particular in north central New Mexico. Jenda made some handwritten notes on a back page of one of the old notebooks she had stashed in the inside pocket of her bag. This was going to be a long journey.

Jenda needed to think. Fully charging the autocar would take almost 20 minutes, but she thought she needed the full charge. Jenda had never worried about distance driving before and she had to query a mediazone to find out how far a full charge would take her. The answer was 500 kilometers, give or take. Jenda unwrapped a sandwich. Consulting the map again, she calculated that a 500 km range would be enough to get her safely to Lubbock, even with modest use of the cool air generator. The journey to Lubbock would take about three hours, meaning it would be dark by the time she got there. "Dark and cooler," she thought. "And surely I'll be able to find a place to spend the night in Lubbock."

Having an interim destination and a plan in mind, Jenda felt a bit more at ease as the autocar made its way out of Weatherford and back onto the primary artery. The clouds had begun clearing to the west, leaving the sun shining directly into the front window. Jenda turned to look out a side window. The undulating landscape was rising gradually in elevation, but not enough to strain the car's engine. Suburbs gave way to towns separated by stretches of well watered, genetically engineered crops. There were also a number of meat and egg factories, supplying the needs of the urban areas Jenda had left behind. She saw a string of transport stages stopped on the monorail line between towns. A semaphore by the side of the rail flashed red.

Jenda's route would take her through Abilene, a fact she had tried to ignore as she laid out her plan in the café. Now she let herself think about it and she wondered about Ben. Surely by this time there must be indications of something having gone wrong at Your Journal and, being a high level executive, Ben would know. What would he think if he knew what Jenda had done, if he knew his insignificant little ex-wife had brought mighty Your Journal to its knees? Jenda liked this scenario. She searched the autocar's audio system for some music that would suit her state of mind – something triumphant but tragic. She finally found an old blues track and settled for that.

Jenda glanced at the road ahead periodically, waiting for the moment when the sun would drop below the horizon and she could enjoy the beauty of an expansive Texas sunset. As she passed by Abilene, the sun's last lingering beams lit up the Your Journal tower, and Jenda saw clearly that the photonic 3-D image at the pinnacle of the building had disappeared. Jenda saw her face reflected in the car window and noted her satisfied smile. As the retiring sun finally spattered the sky with color, Jenda fell asleep.

She awakened disoriented. She stared into the darkened landscape, trying to remember where she was. "Zujo!" she thought. "Have I missed Lubbock?" A quick check of the car's screen showed that Lubbock was just ahead. She quickly entered a command for the car to stop at the next available recharge station. The car still had plenty of charge left – the late sunshine had helped – but Jenda required services. Topping up the car's charge couldn't hurt.

Arriving at the station, Jenda found there would be a wait for charging and she placed the car in the queue. Inside, she found a knot of people around the serving counter.

"It's not just Your Journal and LifeBook," one man said. "Look at this – CorpNet is reporting failures in the air transit control system and FlixNews has gone off the air altogether."

Jenda sat down at a table that gave her a view of the entertainment screen. She was exhausted and the hour was late, but she ordered dinner. She wasn't sure where or when she would be eating again.

She tried to appear neither too interested nor too disinterested in the breaking news being reported by CorpNet. Planes were grounded in all the major continental airports and there were preliminary reports of extensive power outages in Dallas and Washington, D.C.

"Beijing is also reporting a major power outage," the presenter said, "although it is unclear whether there is any connection with the North American outages." Jenda knew these were three of the physical locations where the digital infection had been introduced. There was a connection.

The presenter continued: "We'll get back to you with more details on those outages as soon as we re-establish contact with our affiliates in these areas. In other news, the illness known as Viral Hemolytic Anemia or VHA has claimed its first victims in the US state of Nevada and in Nicaragua. The documented death toll is now approaching the hundred million mark."

Jenda wanted desperately to pulse Luis one more time, to check on him and Meli and the rest. But she knew that was forbidden. Before leaving the shop, Jenda bought a large bag of Nutrichips and a bottle of fortified water. The purchase took longer than usual and the attendant apologized. "We're having to desume a different mediazone," she said. "Ours has gone dead, and connections seem slow all around."

"No problem," Jenda said, fully appreciating the inappropriateness of this stock reply. The inconvenience of a slow mediazone was the leading edge of what was about to be a very big problem. Jenda was grateful the payment system was working at all. She was still a long way from her destination.

When Jenda's car emerged from the queue, she refilled the drinking water dispenser and got back on the road to look for a place to spend the night. She had no intention of being choosy; she was too tired for that. All she asked for was a bed to stretch out on until morning. She stopped at the first roadstead she saw. As the autocar came to a stop, the lighted sign suddenly went dark. Then the lights inside the office flickered and went out. As the autocar door opened, Jenda heard the lock on the front door of the roadstead office click.

"Zujo! What now?" Jenda looked up and down the artery, hoping to catch sight of another roadstead. She got back in the car and tried to screen up NaviGiz on her digilet, thinking it might find something nearby. It wasn't working.

"Now look what you've done, Jenda!" She looked out the windows at the mostly empty parking lot. "Well, there's no point in wasting a good charge wandering around in the middle of the night looking for something I'm not likely to find." Jenda tasked the doors to lock. Then she readjusted the seats. Figuring she shouldn't risk the comfortable oblivion of Duermata, she did her best to stretch out in the tiny vehicle. She finally dropped into a shallow sleep, waking periodically. The night seemed to get progressively darker. All the lights had gone out and as far as Jenda could see, there was only starlight.

Jenda awoke the next morning to brilliant sunshine beaming through the autocar's windows. Although the brightness hurt her sleep deprived eyes, she felt only gratitude and relief. She had slept longer than she would have thought possible. Now she needed a restroom and somewhere to stretch her cramped legs. The roadstead office looked terminally closed.

As she powered up the autocar, a red light flashed and a calm voice announced, "Automatic navigation is not available. Manual controls are engaged."

Jenda's experience with physically managing a car was limited. She took a deep breath and pressed the button confirming manual control, hoping for the best. She set the top speed for five kph below the posted limit and said a quick word of thanks that her contract was permitting the car to keep running even though it clearly was no longer in contact with the autocar corporation. Less than a kilometer up the road, Jenda found another recharge station with a café that seemed to be open. She maneuvered the car into a parking spot and went inside.

The pay point attendant was just positioning a sign that read "Closed". The bathroom facilities, however, were open and that was what Jenda wanted most. After relieving herself, Jenda washed her face and combed her hair. She thought her image in the mirror didn't look much improved.

She went to speak with the clerk, who was still fiddling with the pay point screen. "Why have you closed down?" she asked.

"It's this payment system. It's not accepting charges right now, so we can't sell anything until it's up and running again. Sorry." She didn't sound particularly sorry. She pointed to an open case of fortified water on the next counter, with a sign affixed indicating each customer could take one bottle free of charge. Jenda took one. She wished she had bought more than a bag of Nutrichips at the last station. At least she had bought the large bag. She also wished they still had some kind of physical money in circulation.

Jenda walked around the shop for a bit, telling herself it was for the exercise but looking at all the things she couldn't buy and didn't need. "Although," she thought, "a pair of sunglasses would have been nice. And maybe a chocolate packet or two. Or a bottle of good Texas cabernet." She sat down at one of the tables to drink her fortified water and take another look at her notes about where she was going. She found the extra sandwich she had bought in Weatherford.

From Lubbock, Jenda knew she needed to head north on – she squinted at her hasty notes – highway 840. Jenda knew that was not a primary artery. It would take her to the international border at Clovis, New Mexico. Jenda hoped Clovis was not a frontier that required a passport, since the only passports she had access to were a polyplex one reading "Andrea Nelson" and a paper one reading "Jenda Swain" that had expired 80 years ago.

As Jenda ate her soggy sandwich, made almost palatable by frequent swigs of fortified water, she mentally mapped out the remainder of her trip. Highway 840 would get her all the way to Albuquerque, New Mexico. There she would turn onto a road numbered NM63. She thought that would probably be well marked. From NM63 there were three more turns and Jenda wasn't at all sure about those. In the age of autocars, road signage had become a low priority and broken signs were rarely replaced. The signs that still existed were often peeling and faded and almost impossible to read. She had written down the road numbers for her final three turns, but had failed to indicate which direction to turn. She hoped her mental recall of the map would keep her on track.

Back in the autocar, Jenda easily found highway 840. Maybe this wouldn't be as bad as she had feared. Even manual navigation began to feel less intimidating as rolling hills flattened out into open plains and the road became straight as an arrow. Traffic was almost nonexistent.

The landscape stretched out with monotonous sameness in all directions. Fields of ripening crops alternated with fields of humming windmills, all bearing the colors and emblem of the energy behemoth TotExx. Jenda's attention began to wander…

A loud buzzer made her jump to attention. She saw the curve, but for a moment she couldn't think what to do and it was coming up fast. Then her right hand found the turn mechanism and she veered around the curve, tires squealing. The car swung from side to side as she struggled to steady her hand on the velocity control. At last the car slowed and its course straightened. Her heart was pounding as she pulled off at the side of the road. "Okay, calm down," she told herself. "At least the perimeter warnings are still operating. I have to be more careful. I don't want to end up a mangled heap on the side of the road." She suddenly flashed on her mother's accident and felt pretty sure she would not have any further trouble concentrating on her task. After a few deep, calming breaths, she pulled back onto the road.

With the bright sun, straight flat road, and slow speed, the car was still registering well over half of a full charge as Jenda approached the international border. A flashing red light signaled her to stop at the crossing booth.

"We wanted to warn you, ma'am," the official said. "There are some power outages and communications problems up the road here. We're offering you a free ten minutes of recharge if you need it. Well, as long as our batteries hold out." He smiled and waved Jenda in.

Jenda pulled into the queue for one of the recharge docks. She didn't know if she would need it or not, but anything that didn't require payment was welcome. There would be mountains ahead. She sat at an outdoor table, shaded by an awning, and munched some Nutrichips while her car worked its way through the short queue.

On the road again, Jenda slowed her speed even more as the terrain became increasingly hilly. The only reasons to stop now were her own personal needs, since the shops and cafés all showed "Closed" signs. A couple of times Jenda pulled off and relieved herself shamelessly in full view of the empty road. Then she cleaned her hands with the sanitary wipes, refilled her water bottle from the onboard supply, and resumed her journey.

As she approached Albuquerque, she watched for her turn onto NM63. She began feeling anxious as she left the central inosculation behind. Then she saw a weather-beaten sign pointing both right and left to NM63. She knew this was a right turn, but the sign's placement was ambiguous and she didn't relax until she saw another sign confirming her route.

This road led straight up into the mountains. Jenda pulled off momentarily to check her notes. She congratulated herself as she made the next turn with no difficulty. Her cognitive map told her the following turn should be to the left. She found the road, but after a few kilometers decided she should have turned right and had to backtrack. The manual navigation and multiple stops were making for slow progress. The trip was taking longer than Jenda had calculated. Clouds had built up, too, obscuring the sun and causing the autocar's charge to drop rapidly.

Then it started to rain. Big drops splattered across the windows, threatening a downpour. Between the rain and the late hour, it was already getting dark as Jenda searched for her final turn. Jenda passed one turn that she thought might be the one, but she kept driving, wishing she had included more detailed notes about the distance between points and feeling that the turn she was looking for should be a bit further on. It was several kilometers before the next turn came up. Jenda didn't think it looked right. One or two kilometers further on, she thought better of it and turned around. This time she made the turn onto the narrow road – it only went in one direction – but after four kilometers this road suddenly dropped into an old arroyo and the pavement simply ended. As Jenda turned the car around in the darkening landscape, the charge indicator began to blink, meaning that she had only five kilometers left before the car would come to a halt. She groaned and slumped down into the seat.

"I guess I could stay here until morning," she thought, glancing around the empty landscape and hoping that tomorrow would be sunny. Something caught her eye at the edge of the arroyo. She fumbled for the car's headlamps and, after switching the windscreen wipers on and off, she finally grasped the lamp switch. There was a small sign and it looked fresh rather than old and faded. She pulled up closer to the sign. It contained the location phrase Luis had sent her, and an arrow pointed up the flat bed of the arroyo. There were fresh tire marks along the dirt track.

Jenda took a deep breath and turned the little car in the direction indicated by the arrow and the tracks. The car bounced slowly along the barely discernible path as the last light of the sun was fading. Just as she began to question whether the little sign had been a mirage and to query the state of her sanity in general, she saw what looked like a few houses in the distance. A few moments later she pulled the car into a field alongside no more than a dozen other cars. The little sign had not been a mirage, but Jenda was pretty sure her sanity might still be in question.

30.

Jenda had no idea what to expect as she shouldered her handbag, locked the autocar, and began the short walk toward the line of small buildings. Her last shreds of optimism vanished as she noticed the silhouette of a church steeple with a cross and, a short distance away, a building with a round dome and a crescent moon. "Oh, please tell me he hasn't sent me to one of those Book Communities," Jenda muttered to herself, although it was pretty clear that this was exactly what Luis had done. She had heard about these communities, which had been set up in remote areas by people who became convinced that the use of Chulel went against the will of God, or the will of Allah, depending. She knew there was probably a temple with a Star of David somewhere, too.

Jenda saw a hand lettered sign reading "Welcome" in several languages on one of the houses. There were a few people standing outside, chatting amiably. They smiled and greeted her as she walked up the steps and in through the open door.

She found herself in a brightly lit room painted a pleasing shade of pale green and simply furnished. Behind a table near one wall were two women, one of whom was wearing a bright flowered headscarf. She greeted Jenda warmly. "We were afraid you weren't going to make it," she said. "But then, you had the longest distance to travel."

"Excuse me?" Jenda said. "You knew I was coming? You know who I am?"

"Well," the other woman spoke up, "unless there is some mistake, you're Jenda Swain. From Dallas, Texas. Am I right?"

Jenda nodded as the woman showed her a paper list that had about a dozen names on it. All of them had been crossed off except hers. The woman laid the paper back on the table and drew a line through Jenda's name with a flourish. "And you're just in time for last supper," she said, as a small bell clanged briefly from another building across the way.

"Let's give her the room assignment first," the woman with the scarf said. She handed Jenda a little paper card with a number on one side and a map of the village on the other. She marked the location of Jenda's assigned dwelling and gave brief instructions, complemented by gestures, on how to get there. "How hard can it be in this tiny place?" Jenda wondered, but she thanked the women for their help. The one with no scarf was on the front step, calling to one of the men who was already on his way to wherever it was they were going to have whatever this "last supper" was. He returned, agreeing to help Jenda retrieve her bags from the car and move them to her room.

As they walked toward the car in the darkness, Jenda thanked him for his help. "I think it's you we should be thanking," he replied. "I understand you had a big role to play in all that happened yesterday." He smiled knowingly, but Jenda got the distinct feeling he didn't know as much as he was pretending to.

"It wasn't much," Jenda said.

After they deposited her bags in the room, the man said, "Come on, I'll walk you up to the hall for last supper."

"Oh, I don't know," Jenda said, fearful of getting pulled into some kind of religious ritual.

"Don't worry," the man chuckled. "It's only food. Nothing religious about it. We only call it 'last supper' because it's the final meal of the day in our shared dining hall. Visitors sometimes find that a little confusing. There's a first supper, too."

"Ah," Jenda said. "In that case."

The dining hall was as brightly lit as the welcome house, and the serving table was piled high with simple but delicious looking food. Jenda filled her plate and then looked for a place to sit. She suddenly felt very, very tired. There were long tables with benches, but also some smaller tables that seemed to accommodate families. There were children. One of the long tables had some empty spaces, but Jenda didn't feel like talking to anyone. She sat at one of the small tables, facing the wall with her back to the crowd of strangers. She didn't care what they thought of her. She was tired and hungry and wanted to be left alone.

She ate voraciously but soon realized she had taken far more than she could eat. Her stomach began to feel queasy. As she got up from the table, an attendant came by to ask if he could take her plate. Jenda felt an unaccustomed sense of embarrassment for being wasteful. "I'm sorry," she said, but the waiter smiled. "Our chickens just love people like you."

Jenda made her way back to her assigned room without further encounters. It was a modest room, with a single bed, two chairs, two small tables, and a wardrobe. There were curtains on the window and a rug on the floor. It reminded her for a moment of hers and Luis' room at Isabel's apartment. But that was in Buenos Aires. And Luis was in Costa Rica. And here she was someplace that she so far only knew as a set of EarthSat syllables, someplace that was very far from either Buenos Aires or Costa Rica and pretty far from Dallas. She hoped Granny El had acted on her message and would be arriving soon.

A wave of fatigue and loneliness engulfed Jenda and she sat down on the edge of the bed and permitted a few tears to come. More than anything else she wanted to talk with Luis – no, be with Luis. And she had no idea when or even if that was going to happen. She lay back on the little bed and, giving in to mind-numbing exhaustion, she fell asleep.

Jenda had gone to sleep with her back to the east-facing window, so the sun was well up before its brightness penetrated her weary brain. She blinked, trying to remember where she was. When she remembered, she closed her eyes again.

"What happens now?" she wondered, feeling a bit like someone marooned on a desert island. But here, instead of being surrounded by ocean, she was surrounded by strangers and beyond that a society in a state of universal collapse. She rubbed her crusty eyes and stretched her aching limbs. She looked around for a bathroom. There was none. Then she remembered that the women at the welcome center had told her she would be sharing a bathroom with the other residents of this building.

She got up and tried to smooth the wrinkles out of her crumpled shirt before going out to search for the shared facilities. Her door opened directly onto a long porch and the porch opened onto a vast landscape full of golden and gray-green emptiness, delimited only by a ridge of snowcapped mountains on the far horizon and a cloudless blue sky. The desert-island feeling receded as Jenda's consciousness embraced and welcomed the vast open landscape. She took several deep breaths, filling her lungs with the clean bright atmosphere. Maybe this place wouldn't be so bad. For a while, anyway.

She found the bathroom and it was basic but clean. She relieved herself and splashed cool water on her face. There was no towel. She remembered seeing towels on a table in her room and made a mental note to bring one with her next time. She dried her face and hands on her blouse.

She walked the ten paces back to her room, closed the door behind her and leaned against it, still feeling stiff and unsteady. She studied the small space that was to be her temporary home. Her two suitcases stood unopened next to the wardrobe. She thought about how few clothes she had packed and how unlikely it was that she could acquire any more. Even if there was a shopping court in this community – and Jenda doubted that there was – how would she pay for anything with the payment system shut down?

Jenda heaved one of her suitcases onto the bed to look for clothes. The effort made her feel a little short of breath and she wondered absently what the altitude of this place was. Opening the case, she discovered that not only had she packed precious few outfits, her selections were somewhat inappropriate for the current setting. She had thought she would be with Luis. She selected the most nondescript pants and blouse of the lot. She had not brought any soaps or shampoo or toiletries of any kind. Not even a toothbrush. Even without soap, the shower would be refreshing. When Jenda picked up the towel, she realized it was one of those real cotton ones, although its plushness had been diminished by use and, she suspected, many laundry events.

After her shower, dressed in plain brown pants and a blue knit blouse, Jenda wandered back out onto the porch. She felt a little hungry. It was probably long past breakfast, but all she had left in her room was a half-bottle of water and some crumbled remnants of Nutrichips.

As she anticipated, the dining hall was empty, except for one attendant, who gestured toward a table in the center of the room. The table held a carafe, a few cups and saucers, and some plates stacked with pastries

The coffee and pastry left Jenda feeling queasy again. As she walked back toward her room for a rest, she spotted a sign on one of the buildings reading "Clinic".

She stopped and reflected for a moment. "Maybe I should let them check me out." She assured herself that she was only suffering from exhaustion and stress. "I could use some kind of boost right now, though, and I'm sure they'll have something to offer."

31.

Luis bought a ticket on what turned out to be the last flight out of Liberia airport for Buenos Aires. He had to sign a waiver indicating his acknowledgment that some of the air traffic regulation systems might not be functioning. As he signed the paper he mentally substituted "all" for "some" and "will not" for "might not". He was grateful that he had bought his ticket on the mediazone the night before, because by the time he reached the airport, all the pay points were down. What had started in North America and East Asia and a few other places was spreading rapidly through every connection possible. There were a lot of connections.

The flight was only half full, occupied mostly by nervous looking people heading home to look after family and businesses. Luis had a whole row of seats to himself, so he stretched out as best he could. Inflight entertainment was not operating, there was no connection to the medianets, and Luis had not brought along any Duermata. He unfurled his digilet and scrolled through some photos, mostly photos of Jenda. He hoped she had found her way to safety and that she wasn't too annoyed about having been deposited in a Book Community. He searched his digilet for something to read and found nothing appealing. He closed his eyes, thinking he would try to sleep. "What I need is a good superhero story," he told himself wryly. So he tried to conjure up one of his Batman comic book tales. He finally dropped off to sleep just as The Penguin was about to be devoured by a shark off the coast of Tierra del Fuego.

Luis woke to the announcement of their approach into the Buenos Aires airport. He looked out the window and was relieved to see it was a clear day with almost unlimited visibility. He closed his eyes again and waited for the plane to touch down, wishing he knew some prayers or at least believed in a power that could guide the plane to a safe landing. He decided to simply be grateful for a competent flight crew, and that proved sufficient.

It seemed odd going through the arrivals area with everything being done by hand. Luis gave the official his plastiflex document, screened on to the identity log. The officer looked at it, looked at Luis, and then wrote some numbers and syllables on a piece of paper, which he attached to Luis' passport. As he handed it back to Luis he smiled and shrugged his shoulders. "Don't lose the piece of paper," he said.

Outside the terminal, Luis found that autocars were not available, but that the tranvía alta was still running on a limited number of routes. One of these would take him close to the Plaza Wanxiang and Galería Picaflor.

The electric powered vehicle slid along quietly above the nearly deserted streets of the city. The few people Luis saw below on the street were walking hurriedly, wrapped in coats and scarves, not speaking. He remembered having read about the alarming levels of noise pollution in Buenos Aires back in the 20th century, an era dominated by internal combustion engines. He pressed his ear against the plexi window and listened to the silence.

Well before the stop where Luis had intended to disembark, the tranvía slid to a jerky halt. The train had run out of power. He grasped a handle and pulled the door open, waiting while the only other passenger got out. Then he stepped onto the walkway. It was going to be a long walk.

Arriving at last at Galería Picaflor, he was grateful to see Isabel behind the desk.

"Ah, Luisito!" she cried. "I'm so glad you made it safely. I got your messages, although I wasn't sure what they meant. I still don't know exactly what's going on. Where's Jenda?"

Luis hugged his grandmother. "One thing at a time, abuelita," he said. "And there are a lot of things."

"Then let's close the shop and go upstairs for some sandwiches and you can start telling me." Isabel went to the front window and turned over a paper sign that said "Open" on one side and "Closed" on the other. As she manually locked the door, Luis realized that there was no power in the gallery, the only light coming from the glass storefront.

Upstairs in the apartment, there was even less light, so they dragged a couple of chairs over near the window that overlooked the street. Luis did his best to explain to his grandmother what was happening, taking things step by step.

"So you're saying this isn't going to be just a brief period of the power grid and so on being down?" Isabel said. "Well, then. That changes things."

"Yes," Luis assented, "it changes pretty much everything."

"How do we get Jenda back?"

"As soon as the new 'net is up and running, I'll talk to her and we'll work something out," Luis tried to sound optimistic. "There are supposed to be some small airplanes that will begin to operate, and given Jenda's service, there should be no trouble in getting her onto one of them."

"Good," Isabel said. "You know I've become quite fond of your girlfriend, Luis. I want her back."

"Me too, Abuelita," Luis said.

"And what about Paloma and Ermelinda and Ermelinda's father?"

"Again, we will all be in touch as soon as the 'net is working. The plan is for them to come here and join us, since we believe this area will be safer from the spread of the VHA."

"That will be wonderful. We'll have our own little – what did you call it? A sufficiency community? Well, under the circumstances, I'd recommend that we close up here and go out to join Max and Emily at their house in San Ramon. I have a fully charged autocar waiting outside. I knew we'd want to go see them." Isabel was already rising from her chair, ready to leave at once.

32.

Waiting in the anteroom of the clinic, Jenda recalled her illness during the middle part of her sabbatical in San Miguel and told herself that what she was experiencing now was an episode of the same kind. Her physical harmony was being disrupted by her mental disarray. She looked down at the digilet curled uselessly around her wrist. Luis had said a new 'net – the novanet – would be coming up after the demise of the old supranet and medianets and he had scripted her digilet to receive it. There was no indication yet of any activity.

Jenda was called into the examining room by a woman in a white uniform that bore no insignia other than that of the medical community, the Rod of Asclepius. There were no emblems of healthcare or pharmaceutical corporations. Jenda sat on the edge of an examining table while the woman took her blood pressure and heart rate and temperature with hand-held instruments that Jenda did not remember having seen before. The woman made notes on paper and then, in a tone of practiced optimism, told Jenda the doctor would be in momentarily.

When the doctor entered, Jenda's first thought was that she was from Gen2. But in this community, where people were aging with the passing years, it was impossible to tell. She could as easily be Gen3 or even Gen4.

"How are you feeling?" the doctor asked, studying the paper on which the assistant had made notes about the state of Jenda's body.

"Tired," Jenda said. "A little breathless at times, probably because of the altitude. Also kind of achy. And a bit nauseous."

"Well, you're running a fever," the doctor said as she pulled back Jenda's eyelids to have a better look at her eyes. "I'm going to order a blood test." She buzzed for the assistant to return. "This may be unfamiliar to you, but to do blood tests here, we have to withdraw a small amount of blood. And we won't have the results until tomorrow. Yes, I know, we're fairly backward out here, but at least our processes aren't going to fail just because the supranet and the medianets go down." The doctor smiled and patted Jenda's knee. "We'll send someone to your unit tomorrow to let you know when we have the results. Meanwhile, here's something for the dizziness and I recommend that you drink plenty of liquids and try to get some rest. I'm also giving you an analgesic for fever and pain." She paused. "Do you want anything for anxiety?"

Jenda considered it but then said, "No. Thank you." She swallowed the pills the attendant placed in her hand and drained the cup of water.

As she walked back toward her quarters, Jenda told herself that the blood tests would surely reveal nothing more than a slightly elevated white blood cell count. Following doctor's orders, she lay down on the bed for a nap. Later she had a light supper followed by a shower. She started to unpack more of her things and then thought better of it; she didn't intend to be here long. A handful of Duermata guaranteed her a good night's sleep.

The next morning, she woke to the sound of someone knocking on her door. She sat up quickly and the room began to spin. Hoping she hadn't locked the door she called, "Come in!"

Jenda looked up and saw a man with a familiar face.

"Oh, my gosh! Jonathan?"

"Yep, it's me, Jen – your little brother Jonathan. Or maybe your older brother."

It was true. Jonathan looked almost Gen2, while Jenda was indistinguishable from Gen5. It was clear he had not been availing himself of Chulel for some years. Jenda rose unsteadily to give her brother a hug. "God, it's so good to see you, Jonathan. I've been worried – what with the corporate police and all. Have you heard from Granny El?"

"Wait. Corporate police? What do you know about that? And no, I haven't heard from Gran yet. Pulses are neither coming nor going right now. I was lucky to get the message you sent with the location of this place. If you sent it to Gran at the same time, though, I'm sure she got it. Things are getting pretty strange out there now, you know. It sounds like we may have a lot to talk about."

"I know," Jenda replied. "Well, at least I know a little about what's going on. Come sit beside me, little brother, and I'll tell you what I know if you tell me what you know. I've been awfully worried about you."

So Jenda told Jonathan about Recall and about the digital infection and about her encounter with Selena, the policewoman from Marvaworld with his picture in her digilet.

"I had hoped they wouldn't actually try to come after me," Jonathan said. "Gosh, Jenda, I'm really sorry you had to get caught up in this." He explained that his flick had been pulled back by Marvaworld because its storyline too closely portrayed real events involving some pretty powerful plutocrats. As a precaution, he had decided to take a leave of absence from his academic job and spend time with a friend in Arizona.

"How did you end up in a Book Community?" he wanted to know.

"I don't think it would have been my first choice, but apparently Montagne knew about the place and thought I'd be safe here."

"You could do worse. You know the people in these communities aren't all religious fanatics. Some are here just because they got fed up and wanted to get away. So you're back in touch with Montagne? And who is Luis?"

Jenda explained things as best she could. "I can't believe what a large chunk of my past was missing. I always thought Mom had gone completely crazy with all her stories about things that, as far as I knew, never happened. But it turns out she was right. It must have been painful for her."

"So you're telling me I have a niece out there?" Jonathan seemed pleased. "I'm not surprised that Paloma took care of her."

"Why do you think Mom remembered about my pregnancy when everybody else forgot?"

"Mom was always a bit moody," Jonathan said. "So she was on a couple of mood medications. That may have created resistance to the photonic memory process. I think Mom's art was the only thing holding her together after a while."

"I found a few of her sculptures," Jenda said, "and I brought them with me. I'll dig them out and show them to you later. Maybe you remember more about them than I do – about what they meant to Mom. You seem to remember an awful lot about our childhood. Why is that?"

"Just lucky, I guess. You know I'd gotten into meditation in my early teens. So when I first started getting the Chulel process with photonic memory restoration, being in a room all by myself seemed to me like a good opportunity to do some deep meditation." He laughed. "I had no idea it would protect me like it did. Are you feeling okay, Jenda? You look a little pale."

"I haven't been feeling too great. I went to the clinic yesterday and they should be getting back to me soon with some test results. I'm sure I'll be okay. I'm glad you're here. Are you staying? Have they given you a room yet?"

"Definitely staying," Jonathan replied, "for a while, anyway, if they'll let me. I need to go find out about getting a room. Shall I bring you some lunch so you don't have to go out?"

"Room service would be great. Thanks." Jenda gave her brother a smile and a hug.

While Jonathan went to find a room and settle in, Jenda sat on the floor next to her suitcases and rummaged through her things, looking for their mother's sculptures. There were only three. Jenda unwrapped them and set them on the desk in a line. They were all female figures and one of them seemed to have a slightly pregnant belly. "Why hadn't I noticed that before?" Jenda wondered.

She picked up the wrappings that had protected the figures. They were clearly some of her old Vintie attire. She shook out one of the blouses, which seemed to be made of a sturdy cotton, tightly woven and still strong after so many years. It had embroidery around the neckline and sleeves. Jenda held the blouse up to see if it still might fit. The embroidery, she realized, was hand done. As she examined the garment further, she discovered an area along one of the side seams that had been mended long before Vintie Jenda had gotten hold of it. She knew this because the stitches – although clearly executed by hand – were small and regular, the mark of someone who was caring for a garment rather than making a political statement. Jenda suddenly wished she knew where the blouse had come from, who had made it, who had worn it, who had mended it. She felt the blouse had a story and she wanted to be part of it. She took it down to the shared bathroom and washed it carefully in the sink. She squeezed it out and draped it on a towel over the porch railing to dry.

The effort of washing the blouse tired her out. She lay down on the bed for a rest and was about to drift off to sleep when she heard a knock on the door. Thinking it was Jonathan bringing lunch, she called, "Come on in, it's unlocked."

It wasn't Jonathan. It was the doctor.

"Feeling a little unsteady?" she asked Jenda.

"Yes. I'm sorry. I guess I sat up too quickly." Jenda wanted nothing more than to lie back down.

The doctor dragged the desk chair over next to the bed to sit down. "We got the blood test results," she said. "Your white cell count is high."

Jenda looked up quickly, feeling hopeful.

The doctor continued, "Your red cell count is low. Very low. Anemic."

Jenda braced herself on the edge of the bed with both arms as her head and shoulders sagged. She didn't want to look at the doctor. She didn't want to hear what came next.

"I'm truly sorry, but it looks like you've contracted the hemolytic virus," she said. "There isn't a specific test for the virus yet, but you have all the symptoms. And given that you've recently traveled in Central America, well, it seems clear."

Jenda looked up at the doctor. "So what you're saying is that I have something that's going to kill me," she said, surprised that her mind had gone so quickly to this conclusion.

The doctor took a deep breath. "Thus far, to the best of my knowledge, this virus appears to be 100% fatal. So, yes, to be perfectly honest, this is most likely the thing that will end your life." She paused. "Do you have any religious preferences? We have a priest… a rabbi…an imam?"

"No. I've never been a Book person," Jenda said. "More of a Buddhist. Sometimes, anyway." Jenda couldn't think of anything to say. This was not part of the plan she and Luis had worked out.

"I've brought you some more medications that can help with the symptoms," the doctor was saying. She placed the bottles on the table next to Jenda's bed and reviewed instructions for their use. She shook a few tablets into a cup and handed them to Jenda along with a cup of water. "I brought the water jug and cup, in case you didn't have anything available to keep you hydrated. The jug can be refilled from the tap. I'll bring in an oxygen apparatus tomorrow. You may not need it yet, but you'll soon find it useful."

Jenda nodded obediently and swallowed the medications.

"Do you have any questions?" the doctor asked.

Jenda slowly raised her gaze to look up at the doctor, her head cocked to one side. She almost smiled as she heard the echo of Malia Poole's voice telling her, "You need to ask more questions." She had so many questions now, but she didn't think the doctor had the answers.

There was another knock on the door and the doctor opened it to let Jonathan inside. They didn't have to tell him anything. He knew by looking at the doctor and at Jenda's stricken face what the diagnosis was. He set down the lunch tray and moved toward his sister.

"Won't he catch it?" Jenda asked the doctor, looking anxious as Jonathan moved toward her.

"No, dear," the doctor said. "All indications are that only regular and especially recent Chulel users are susceptible. He'll be fine. As will most of the people here. We'll warn a few of our newest arrivals about this, and for their sake we'll have to ask you to limit your movements."

Jenda said she understood. Tears had begun flowing down her face, but she didn't collapse into hysterical sobs as she might have done in the past. She felt oddly calm as her brother came and sat beside her on the bed and put his arm around her shoulders. She flashed on a toy she thought she must have had as a child, a tube you looked through toward the light to watch how the colored patterns changed as you turned the tube. She felt like her own pieces had suddenly fallen into a different pattern.

The doctor rose to leave, indicating that she would return in the evening. She set the chair back in its place and moved toward the door.

"Doctor." Jenda called her back. "I do have one question: How long?"

"Of course," the doctor said. "So far – in most cases – about a week. At most two weeks."

"Okay," Jenda said. "Thank you." She leaned against her brother's shoulder and looked down at her digilet, wishing desperately for it to give her some sign that she would be able to at least talk to Luis while there was still time.

"I brought your lunch, Jen. Do you feel like eating anything?"

Jenda said she didn't, but thanked him anyway. "Maybe I'll eat a little bit later," she said, looking up at her brother and trying to smile. She noticed that he had tears in his eyes. "I'm glad you're here, Jon. I don't know what to say right now. I don't even know what to think."

"We don't talk about these things in our world, do we Jen? We did in my Buddhist training in Tibet. But the real thing is always different. We'll find a way through this. I'll be with you."

"I think I may need to lie down for a while now. The meds are making me feel drowsy."

When Jenda woke, her brother was gone and it was dark. She thought she might be feeling a bit better, so she reached over to turn on the lamp. That made her feel a little dizzy, but it didn't make her want to throw up. The lunch tray was gone, but there was a glass of apple juice and a bowl of Nutrichips on her side table. Jenda arranged her pillows and, sitting cross-legged on the bed, she ate a few chips and drank the juice. Then she picked up the pill bottles, one by one, trying to remember what time it had been when the doctor brought them to her. She swallowed one more of the dizziness pills, one analgesic, and more Duermata. Then she turned off the lamp and lay down. She stared into the darkness, trying to see more clearly this new pattern her life was taking. There were fewer pieces; she knew that. The pieces that stood for Luis-Martín Zenobia shone bright as crystals in the sun, but they seemed small and so far away. By the time she fell asleep, her hair and pillow were wet with tears.

33.

The limitations on Jenda's movements meant she was pretty much confined to her room and its immediate environs. Her meals would be delivered. "As long as you're able," the doctor told her, "you can take walks in the garden next to this building." The clinic put a hand lettered sign at the entrance, warning new arrivals to stay away.

The day after her diagnosis, Jenda and her brother explored the garden. As they approached the first bench, Jenda was beginning to breathe heavily and asked to sit down. One of the oldest community residents was already occupying the bench, but he slid over to make room for them. He introduced himself as Lucas and offered his sympathy for Jenda's illness.

"You know," he said, in his slightly hoarse old man's voice, "this is what God ordained from the beginning. You remember the story of the Garden of Eden? In the Garden human beings were at one with the Lord, but he chose to give them free will and they chose to disobey Him, to give in to the serpent's temptation and eat the forbidden fruit. From that day to this, human beings have been subject to old age and death. This Chulel thing offended God, you know." He paused. "I don't mean to say… I mean I'm genuinely sorry for your illness, miss." Neither Jenda nor Jonathan said anything, only nodding in acknowledgment of his story. "Well, I must go," Lucas said, as he stood up and walked slowly down the path, leaning on his cane.

Jonathan and Jenda exchanged a quick look of mutual understanding. "Gosh, I haven't thought about the whole Garden of Eden thing in a long time," Jonathan said. "I used to wonder if maybe we all wouldn't have been better off if those two had taken a few more bites out of the apple. Seems we're still unclear about the difference between good and evil." He glanced at Jenda and his eyes held a mischief that Jenda found familiar. "And how come the snake had to be the bad guy?

Honestly, I think knowing is always better than living in even the most blissful ignorance." Jenda smiled in agreement.

It wasn't long before Jenda had to confess she was too tired to continue and Jonathan walked her back to her room. She lay back thankfully on her bed and took in a few deep breaths, trying to send more oxygen to her debilitated red cells. She felt as if her head was wrapped in cotton batting. She couldn't think clearly and she was sure her lungs had shrunk. Only deep breaths pulled in enough air. She sat up slowly and reached again for the collection of medicine bottles on her table. She shook out a few tablets and swallowed them down with gulps of cooling water. Then she felt a sensation on her left wrist. Her digilet had come to life.

Jenda's heart pounded so hard she was afraid she might pass out. She closed her eyes for a second, willing her heart to behave, willing the digilet to produce a message from Luis. Then she unwrapped the digilet and snapped it flat. There was an image on the screen. Jenda tapped it and the familiar symbol of Interloc emerged. Jenda stopped for a moment, her finger poised over the screen as she tried to recall the new access phrase Luis had given her. Then she remembered: "kukulcan&picaflor," the names of Luis' and Isabel's art galleries. Jenda tapped the syllables into the device with trembling hands and waited as the message screen came up. There was nothing for her. Tears came to her eyes. She wanted to shout into the digilet to get Luis' attention. Time was running out. "I need to be rational," she told herself. "It may take longer in rural Costa Rica for all this to get up and running." She had no way of knowing that Luis was in Argentina, settling in at Max and Emily's cottage near San Ramon.

Jenda needed to leave a message, but she couldn't think what to say. How would she tell Luis? She decided to start with something easy: "Arrived safely. My brother is here too. Sad to be away from you. Hope you are well." It wasn't much, but the rest would have to wait. Next she sent a message to Meli, and one to her grandmother. Jenda coiled the digilet back around her wrist.

She continued sitting bolt upright, her eyes wide, her heart shattered, her mind in turmoil. "One week," she told herself. "Maybe two. I may never see Luis again. I will never get to know my daughter."

She lay down, trying to arrange her aching limbs comfortably. Tears welled up again as she hoped against hope that no one else would be sick. "What if Luis caught it, too? What about Meli? And Montagne? Paloma will be okay. She stopped taking Chulel years ago. I'm glad now I didn't go see Granny El. I wouldn't want her to get this illness. What's wrong with me anyway? Why am I just now thinking about how contagious this thing is?"

And then Jenda thought about all the people she worked with and about all the people in the café where she ate the grilled cheese sandwich and about everyone else she had been in contact with over the three days between leaving Costa Rica and arriving here at – she reminded herself she still needed to ask if this place had a name. As she finally fell into a light sleep, Jenda was also thinking about the infection she had introduced through the YJ screens and remembering having read once about someone called Typhoid Mary.

Jenda woke to the familiar chiming of an Interloc message on her digilet. She picked it up and smiled.

MURCIELAGO: ¡Hola, querida! ¿Qué tal?

Jenda took her time sitting up to avoid the dizziness, positioning a couple of pillows for support. Then she responded.

POLILLA: Luis! So good to hear from you! Are you okay?

MURCIELAGO: Yes, fine here. So glad you made it to Lechuza safely! How are you doing?

So that was the name of this place. Jenda paused as she filed that bit of information away and tried to think what to say next. She couldn't lie. There was no time for lying.

POLILLA: You sent me to a good place. But I'm ill.

Sitting in the warm sunshine under the vast blue sky outside the Feldmans' little cottage at the San Ramon estancia, Luis felt an icy shiver of dread. He refused it.

MURCIELAGO: I'm sure you'll be fine in no time. Did you see a doctor?

POLILLA: Yes. She says it's the VHA.

Luis' world shattered. The blue sky went dark and his heart plunged into a black hole of sadness.

In her little room at the Book Community of Lechuza, Jenda's face contorted as she struggled to contain her sorrow.

POLILLA: Are you sure you're okay, my love? Please be okay!

MURCIELAGO: I'm fine, querida. Except my heart is breaking. I haven't had Chulel in almost three years now. I'm sure I'll be okay. Are they taking good care of you? I can't believe this is happening.

POLILLA: What about Meli?

MURCIELAGO: I'm in Argentina now. I came to see about Isabel. Meli and the rest will join us here as soon as they can.

POLILLA: And everybody there is okay? Have you heard from them to know that they're okay? I don't know where I picked up this illness and I worry.

MURCIELAGO: You most likely picked it up on the airplane. I haven't heard from Montagne since I left, but everybody was feeling fine then. Don't worry about us. Just take care of yourself. How is your brother?

POLILLA: He's fine and being very kind to me.

Just as Jenda touched the screen to pulse this, a notice came up: "Connection lost. Please repair connection and try again." And then the screen went dark.

Jenda continued staring at the dark screen, trying to maintain her connection with Luis. She knew Luis was doing the same.

He was. And he knew she was.

Both of their faces were tear-streaked. They both sat where they were, their hearts torn open.

There was a knock on Jenda's door. She reached for a tissue from the bedside table and dabbed at her face. "Come in," she called.

It was her brother. "You have a visitor," he said. Jenda scowled. This was not a good time for visitors. But as the door opened further, she saw that the visitor was Granny El.

"Granny, no! Jonathan, take her away. Please! No, you'll get the illness, Gran. Don't you understand? Jon, please…" Jenda was becoming hysterical. She pulled the bed sheet up in front of her face.

Granny El stepped forward. "Will you just calm down, Jenda?" she scolded. "I know exactly what I'm doing." Then her voice softened. "This is my choice. You know I wouldn't make a very good old lady. Other people may age gracefully, but I'm pretty sure I never would. No, better to go this way. I've had 165 years, you know. I'm okay with the idea that I'll be coming along right behind you." Her voice was quivering. She sat down on the bed next to Jenda to embrace her.

"Oh, Gran, why are you doing this?" Jenda held back for a moment and then returned her grandmother's hug. "Crazy old woman," she mumbled, as they clung to one another.

Granny El poured a glass of water for Jenda and examined the bottles on her bedside table. Jenda could see that Granny El intended to take charge of her care. Jonathan could see, too, and took his leave, promising to check back later.

Granny El pulled up a chair next to the bed. "So have you heard from that boyfriend of yours?" she asked Jenda.

"How did you know?" Jenda began, trying to remember if she had ever confessed to her grandmother that her affair during this last sabbatical was no mere dalliance.

"Oh, come on, Jen." Granny El's face crinkled into a smile. Jenda loved those crinkles. "I could see it in your eyes that something was different this time. Are you going to tell me his name now?"

Jenda smiled. "Luis," she said softly. "Luis-Martín Zenobia." Jenda even loved his name, and she loved saying it out loud to Granny El.

"Nice name. Now, if you're not too tired, maybe you'd like to tell me a little bit about him." And Jenda spent the next half hour conjuring up the living presence of Luis-Martín Zenobia, aware that her grandmother knew this was the best medicine she could offer.

"Do you know anything about Dad?" Jenda asked her grandmother, thinking maybe she had said enough about Luis for the time being and that perhaps the revelation that Granny El had a great-granddaughter could wait for later. "Do you know where he is?"

Granny El shook her head. "I haven't been in touch with him in years, Jen. Have you asked your brother?"

"I asked him yesterday," Jenda replied. "He said he only has an old contact phrase. He sent the location, but hadn't heard anything back."

After her conversation with Granny El, Jenda napped, waking up only when she heard someone rapping on her door with a meal tray. She ate what she could and then went to the desk where she had piled some of the books and papers from her suitcases. She gathered up some of them and sat down on the floor, leaning against the side of the bed, facing the window, its blue curtains pulled back to let in the light.

She was still searching for something, but she hardly knew what it might be. She had brought such an odd assortment of things, such a jumble of puzzle pieces. She wanted desperately to fit more of them together while there was still time. She glanced through a few of her childhood journals. She picked up a sketchbook, one of the last ones her mother had used. It was filled with drawings of the girl depicted in the three statues as well as a mischievous looking boy. Jenda knew they were drawings – memories – of her and Jonathan. She turned the pages slowly, trying to imagine herself and Jonathan as the children in the sketches. She held the book up to the light to get a better view of one of the faded drawings and as she did so, a few pages fell into her lap from the center of the book. She picked them up and knew at once these were not pages of the sketchbook. They were pages written in her own hand, pages from one of her old journals. She looked at the date: April 20, 2030. These were pages from her missing year, from the days just before her journey to Argentina. Her hands shook as she smoothed out the folds and began to read:

These are hard times. Montagne says we must remain firm. We want a better world for our child than the one we live in now. The corporations press us all to destroy the beautiful treasures in our lives – the paintings, the books, the printed photographs of friends and family. They entice us into buying the shoddy goods they know will not last. We resist. Tonight Montagne and I and a few more friends will go to the 3Dec headquarters and put in place the installation I've been creating in Leticia's parents' garage. I'm doing this because I know I must do something. The corporations are killing us, seducing us into serving their needs and forgetting our own. We can't give in. We are the Vintage ones – we must keep sculpting light!

Those were the words she – Jenda Swain – had written more than 95 years ago. That was who she had been – a young woman trying to change the world, to shake people into awareness of what was happening, to stop the insidiously expanding control of the corporations.

"It didn't work, did it, Jenda?" she mused. Or maybe it just took longer than they had anticipated. Maybe it took something more than art installations. And yet... weren't those kinds of things still remembered and honored by the very ones who had brought about this final takedown? Wasn't it all part of the same pattern?

Jenda felt the kaleidoscope of her mind shift once again. The new pattern felt immense and powerful. The pieces fit. She placed the journal pages back inside the sketchbook and held it between her hands, feeling a strange composure, an unaccustomed peace. She felt ashamed for having been so focused on her own personal predicament. "I'm only one piece of the whole," she thought. "But at least I'm part of it – and an active part." She felt more certain than ever that what she had done at YJ was right, that what was happening in the world outside this little community was necessary, despite all the pain and suffering. She suddenly remembered a moment from her past: Grandpa Ned was in the hospital, dying. He was on life support and the family had finally reached the decision to pull the plug.

Maybe that was it. That was what they had done.

She got up and cleared away everything from the desk except her mother's three sculptures and the two paintings of her own. When Jonathan arrived a few minutes later, she directed him to the table.

"I see you found your 'lady in blue'," Jonathan said, picking up the painting of the Virgin of Lujan. "You told me about how you were haunted by this image when you came back from South America. Gosh, you even got a tattoo of her."

Jenda explained to Jonathan about the Virgin of Lujan and why the image had affected her so.

"I'm glad you finally tracked her down," he said.

He picked up the other painting. "I remember this one, too. The clouds, with those strange swirls of syllables, are like a watercolor of Grandpa Ned's that used to hang in our hallway." Then he turned his attention to the sculptures, picking up each one and turning it over in his hands with obvious affection.

"What can you tell me about them?" Jenda asked.

"I think these were Mom's favorites of all the pieces she made of you," he said. "You were her dancing girl, dancing like that whenever you felt happy. Sometimes even when you were sad you'd dance this graceful, swaying dance. I'm not sure you ever took lessons, but you always danced. And this one – you were always reading books. Dad used to scold you about carrying around all that paper, all those old-fashioned books instead of using your screen." He picked up the one of the girl with the softly rounded belly. "You know, I wasn't at home that much around the time of your trip to South America, but I remember once when I visited – not long before Mom's accident – seeing her in her studio, clutching this statue and crying." Jonathan set the pregnant sculpture down and picked up the dancing one again. "Mom had trouble expressing affection," he said. "It was the way she was. She put all her emotion into her art. I think these pieces are how she loved you."

Jenda wiped away a stray tear. "I can't imagine how hard it must have been for Mom when other people's memories started disappearing. And we thought she was the crazy one!"

"I wish I'd been around more. She may have had problems, but she wasn't crazy."

"Can we talk a little about things that you remember from when we were children? Do you remember a classmate named Malia Poole?"

34.

Jenda woke early the following morning to the sound of her digilet telling her Recall was back. She unfurled it without sitting up. There was a message from Luis. She felt dizzy. It had been too many hours since her last medication or else the dizziness was just getting worse. Maybe both. She fumbled for the oxygen apparatus the doctor had brought and took a few nourishing breaths.

Luis' message indicated that he thought a voice connection was now possible and he left instructions. Jenda took her pills and arranged her pillows. Then she followed the instructions Luis indicated. She heard a buzzing. And then she heard Luis' voice.

"Hello? Jenda?"

"Yes, it's me. God it's so good to hear your voice!"

"I've missed your voice too, querida. How are you doing?"

"Okay, I think. Granny El got here yesterday." She explained how Granny El was intentionally exposing herself to the illness and how Jonathan had not been taking Chulel for many years now so he would be safe. "How is everybody there? Have you heard from Meli yet?" Jenda needed to know.

"We're all fine, Jen. Everybody is fine. I talked with Montagne earlier today and he and Meli and Paloma are all in good health. Tao-Min is there now with Meli. She had been on a business trip to South Africa. I should tell you, though, Paloma refuses to leave Costa Rica." And then Luis explained to Jenda how Paloma said she could never leave the town with the technical college she had built with the money from Jenda's parents and the street they had named after her, and of course Meli refused to leave without Paloma, and so Montagne had decided to stay as well and finish setting up the sufficiency community to ensure that they all made it through.

Jenda said she understood and that she hoped they would all be okay.

"They all said to tell you they send their love. You can call them, too, if you like."

"Yes, I'll definitely do that."

"Are you really okay or are you just saying that. You can tell me, you know."

"I know, Luis. But I do think I'm okay." And she told him about the pages she had found in her mother's sketchbook and how she had felt when she read them. "So, yes, I'm sick," she said finally, "but so are thousands of other people. And our whole society has been sick for decades. This is how it ends for me, Luis, but I refuse to go out feeling sorry for myself."

"Montagne was right about you, Jenda. He told me that back in the day you were one of the strongest and fiercest women he knew."

"Do you remember when I asked you how long you expected to live?" she asked.

"I do. And do you remember what I told you?"

"I do. You said you expected to live to be a very old man. Well, it looks like that will happen. But not me. I'm kind of sorry that I'll never know what it's like to be an old woman. I mean, I may be 112, but I've never been old. And now I never will be. I've lived a lot of years, but I always felt like I was young, with my life still ahead of me. Not much ahead of me now. What do you think comes – you know – after? Can we talk about that?" she asked.

"That's one of the great questions of all time, querida. I've read a lot of stories about the things people believe in different cultures, in different religious traditions. But as for me... I guess I used to think it would just be the end. Like shutting your eyes and everything being gone. A natural enough process, but not leading anywhere. Now I think I may have some of the same questions you have."

"Remember in my childhood journal when I wrote about my cat Milly? And how she died and I was hoping that the Buddhists were right and that she would come back again in a new life? I still think I like that idea, only – I don't know if it's

274

true or not. I think I'd like to come back and see what happens after all of this gets sorted out."

"Let's both come back, okay? I'll look for you."

Jenda laughed and agreed.

"I tried to find an airplane to bring me back to North America to be with you. But there's nothing running. Nothing at all, Jenda."

They both fell silent for a moment.

"Well, there is one thing," Luis said finally. "I think they've got things set up where we could do at least a brief session visually. Kind of like what used to be Chat^2. Shall we try?"

"By all means," Jenda replied. "I'd love to see your face. Although mine isn't going to look so good." She was searching for her hairbrush.

"Okay, just a minute and let me see if I can get this to work. Hang on. You'll need to switch on your camera."

There was silence at the other end and Jenda did as she was asked, combing her hair with her fingers as she waited. And then, suddenly, there was Luis' face on her tiny digilet screen.

"Oh, gosh, look at you. Your beard is getting long," she said. "Can you hear me okay? Is the picture coming through from my end?"

"Clear as a bell, querida. You look good. I can see you're a bit pale, but you're as beautiful as ever. What is that you're wearing?" Luis was smiling.

"Oh, this old thing?" Jenda offered a weak smile in return. "I guess it's one of my old Vintie outfits. It was wrapped around one of Mom's sculptures in the stuff I brought with me, so I washed it out and decided to wear it. Do you like it?"

"It looks beautiful on you. I think it suits you. Abuela Isabel and Max and Emily send their love. The Feldmans have started to have some success in piecing together Abuela Isabel's lost memories. She's remembering a little bit about Abuelo Arturo and about my mother and my uncle Julian. And do you remember she had those two books by a California author in her collection? Well, it turns out that this author – Martin Jameson

– was a professor she met at the college where she was teaching and apparently Isabel and Martin had quite the love affair."

Jenda smiled, imagining a young Isabel experiencing the kind of intense love she had for Luis. "Well, that's a good thing to remember, isn't it? It's always good to remember love."

Luis paused, and Jenda could tell by the rhythmic movements of the image that he was walking.

"You remember when we found the little dove on the sidewalk in San Antonio, querida?"

"I remember. You told me an old story about a bird and a snake."

"That's right – about a contest to see who human beings would be like – the snake that sheds its skin and lives forever or the bird that has to die."

"And the bird won, right?"

"Yes. The bird won."

"I've thought about that, Luis. You know, snakes don't really live forever. Why did those people ever think that?"

He laughed. "Wishful thinking, I guess, querida."

"Yeah, just like us. I think I'd rather be a bird. Or a bird-like human. Knowing."

"That's kind of what the legend meant to the people who told the story. It's the knowing that's important. I think I've begun to feel it since I gave up Chulel. I wish you were going to have more time to experience it. I wish we could experience it together."

Jenda saw his eyes glittering with unshed tears.

"I don't know how long this connection will last, mi amor, so I will say this now: I love you more than I have ever loved anyone in my life." His voice was shaking.

"And I love you, Luis-Martín, more than I ever believed I could love. You've given me my life back, helped me find myself again. If I could, I would be with you for a thousand lifetimes! Will you look after Meli for me? I know she has Montagne and Paloma, and I know she's a grown woman, but…"

"Of course I'll look after Meli – as if she were my own daughter. I promise. Listen, our connection is fading. I'll call you back tomorrow, okay?"

"Yes, please," Jenda smiled weakly, feeling suddenly exhausted. "And the tomorrow after that."

And so Luis called Jenda every day until the day she didn't answer.

~~~

Luis was able to keep the community in San Ramon abreast of developments via the newly independent novanet. They watched the story unfold about the collapse of the old order and the emergence all over the world of a variety of new orders. They couldn't be fully aware, however, of how the world outside their little community was disintegrating even more completely as people continued to succumb in massive numbers to the lethal blood disease. The fortunate ones were able to choose to do as Luis and his family and friends did – and as Jenda would have done – and resign themselves to eventually dying from old age, giving up Chulel to protect themselves from the fatal illness. Others chose to do what Granny El did and deliberately expose themselves to the illness in order to care for one another or to avoid the uncertainties of old age in a disordered society. Still others took more direct action via drug overdoses or other means.

As the years passed in their little community Luis and his grandmother and their friends Max and Emily – and, after the death of Silvestre, Rosalí as well – would sit around in the evening reading from one or another of Isabel's precious books. Or they would look at the paintings Luis was working on. Many of his paintings were images of a superhero, a dancing female superhero who looked a lot like Jenda and who wore a beautifully embroidered billowing blue superhero cape.

Or they would tell stories. And as one of them would begin to forget, someone else would remind them by telling them a story and then that one would pretend to remember. One of their favorite stories was about when Jenda was a little girl in San Ramon and had a white cat named Milly. They all remembered

Jenda's cat, and they would nod and smile, remembering. And then one day the cat had died and Jenda and Paloma and Rosalí had buried it in the back garden, in the shade of the jacarandas and fruit trees that Silvestre and his father had planted.

"But that was after Meli was born, wasn't it?" Emily would ask.

"Oh yes," Rosalí said. "Because the cat was there when Meli was born. It was such a beautiful white cat." Isabel remembered that, too.

After a while even Max and Emily remembered that one, and when he was the only one left it was one of Luis' most treasured memories.

Acknowledgments

Way of the Serpent has its roots in a lifetime of studying humanity and a lengthy career in anthropology, but the story began to take form only around mid-2014. I have been encouraged and assisted (and occasionally chastised) in the process of writing the story by a host of friends and colleagues, including Maria Elena Sandovici, Sangye Teresa O'Mara, Richard Crossland, Patt Brower, Valerie Pheasant, Teresa Roberson, Cheryl Rooke, Catalina Castillon, and Steven Zani. I am deeply grateful to each and every one of them. I also owe a debt of gratitude to Madeline Caldwell, who provided valuable editorial insight on an earlier draft of the book. None of these people is responsible for the final outcome; I accept that burden fully and happily.

The story referenced in the epigraph is Silvina Ocampo's "Forgotten Journey," recently published in English in *Thus Were Their Faces: Stories*, translated by Daniel Balderston (New York Review Books, 2015). I also refer to a documentary film about the Dani people of New Guinea entitled "Dead Birds." It is by legendary documentary filmmaker Robert Gardner and available from Documentary Educational Resources. I would also like to acknowledge Jason Wilson, author of *Buenos Aires: A Cultural History* (2012: Interlink Publishing). His book helped me greatly in imagining what that city might be like in the 22nd century world I created.

I can be found online (with my artwork and occasional blog) at donnadechenbirdwell.com, on Facebook, and also on Twitter @wideworldhome.

Made in the USA
Charleston, SC
23 July 2015